Praise for Auburn McCanta's Illuminating Debut Novel

ALL THE DANCING BIRDS

"Touching and informative, *All the Dancing Birds* offers valuable insights into the subjective experience of Alzheimer's disease."

—Daniel Kuhn, author of *Alzheimer's Early Stages:*
First Steps for Families, Friends, and Caregivers

"*All the Dancing Birds* offers a powerful and painfully beautiful peek into the mind of Lillie Claire, a vibrant woman struck in her mid-50s with Alzheimer's disease. In this perceptive novel, author Auburn McCanta renders a fictional tale with factual punch as she shines light on the ways this tragic illness touches friends, family and the critical "second family" of nurses and caregivers. Alzheimer's eventually robs Lillie Claire, a poet, of her treasured words. But her story, so lovingly tendered with clarity and wit, demonstrates the triumph of love. *All the Dancing Birds* offers great insight to, and love for, those touched—and ultimately changed—by the mystery of a mean disease."

—Drew Myron, poet, *Beyond Forgetting:*
Poetry and Prose about Alzheimer's Disease

"If your life is touched by Alzheimer's, you need this book. It will help you understand the experience of having Alzheimer's—and inspire you to interact with loved ones touched by it in more meaningful ways.

—Cynthia D'Amour, bestselling author,
national speaker, advocate

"In *All the Dancing Birds*, Auburn McCanta accomplishes the near impossible. By allowing Lillie Claire to tell her own story, McCanta gives us an amazing inside glimpse into a disintegrating memory. Truly a touching, disturbing story—wonderfully told."

—Susan Springer Butler, author

"Auburn McCanta's haunting story invited me in to see how Lillie Claire (and my parents) coped with a disease that first took their memories, then slowly took their lives. Lillie Claire's story mirrored the journey my parents took and she became part of me emotionally. I laughed and cried as if I was one of her family members. I sang along with Jewell. In the end, I was grateful to learn that Lillie Claire could still understand and love her children, if even only silently."

—Daniel Joseph, son, caregiver,
Alzheimer's advocate

"Rarely is there a writer with the combination of talent, life experience, true compassion, and raw nerve able to tackle a topic so shrouded in mystery and bathed in fear as Alzheimer's disease. For the many who have, or will be affected by this robber of those things that make us who we are, Auburn McCanta is just that rare individual. Having lost loved ones to Alzheimer's and being a statistically miraculous survivor of brain cancer herself, she is uniquely qualified to speak for Lilly Claire, while bathing her story in the compassion and truth that is McCanta's own heart song."

—Lisa Nicholson,
special needs and brain illness advocate

*All
the
Dancing
Birds*

a novel

Auburn McCanta

Marcanti Clarke Literary Press

All the Dancing Birds
Auburn McCanta

Printed in the United States of America.
Marcanti Clarke Literary Press
P.O. Box 10353, Glendale, AZ 85318.

For more information about this book, visit www.AuburnMcCanta.com

Edition ISBNs
Trade Paperback 978-0-9850700-0-7
Hardcover 978-0-9850700-1-4
e-book 978-0-9850700-2-1

Library of Congress Cataloging-in-Publication data is available upon request.

First Edition 2012

This edition was prepared for printing by The Editorial Department
7650 E. Broadway, #308, Tucson, Arizona 85710
www.editorialdepartment.com

Cover design by Carol Ruzicka
Interior vector art by Novi Candrasari
Book design by Christopher Fisher

To Dan, the love of my life

For Mom and Pop and Dad
And for all my little ladies and gentlemen

It Took so Long

In days of debris,
We sifted for angels.

Now we know:
It's futile to search for solid joy.

Happiness is a vapor, powerful
As wind, but just as shifty.

We do not hold
Keys or answers

But vision,
Memory, hands.

Mine in yours, every
Squeeze says *loved*

Says *I am I am I am.*

—*Drew Myron*

"The mind in its own place, and in itself
Can make a heaven of hell, a hell of heaven."

—John Milton
(*Paradise Lost*, 1:254-255)

All the Dancing Birds

Auburn McCanta

Chapter One

Now here I am, a small flickering light, sputtering softly in my chair, shifting, winking on and off. I've been trying to think my way out of this paper bag of a morning, but so far, I've only come up with the notion that, somehow, my mind is structured slightly differently than it was yesterday.

I've turned oddly forgetful.

I'm consumed with the thought that insects—scurrying black ants—are busy chewing the log of my brain into sawdust, grinding tunnels into blind passageways. Maybe these little buggies are making holes where all my thoughts are falling, tumbling, down and down. Of course, I tell no one about my bugs, or that I'm chronically consumed with half-baked daily riddles. Today's perplexity is this: where did I place my little wallet with its ring and clip that holds my keys? I need them and they're gone. Vanished!

I'm going to be late for dinner at my daughter's house and here I am.

Stuck.

Certainly, I can't talk with anyone about this new mysterious life. Not now. Maybe never. Of course, I should call my daughter to explain why I'm late, but what could I say?

Just approaching my mid-fifties (with only a few gray hairs, I might note), a mother doesn't just casually mention she's suddenly and forevermore deteriorated into a frightful and incorrigible dunderhead. Certainly, it would be inappropriate to startle my children by blurting out, *there's nothing to worry about…your mother's just losing it, but that's not a problem, my dears.* Indeed, how could I explain that their mother has recently turned into a mess of sodden, tearful forgetfulness?

Of course, the day had started kindly, as they often do—cloudless and just sharp enough to outline the faint edge of my breath during the short walk down the drive to retrieve the morning newspaper. It was nice then: coffee, the *Sacramento Bee* and no cares other than the day's miserable headlines.

Then one after another, clouds rolled in overhead as if to call attention to the sudden, frantic search for my keys: drawers yanked open and pawed through, only to be left hanging open like mouths in mid-sentence, chair cushions flipped and left upended, even covers on the bed torn down, only to be left all higgledy-piggledy across the floor.

After two hours, I abandoned the hunt, still without finding what I most desperately needed.

My little wallet and my car keys are gone!

Now, as early afternoon overtakes me, I realize I've been sulking deep into the folds of my chair for the better part of the day, curled into the shape of a despondent question mark, grateful there was no one to witness my fretful search, my wild-eyed rummaging through every nook and cranny of the house.

Have you noticed how odd Lillie Claire has become? Such a question would certainly be appropriate, given this morning's cursing and crying.

Yes, the obvious response would be. *Odd. Very odd. That's the only proper word for it—odd.*

Only now do I realize how cleverly I've insulated myself from such hurtful comments and questions. It's been at least six months since I've laced up my tennies, thrown my purse strap across my shoulder, and wandered the six blocks to our neighborhood coffee shop with its deep, cozy chairs arranged like conversation nooks in a home. Once I relished strolling along Sacramento's tree-lined Midtown streets, popping into its eclectic shops or meeting friends for empanadas at *Tapa the World*, or even going a few blocks north on J Street for a plateful of spicy fries at *Hamburger Patty's*, but I've taken now to embracing the solitude of my own company. After spending an entire lunch with the name of a long-known friend bounding away from my grasp, leaving me terrified all through our meal that I might need to introduce her to someone, I decided to simply stay home.

From that day on, I answered every lovely invitation with an equally lovely declination. *I'd love to, but I promised my daughter…I think I'm coming down with something and I'd hate for you to catch it… My son's coming into town, you remember Bryan don't you?* Each excuse was layered with a smile and a promise for a rain check…*very soon, I promise.*

After a while, the phone gladly stopped ringing and (except for occasional outings with my children whose names are seared into my bones) I've simply stayed inside like a recluse, grateful to never again spend two hours with a dear friend's name rolling around like a worry stone in my mouth.

With effort, I pull myself up and shuffle toward the kitchen. Maybe a nice sandwich will mend this recent and persistent *oddness* I seem to have caught.

The cool of the refrigerator seems to snap me from today's funk. I pull out sliced luncheon ham, a bottle of dark, spicy mustard, half a loaf of bread, a tomato gone all soft in the head (much like me) and lettuce that should have been tossed days ago.

And there—beneath that wilted lettuce and alongside a watery cucumber left over from last Wednesday's riata dish—sit my little purse and keys, now all cold and slimy.

My wallet! My keys!

YOU LAUGH. You laugh when you find your wallet in the refrigerator. In the refrigerator crisper drawer, of all places. Your laughter is not so much funny-ha-ha laughter, but more like when a sound escapes in the cool of the kitchen and hangs in the air, illuminated by the refrigerator light. You've spent the morning frantically tearing the house apart, moving from room to room, frightening yourself with images of thieves in the night, gremlins under the bed. But it turns out you are the thief and the evidence rests cold and leathery damp in your small and grateful hand. Mystery solved.

I check inside the folds of my wallet for damage: I pull out my driver's license, a couple of credit cards, my library card, my medical ID and a few old dog-eared photos of my children, mugging and grinning for the camera. Although a bit cool, everything seems in order. Still attached to the outside is the removable clip that holds my car keys. I've got no idea—not one single thought—how I could have considered tucking my wallet and keys into the vegetable bin, under a well-wilted lettuce and half a decaying cucumber, instead of into my purse. Not a clue.

Here in the quiet of the kitchen, I'm struck with a roughened whirlwind of worry that ties my stomach into knots. Somehow I know that this growing forgetfulness—this heart-squeezing, gut-prickling, fearsome knowledge that yesterday I knew things and today I don't—is something I'd best keep hidden.

The phone rings. I absently answer. "Hah!" I say, picking at a small piece of slithery lettuce stubbornly stuck tight to a notch on my keys.

"Mom? Are you laughing? What's... what the hell's going on over there?"

Ah, my Allison. My daughter's voice is comfort food, like mashed potatoes drizzled over with cream gravy and crumbled sausage. She always manages to settle me by saying something very simple like, say, *hell*, or *oolong tea*. She makes me soft in the knees, the way she lingers over each vowel with her lips pursed into a kiss, while consonants tap against her teeth and throw themselves toward the back of her throat like the sound of someone skipping down a hallway.

I modulate my voice. "Oh, no. *No.* I'm sorry, honey, oh...of course not. I was just thinking about something else and the phone apparently caught me mid-thought."

"You were thinking of something else? Apparently? You were supposed to be here an hour ago and...well, hell...we were getting worried." My daughter sighs and recalibrates. "You realize dinner will be totally ruined because of you now."

"You should be nice to your mother," I say, carefully working my mouth to continue its level tone. "I represent your inheritance."

I smile at my small triumph.

A defensive pose is obviously rudimentary, but still seems more dignified than flapping about between my current moments of blustery panic and the more flat-lined despondency of this day.

"Be nice?" Allison retorts. "For all we knew you could have had an accident or…or something." I picture my daughter and how she's likely managed to make her lips look like little wavelets of concern, all the while causing me to suffer over those delicious vowels that continue to swirl and slide from her pouty mouth.

She bedevils me like that.

"You are coming, aren't you?"

"Of course," I say. Then I toss out a mere half-truth, hoping it's at least something good enough to turn the conversation around. "I know…I should have called. But my wallet and keys turned up missing this morning. Not to worry, though, sweetie. I just now found them and…wouldn't you know they were in the bottom of my purse all the time? I'm just on my way out the door now." My mouth puckers with the acerbity of the lie

"Go ahead and open the wine, if you haven't already," I say. "And I hope you have my favorite red this time."

I look out the kitchen window in time to see a robin flutter into a small Chinese pistache tree. The spindly tree, planted only last spring, barely managed to gasp and struggle its way through its first Sacramento summer—and it had been a hot one. Now it defiantly prances in the day's stiff breeze, its leaves turned red and stubborn against the cold as if it were fully grown and thick in the trunk. Its crimson leaves look like flying embers hot enough to burn the feathers of any bird foolish to rattle into its branches. I think of that robin, now swallowed up into the tree's center and, for the merest moment, my throat catches. Overhead, clouds are now forming into giant sculptures of dragons and angels, with fire-spitting dragons winning the day.

I am very, very close to bursting into tears.

"I've got red *and* white," Allison says, her round voice again pulling my clotted thoughts back into a threadbare semblance of normalcy. "Try to hurry, Mom. Seriously, dinner's almost ready."

Her voice becomes a papery whisper; she's cupped her hand around the phone. "I should warn you that Bryan's a bit grumpy, so be prepared." Then louder, she says, "So, I hope you get here before everything is totally overcooked."

In spite of her warning, I look forward to an evening with my children. Our conversations are always fierce and bombastic, punctuated here and there with squeals of brilliant laughter. Allison especially relishes egging things on toward heightened velocity, complete disruption. I preside over it all with a mother's presumed calm.

"I'm already out the door, dear. And don't worry," I say, raking my fingers like a comb through my hair. "I'll help when I get there." I think of my daughter hovering with uncertainty over a steaming pot of pasta, urging the water along, now and then poking a fork into a clump of swirling noodles.

"Just hurry up and get here," she says, "for, you know… the other thing."

"Oh, you mean Bryan? Well, of course, dear. I can't *wait* to see him." I make the first completely true and honest statement of our conversation. It's hard to locate the last time I've seen my boy.

My boy. My heart of hearts, my love of loves.

Allison makes a groaning noise. I can see that, once more, I shall oversee the friendly dissonance of my children; I'm delighted with the prospect.

We hang up and I decide to also hang up the last of my horrible day. After unclipping my car keys, I wipe my wallet clean from any remaining scent of lettuce and shove it into my purse. I give my face a fast swipe of lipstick and then hurry to the car. I pat the hood as I cross to the driver's door. "Good old paint," I say. "*You*, at least, decided not to crawl into the lettuce drawer."

Within a few minutes, I squeeze into an opening just large enough for my car on the ramp of eastbound Interstate 80, heading toward Fair Oaks. The sky stays busy shuffling clouds around and around until I feel nearly dizzy from the constant movement. In front of me, I see a long, dark line of rain; behind me, the sun works its way toward the horizon. I'm somewhere between the rain and the sun, firmly wedged into a lane of stop-and-go cars. I float along within a stream of sour-faced commuters.

The traffic is agonizingly slow, but my mind thankfully whirls with thoughts of my Allison—my first, and in some ways, my best. She is beautiful. Yummy. She is what I once was and I am what she will become. After thirty-two years, I still feel the astonishment of her birth, the moment of her exit from my body, the continued string of our connection. We share structure and cells and even the peculiarity of subtle mannerisms and vocalizations: the way we tilt our heads just slightly to the right when we puzzle over something; how the understructure of our speech is a composite blend of the drawling, warm butter drizzle of North Carolina painted over with a clipped northern California influence; the way we bite our lower lip when pensive or disquieted; the looping gestures we make with our hands.

We also share the odd quirk of our names. I am Lillie Claire Glidden. She is Allison Claire Colson. We laugh that our first, middle, and last names each are peppered with little ells. We call ourselves the La La La Girls and fall over our tongues trying to say our names three times quickly. We have yet to do so with success.

She's a beauty for certain, yet she breaks my heart. I still carry the disbelief that any man, most especially her former husband, would be foolish enough to leave such loveliness. I guess there's no accounting for taste, nor is there any guarantee that a woman's good looks make a compelling argument for marital longevity.

When I arrive forty-five long minutes later from what should have been a twenty-minute drive, Allison greets me with air kisses and waves me into the living room. I'd like to fall into her arms and have a good cry over my abysmal day and how now even her neighborhood appears slightly off kilter and out of perspective, as if someone has moved the street signs and rearranged all my landmarks. I decide instead that a nice glass of wine or two might set all my worries aside for the rest of the day. Allison's hands are comically pushed into man-sized, heavily padded oven mitts. Her cheeks are ruddy and moist from the effort of cooking.

"It took you *forever* to get here," she says, her lips pushed into a complicated pout.

"Friday traffic…you know how it gets around here. I hope you're not going to too much trouble." I try to keep the irony of my statement from showing in my voice.

"Oh, no. No trouble at all." She pushes at a wisp of fallen hair with one giant-mitted hand. The lock immediately falls again across her forehead. "Wait." Allison sniffs at the air. "Uh oh. I think…do you smell something burning?"

"Go. Not a problem," I say to her already retreating form.

I'm left to pour my own glass of wine, which, given the state of my day, suits me just fine. I serve myself an extra generous portion and then look for my son. He sits in the den, scowling at the television.

From the sound, I gather he's watching a basketball game, and from his demeanor, it's easy to conclude things aren't going well for his side.

But then again, my Bryan Ivan Glidden is of the sullen variety to begin with. He's been this way since the day he was born. Maybe he's just mad after discovering his initials—B. I. G.—spell a word he doesn't feel he measures up to according to the length of his own yardstick. Maybe he's angry because his sister, older by only one year and wild in the business of her own babyhood, stole me away from him for great long moments at a time. Perhaps he was simply a fumbling baby who grew to be a man of graceful charm and the confusion of such an unlikely juxtaposition filled him with constant sparks and clouds.

For whatever reason, Bryan has fussed at me from the first. My breasts were never tasty enough; my arms never comfort enough for his lusty lungs and kicking legs. He fumed and gyrated from the beginning and, from all indications, he is still eluded by the simple satisfaction of an ordinary day.

Still, in spite of his frowning eyebrows and lip biting, he is beautiful and I ache for the days when I could have pulled him to my lap, singing *Skidamarink a dinky dink, Skidamarink a doo*, which always made him clap and laugh and beg me to sing it again and again.

Bryan waves me in, barely taking his eyes from the game. I settle myself in a chair across from him. He jiggles his legs up and down, a habit born, I suppose, from always hurrying. Even seated in a comfortable chair, my son seems to run places without ever leaving. A defiant glass of yellow-white chardonnay (in direct opposition to my lovely, rich cabernet) rests cupped in his hand.

"Hi, sweetheart," I say. "Wow, it's good to see you."

"Hey, Mom. Good to see you too." He greets me without looking up from the game. The last light of the day crawls over his shoes.

I try again. "I'm so excited. Your sister tells me you're moving back to Sacramento."

That does it.

"Allison!" Bryan yells toward the direction of the kitchen. "She's such a butt," he says into his wine when she doesn't answer. "It's not a certainty…I'm still negotiating with the law firm."

"A law firm? How wonderful. In Sacramento?"

"Good God, Mom. Of course it's a law firm. I'm a *lawyer*."

"Don't be so cheeky with your mother, Bryan. I can only thank God that your *father* isn't alive to hear such language."

I watch my son's face fold inward for a brief moment and I know my words have stung like needles. A mother's words, especially when spoken through a well-puckered mouth, punctuated with narrowed eyes and a slight tilt of the head, carry more weight than any well-articulated swat.

"Oh, gosh, Mom, I didn't mean to be rude. I'm sorry," Bryan says, lowering his face. "I only meant—"

"I know what you meant, dear. It's just—"

"Well, still...I don't think it was Allison's call to spill my good-news beans." Bryan swirls his wine, then watches it settle back. "If she ever gets a job, I hope she'll give me the honor of jumping into the middle of her announcement."

"Allison would be the *first* to tell you she married well and divorced even better, so perhaps we'll need to wish for other good news for you to spill on behalf of your sister." I smile, but I'm not certain my point was received in the manner I intended.

"Right...I forgot her job is *shopping*. Not much to spill when her only source of world news is the Saturday Macy's ad."

I decide it's that nasty white wine that's constricted his mouth and soured his mood. I tip my head rightward and bestow a smile on my son, in spite of his fundamental arrogance. I wait until he can no longer stand my silence—another effective motherly tactic.

"Sorry again. I didn't mean to be rude. Not to you." Bryan leans his head in the direction of Allison, who's now fussing over the dinner table. "I *meant* to direct my rudeness to She-Who-Must-Not-Be-Ignored." Bryan raises his voice toward Allison, who is unsuccessfully trying to stand a narrow bouquet of dyed blue daisies within the neck of a too-large vessel.

"Whatever, Bryan," Allison says, giving up on the flowers and allowing them to flop in an ungainly clump down one side of the vase.

"Okay, kids," I say. "Let's not make my day worse than it's already been."

I stop myself before spilling my own secret-news beans about the recent state of my memory.

"No worries," Bryan says. "Anyway, I wanted to surprise you at dinner, but the deal is this...I'm negotiating with Brown and Sauter."

His mouth curls over the name of the law firm like a child screaming delight over a shining red bicycle on Christmas morning. "They've opened a spot to bring on a water guy like me, actually they've decided to start up an environmental department, and it looks like I'm their dude. It's a perfect fit and I'm really, *really* ready to move back here."

I clap my hands. "Oh, well, dear, that's wonderful news. Just wonderful!"

"Don't get excited yet. I probably won't know anything for at least a month."

"But still, it's wonderful. We'll *all* hold good thoughts for it." I point my voice toward the kitchen. "Won't we, Allison?" Returning to Bryan, I ask, "How does Katie feel? Is she excited?"

"I really couldn't say. I don't talk to her."

"You don't *talk* to her? Why on earth?"

"Mom, of course not. Why would I talk to Katie? We're through with all the haggling over who gets what, no kids to fight over, no designer dog to split down the middle. It's just a matter of toughing out California's stupid six month and one day waiting period for the divorce to be final. We're almost there, though...actually, the middle of next month."

"Divorce? *Divorce*? My God, Bryan. You never told me." My hands flutter across my lap like wounded sparrows shot from the sky. "How could you not tell me?"

"Of course I told you. We talked on the phone about it. You cried all over the place. Told me I was a jerk and I should try to work things out. How could you forget?"

"Oh, well...of course," I say, my eyes widening as if I were just caught being naughty. "No, actually...I just meant—"

YOU SEARCH. You search like a wild woman through every tangled memory you've ever had for something—anything—that reminds you of a significant conversation. You look into the deep of your wine, like it's a witch's gazing pool and think yourself crazy not to remember your son announcing the end of his five-year marriage. You run through the halls of your mind to whatever synapse or structure might hold the memory of a conversation so meaningful that it most likely stole your breath away and made you twist a hanky between your fingers for the sheer agony of it all. Your mind is mean. It has taken a moment from you—a huge moment—and in a bully's game of keep-away, it won't give it back. You hope your eyes don't make a clamor that would call attention to the wild foray going on inside your head. In the end, you lamely mutter an apology. Tears well in your eyes and you excuse yourself to the powder room before those too are discovered. You stand over the sink and berate the face you see in the mirror. When you've sufficiently recovered, you finish the evening with a half-frozen smile pasted to your face, all the while spreading vows throughout every nook and cranny of your mind to keep future diligence over your conversations. By the time you leave, your only issue is where—once again—you've placed your car keys.

On the way home, I make a wrong turn onto the freeway. I've headed toward Lake Tahoe, when I should have turned in the direction of San Francisco. Stupid. Silly. I realize I'm well far away from where I should be, but in all honesty, I could say that about myself in most everything these days. "My God, Lillie Claire," I say into the dark of my car. "What in the world is *wrong* with you?"

For the umpteenth time in one day, another sting of tears starts up behind my eyes. I've been tilted on my axis, only to be soundly dumped onto my sad and ridiculous chowderhead.

I correct my direction at the following off-ramp and then spend the next thirty minutes paying close attention to my hands, gripping them tightly to the wheel to keep them from making another wrong turn. I only find familiarity when I finally pull into my driveway. I turn off the ignition and sit wordlessly in the dark before asking my legs to tremble their way out of the car. I start toward the house, but stop, standing gawky and slew-footed in the middle of the drive.

For a brief moment, the day's clouds part like a ruffled, purple peek-a-boo skirt. I look up and whistle at a round and yellow moon.

The moon whistles back.

Chapter Two

I stand beside my bed, wondering if I should straighten the covers or crawl back in its downy softness. I run my hand over the sheets. I don't know when it was I decided lace-edged pink sheets would be my signature bedwear. I think it occurred during a shopping trip about a year after my Ivan died so suddenly that it took at least that long to stop expecting him home every night for supper. Even now, I'm still caught up improbably thinking I can hear him singing in the shower, or clanking dishes about in the kitchen, or humming some made-up ditty while spreading strawberry cream cheese over an onion bagel or pouring glasses of wine for dinner. Then I realize he's been gone ten years. Ten years!

It's odd I can't remember where I kicked off my shoes last night, but I can remember every moment of Ivan as if he were still here, sitting in the bedside chair pulling on his shoes, tucking his shirt down over his narrow belly and talking about some client's spreadsheet as if it were the most exciting literature ever written. I would be making the bed—the one that now has pink ruffled sheets, covered by a poplin rose-embellished quilt—nodding my head as if spreadsheets were the best thing since Poe's *Sonnet to Science*.

In those days, I would throw open the drapes, letting light flood every corner of the room to fall upon Ivan's papers like a glorious benediction. He would look up—appreciative. I never understood what he meant by that look, but I certainly understood the nuance of light and shadow. I studied it. I wrote of it, quizzed my students about it and made up rhymes for Bryan and Allison regarding it. We were a family enamored with light.

I keep the bedroom drapes tightly closed now. The rest of the house can fend for itself against the sun and clouds, but the bedroom has become mine alone and, without Ivan, it has no right to claim any light for itself. It's now a room of dark and shadow and I want it that way. I think, in fact, the room remembers Ivan as much as I do. It took me months before I could bring myself to vacuum away the outline of his footprints or clean his side of the bathroom vanity, and even longer before I could angrily pack away his clothing for charity, cursing every shirt and pair of pants for no longer wrapping themselves over his body. I hated his ties. The scent of his cologne made me cry until I threw up into the toilet. I recall one day sliding my bare feet into his leather lace-up shoes and walking through every room of the house before finally hugging them to my chest and then sending them off to the Goodwill. Perhaps there was another Ivan out there who needed his mostly beige slacks and ties to become a successful statistician and economist. Perhaps the world needed another settled and sedate financial man who played a guitar and sang and held his wife until the cows came home.

Two years after Ivan's death, I began stacking my books and papers on his side of the bed. It was like I was screaming to the Universe that if it had to take my beautiful fair-haired Ivan away, then the only proper person for that side of the bed was a man I called Mr. Literature. Of course, he would be dark and filled with the essence of Stephen King, Mary Shelley, Bram Stoker, and the very woeful Poe. It seemed only fitting.

I've since placed my books and papers where they belong. My days with Ivan are long past and I've grown to that acceptance. But, even now, I still spend several minutes a day recalling my husband's husky whisper in my ear, the scent of his morning hair, his hands pressed on my body.

Oh, God, those hands.

My memory of Ivan is most likely either larger or smaller than he was in his true life, but it doesn't matter. This is a widow's perfect memory and, whether any of it is true or not, it's a daily thing that helps get me standing on my morning feet. One day, I'll tell my children that for the past ten years, I've missed my husband, their father, and hated myself for not saving him from his suddenly failed heart. Not today, though.

Not today.

The backs of my hands are threaded through with bluish veins like small streams and tributaries across a crêpe paper landscape; light brown dots here and there mark me a woman who spent too much youthful time lolling in the sun. I turn my hands over and ponder the criss-crossed lines on each palm, the life lines, the heart paths. I think of the many times I ran my fingers across Ivan's palms, tracing every crease and marveling at the warmth radiating back at me. By the time he died, I had nearly memorized the placement of every line, every swirl and loop across the tip of each finger, the length and breadth of them.

Now I don't remember one detail of Ivan's hands and I hate myself for it.

I know what to do.

I go to my closet and pull down a cedar letter box from the upper shelf. It's where I keep my favorite poems and letters, all of which I've written and each of which is addressed to my children. I don't know why I keep them secreted away in my father's handcrafted box, when I could as easily share these dear little writings as they occur.

Still, I continue to add new letters and little scraps of thought. At least once a week, I sit at a small secretary's desk tucked into a corner in the living room. I select a piece of stationery—usually something flowered, occasionally a slip of gold-edged creamy paper I keep for special occasions. The paper is important because it's the first impression and sets the tone for the words I'll place on it. Many of the older notes are undated, but since I've noticed little memory dings creeping along the edge of my thoughts, I've started adding the date (provided I can figure it out, of course).

I started writing when it occurred to me that children never really know their mothers: first they're too young; then they're so busy dividing and branching out into the person they will soon become, their ears are closed to any wisdom a mother might offer.

Then they leave.

And thus I write.

The thought that my children will find these poems and letters after I'm gone is somehow pleasant to me. I picture the mouths of my very grown-up babies (surely saddened by my death) slowly tilting upward as they read my letters, my poems. *Look at this,* one will say to the other. *This is so lovely,* the other will say. *I didn't know this about Mom. Here, read this one.* On they will go, together, like when they were children and we would take discovery walks through the arboretum or the zoo, our hands twined together like slender twisted cords, little *oohs* escaping our lips because we were seeing the world's wonderment. They will discover me. I won't be lost.

I will be the day's wonderment.

I open the box and pull out an early letter, hoping it can help me remember my Ivan's hands. I unfold the paper like one would open the wings of an origami bird, careful to retain the paper's memory of each crease, every fold.

The closet is unusually large for a mid-century house—a walk-in, actually, that may have served initially as a baby's cradle nook or a small reading corner. It was Ivan who transformed the nook into a closet; I can still see a slight ridge where his hammer missed its mark, hitting the wall. It looked like a smile to me and I told Ivan to leave it. It's been this way since.

The size of the closet allows me plenty of room to stand in its center with all my blouses and skirts and slacks hanging loosely on three sides, like narrow, wrinkled people. There's floor-to-ceiling shelving for shoes and folded items on each side of the entry door, a naked bulb light overhead with a pull chain instead of a wall switch.

I begin to read; it takes a while until I fall into the rhythm of my words. I follow the words until the end, and then I read the letter twice more, until its meaning, its memory, soaks deeply into my skin and remembrance falls over my head like soft rain.

My dear children:

I wish you could have seen this morning's sun as I saw it. I love the way it comes into my room in the early mornings, sliding up over my body and into my sleeping mouth like it's the first meal of my day. Then it opens my eyes and lets me love it or curse it, depending on how well I slept the night before. This morning I loved the light, because it woke me to thoughts of you, my dear children.

You're now so grown and adult, it hardly seems fitting to call you children; still, I'll always see the child in you each, in spite of your well-grown bodies and faces. As odd as it sounds, I wish you could know me, as well, for the child I once was. Maybe someday we can travel to the house where I grew up with my Ma and Pa (your MeeMaw and PaaPaw).

I could show you North Carolina—my cradle of green— and how its trees are tall and straight and slim like me. I could show you how I walked, swinging a bucket of frogs at the end of my young arm. You would laugh, of course. We could sway within the languid rhythm of the local dialect, slow and dreamy like a sultry summer's day, every word thick with sweet tea and milk biscuits. We could eat grits and eggs for breakfast and pop fried okra into our lunchtime mouths. For our evening meal, we'd have Southern fried chicken with collard greens cooked up on the side, biscuits with cream gravy, and another side of corn, fresh from the cob. A berry pie would wait for us on the sideboard and a thin dog would skitter around the edge of the table, wagging its tail to the rhythm of our conversation.

Then we could walk across the yard, with its clay soil, deep and rich like the layers of one's soul. I'd have you dig your fingers into that hard Carolina clay, textured and striated with history, so you could hold it in your hands. I'd show you how I'm filled with layer upon layer of pine dust, folk music, and ancient yarns, all evoked from atop a porch on a Sunday afternoon.

I could show you the precise spot where the blood of our people soaked into the earth. I know where it is because one day, your PaaPaw dug a deep hole in the yard, just beyond the house and back of Ma's clothesline. He wanted me to see the colors that lay deep within the Carolina clay. He told me how the ground carried deep within its folded layers the hardened gray of its soldiers' uniforms, the red of the blood shed on its land in battles you will never understand for things that are now long different.

Yes. I'd especially show you the dirt. We'd dig our own hole so you could see for yourselves the colors and lessons of history and Southern courtesy far beneath the surface of what you see. You could scuff your feet over the place where our family lived and drop your spittle onto it. You could stand over the wetness and watch it slowly seep in to mix with the fluid of our people. Your people.

There is mystery in watching how the earth accepts the gift of moisture from someone's spit.

I wish I could show you, but we're probably too old for spitting now.

With all my love,
Your Mother

When I'm finished, when I'm tenderly turned within the melancholy of this memory, I refold the letter to its original crease and return it to the cedar box. I didn't find what I was looking for (something about Ivan's hands, I think). I think again about the moment of discovery when one of my children—probably Allison who is always rather snoopy—will pull down her PaaPaw's cedar box from the shelf and find my poems and letters tucked dearly inside.

And now, lifting the box back to its place on the shelf, I realize I've found another and even more ingenious use for my letters, a present and highly purposeful use: I shall learn once again of myself.

I know I'm the one who sat at my little writing desk, the one who selected a piece of stationery, flowered or plain, depending on my mood or the light falling across my desk. I know I'm the one who then wrote thoughts and poems and little stories across each page, all in my scrawling hand. Still, it seems now that someone else captured my essence—a stranger, someone with perfect memory and an organized mind.

An apologist for my side of things.

I smile. Tomorrow I'll look for something about Ivan's hands, if only I remember.

"Do try to remember what you're doing, you silly, silly woman," I say, softly closing the closet door behind me.

Chapter Three

I wake this morning, as always, with the sun hugging my body, but once again I'm visited by the thought that something is terribly wrong with me. Again, I'm puzzled.

I peel away my tangled blankets, unclasping the sun from my arms, my legs, my rumpled face. I feel my mind disengage from the night and move into another agonizing wakefulness. I suppose if someone lived with me, they wouldn't notice any difference at all. Still, I notice. I'm moody. I try to think my way to my feet, but a new fractured sense leaves me befuddled with the distance between my feet and the floor.

The floor doesn't look right.

"Come on, Lillie Claire," I say into the quiet of the morning house. "Let's get on with the...the—"

I'm suddenly at odds with a word that should be familiar; a word that should easily spring to mind, but now makes me search for it like I'm a common beggar. There are blank spots and spreading holes where once my mind was seamless and fluid; the movement from thought to thought now comes only with effort, in spurts and spasms.

"Program," I say at last. "Let's get on with the *program*."

In spite of locating my missing word, I nevertheless seem to have allowed my memory gene to slip from my hand, letting it clatter in noisy shards across the floor. The proof is in unexpected moments when my mind turns suddenly dark and empty, like the momentary blank television screen between the end of a commercial and the start of the next program. Sometimes it's only a fleeting space, but other times the black screen in my mind makes me wonder if I've gone off the air for good. Sometimes I roll my eyes upward toward a surprisingly flaccid brain, waiting and waiting for whatever I'm trying to recall. I increasingly find myself in little arguments with books, repeatedly reading even small passages because I get lost in loops of thought that refuse to leave me alone. I forget a new person's name as soon as it's given to me and—just yesterday—I turned my car again the wrong direction on a familiar road.

I find daily regret and annoyance for every narrow misstep, every teensy moment of omission. I often lose my way. I forget where I parked my car only to fight tears while I wander up and down the parking aisles, clicking my remote every few seconds, hoping I'll hear a friendly answering chirp. Everyday things feel shifted from their normal place.

I'm now even befuddled by my cell phone, which coincidentally went missing yesterday, adding to my growing list of daily mysteries. All day I wondered where it could be, with its dead battery and its increasingly confusing buttons and mechanisms. I found it only by accident, stuffed into one of my socks at the back of the sock drawer.

Naturally, I hide these small forgetful moments, but today, even the behavior of hiding deficiencies serves to disorient me.

My skin chafes against the morning and I don't know what to do to make it better.

I shuffle through the process of making coffee, all the while wildly calling some semblance of happiness to me like one would whistle over a lively little dog. The kitchen is silent except for the gurgling of the coffeemaker. At last, I decide I like the familiar hug of the sun as it slides through the kitchen curtains to wrap itself around my shoulders.

Good old sun.

I drink a second cup of coffee while I make a scrambled egg and a piece of toast, which I accidentally burn because I can no longer figure out the workings of a toaster I've known for five years.

After breakfast, I change from my pajamas to a pair of khaki slacks and a yellow shirt. The shirt is long and bright and fluttery like a flag on a breezy day. It's my favorite because of its cheerfulness and the indulgent way I feel when I slide my arms into its crisp sleeves the color of a canary's wings.

It's my lucky shirt!

The lucky shirt does the trick. My day carries on and I carry on, and at last, happiness is wrapped about my body like a bright yellow banner flowing into the day.

I smile and people smile in return, which is amazing, especially walking through the grocery store, as I do now. Most people stay set to their business in the store, pushing carts and pulling items from the shelf, stopping to read the label, or placing the item directly in their cart before they push on ahead to their next stop. Today, however, in spite of everyone's bustle, people smile at me as if I'm altogether acceptable.

I smile back.

I know it must be my brilliant yellow shirt that causes them to look up from their grocery lists and their hurried feet in time to notice me.

To smile.

I love the grocery store, with its scents and colors and especially its freezer aisle that cools me to my bone. I read my shopping list and gather things into my basket.

In the produce department, I pick out a bunch of slender asparagus, a head of romaine, some Roma tomatoes, and a couple of sturdy cucumbers. Then along the meat aisle, I browse until I find two little lamb chops that won't ruin my budget. I use my list carefully, but still extra items appear in my cart: a bag of chips and a bottle of chocolate sauce, a four-pack of yellow bug lights, a little travel packet of assorted threads and needles. I don't need these items, but they catch my eye and I'm powerless to resist.

By the time I reach the checkout counter, I've circled the store several times. My basket is filled with boxes and cans, three bunches of bananas, a bag of blood oranges, clumps of organic broccoli rubber banded together like a bride's bouquet, several chuck roasts and two large packages of frozen chicken tenders, bags and bags of pinto beans and four, maybe five packages of angel hair pasta. There are three tall, white pillar candles I'm sure I'll use someday, a red plastic spatula because I can't remember if I have a spatula at home and certainly I might need one of those, three bottles of my favorite shampoo because I don't want to run out, two or maybe four air fresheners, five bottles of Ménage à Trois red table wine, and a large box of biscuits for the neighbor's dog.

My small list is gone, fluttered from my fingers somewhere along the way, and without its guidance, I find myself now with a basket brimming with variety and color, shapes and textures. Just before selecting a checkout lane, I toss in a fresh bouquet of red and white spider chrysanthemums. My basket is magnificently filled and I'm dazed with all I've done.

The checkout girl smiles at me; I beam back at her.

We're both wearing yellow, which makes my lips pull into a wide display of happiness for us both.

We are happy in yellow.

She runs my items through the scanner while we chat about the weather and how she's hoping to get off work early today. As we talk, she passes item after item through her agile hands. A young man with long wisps of blonde hair floating just over his upper lip loads my things into bag after bag. He smiles and chats along with us. All around are the high-pitched beeps of electronic scanners and the idle chatter of people. I'm nearly frantic with joy because of all the activity; I hold onto the edge of the counter to steady myself. When the last item is accounted for, the smiling, chatting, dizzying checkout girl, who is wearing yellow just like me, gives me my total.

Three hundred twenty-three dollars and sixty-five cents.

YOU HEAR. You hear the amount of your purchase and you're stunned with the figure. Three hundred twenty-three dollars and sixty-five cents! Your face becomes a frozen smile. You don't know what else to do but pull your checkbook and a pen from your purse and place them on the little check-writing stand, all the while vowing in your head to forever be more watchful over your purchases. All around you, scanners are beeping and people are talking and the wheels of shopping carts are making tiny scraping noises across the floor. You hear it all, but the noises blur together like wind howling across the leaves of a tree. You look at your checkbook and none of the blank lines make sense. You're confused by the ordinary and the more you force your hand to cooperate, the more addled you become. You take a deep breath and try once more to begin a simple task you've done so many hundreds of times. Your hand hovers. The wind howls. Finally, you look up and ask the checkout girl what day it is. She tells you it's Wednesday and you write Wednesday on the upper right line. You ask her again for the amount and she tells you. You start to write the number and realize halfway through that you need to ask again. A number so long is just not sticking. The cashier tells you one more time and a lull in the wind lets your ears remember the number long enough for your forgetful hand to finish its task. At last, you write your check and hope to goodness it's in proper order. You leave the store with your packages and your yellow shirt waving behind you like a flag on a breezy day. You leave, knowing for certain you will never tell a living soul what has just occurred.

I drive home with my bags and bags of groceries. Tucked inside each bag is the gathering knowledge that I've not only spent a frightful amount of money, but I've also added another secret to my growing list of concealments. My beautiful yellow shirt has failed me and, from this moment forward, it is no longer my lucky shirt. I look at the drape of it over my lap, wondering how long it might take to catch fire if I should hold a match to the corner of its hem.

By the time I'm home, I forget about burning my disloyal shirt and, rather, concentrate on pulling bag after bag out of the trunk to carry into the kitchen.

It's a wearisome task.

I fill the pantry and refrigerator with cans and bottles and, after I empty each bag, I fold the sack and slide it into the space between the refrigerator and the wall. When I'm done, I have an impressive paper tower reminder of the morning's adventure.

The day fritters on. Soon, I find myself in room after room, wondering whatever I should be doing. As early evening comes, I decide to put on my lounging gown to watch the local news. I'm just settled into the depths of my chair when the doorbell rings.

I open the door to find my lovely Allison on the other side.

"Mom, you're not ready!"

"Ready?" A small tic of something puzzling flirts with my left eye.

"It's dinner night for the La La La Girls." Allison sashays into the living room, plopping her purse on the coffee table. "Better get to it, chop-chop. I thought we'd do Chinese tonight."

"Perfect," I say, knowing my next sentence will be yet one more lie to tie onto the great string of lies I have already told over recent months. "Of course I didn't forget our Wednesday dinner." I say this newest untruth easily, without hesitation or even a pinch of regret. I go on with my whopping fib. "I was just about to get dressed," I say, smiling like a black-hearted weaver of tales.

Before Allison has a chance to figure out my deception, I run to my bedroom and grab my black pants outfit from the closet. I dress quickly and then find a hole in all the sticky notes I've pasted on the bathroom mirror. There must be fifty little rectangles of yellow paper stuck to the mirror, each note holding reminders written in my scrawling hand. I peer through the one available spot to stick my face and slide on my lipstick.

Written upon each little piece of paper are the same words: *Don't forget about Wednesday.*

I vow future efficiency and write a note to buy more sticky notes. I poke it in the only available hole.

Breathlessly, I rush back to the living room where Allison has been thumbing through the latest *People* magazine she apparently brought with her. For a few moments, we bicker about who will drive. In the end, I win. My car, although slightly older and less prestigious than Allison's bronze Lexus convertible, contains the one thing that always sways my daughter—it has satellite radio, which means we can listen to music without commercial interruption.

I drive to our favorite Chinese restaurant, *The Bamboo Café*, my ears stinging with some classic rock Allison has dialed in. I'm sure the pounding rhythm disrupts my natural heartbeat; the volume makes my fragile eardrums vibrate in protest. The drive takes only a few minutes, still I'm relieved when we pull into a parking spot.

Inside, we settle into a booth and order beverages while we look over the menu. Soon, I'm sipping a glass of plum wine, which finally settles my thumping heart and allows me to take in the loveliness and liveliness of my daughter. She roars through a glass of *Tsing Tao*, waving to the waitress for one more, each.

"So, Mom, I was thinking," Allison says, her voice round and husky as she takes a breath from her beer. "What would you say about going to Canada this summer?"

Chapter Four

Allison looks at me with wide-as-an-ocean eyes that are never refused. I wonder if that could be one reason why she's now divorced. An uncompromising woman rarely fits for long within the confining curve of an ungenerous man's hands.

To be fair, I recall Jim Colson was generous with his money, but stingy with the one thing Allison needed from him—devout attention to her *every* whim. Outwardly, she was the caricature of a successful older man's wife: young, beautiful, blonde, and seemingly aloof. But Allison possessed the one thing that belies a trophy wife—she loved him fiercely and without compromise.

By all accounts, when she discovered his playful notions with other women, she handled the situation with her chin in the defiant pose of one not to be discarded. In the end (and most likely because of that pointedly strong chin), he left her with a large settlement that nevertheless did nothing to restore her innocence or trust.

I suppose it was during the tumult of Allison's divorce when we silently agreed to cast off our mother-daughter roles and strike up a friendship with our weekly La La La dinners and tight-as-twins secret language. Perhaps I should have kept my distance from such nonsensical girly behavior, but a mother's compulsion to fix her children's boo-boos doesn't necessarily end when they're grown.

During Allison's unfortunate divorce, our conversations changed;

we collapsed the difference in our ages and began to wildly regard each other as joyful, newfound friends. I lifted my daughter up as my colleague with the altruistic purpose of easing her shame. She, in turn, sacrificed for herself whatever motherly wisdom I might have provided, while replacing it with a giggly girlfriend. I thought our new arrangement might be only temporary, but it lingered and stuck.

It works for us.

Since my widowhood and Allison's divorce, we've made it our habit to take unusual vacations together; the distraction of obscure places is as much a goal as the destination. One year we cruised through the Panama Canal. Another, the Suez. We've been to Australia and China and to falling-down, rattle-trap castles in Ireland. Once we stayed in a yurt in Oregon for a week. For all her beauty and money, my Allison is generous and adventuresome. Her Jim was a fool.

The sound of Allison's delicious, round voice now floats across the table. "Nootka Sound. Isn't that a gorgeous name ... Nootka?" She impossibly elongates the word until it sounds like, *Nooooot-kaah.* "They have this really amazing floating fishing lodge there," she says, her eyes flaming wild with possibility. Her hands fly through the air and her voice trills in my ears with its high and delightfully varied pitches and tones. "You can fish for Chinook and Coho salmon, snapper, ling cod ... right out of your room if you want. Or you can take a guided fishing trip out into this totally huge and wild water where pods of killer whales steal the fish clean off your line as you reel in. I read it on the Internet. Isn't it incredible?"

"Oh, I don't know...fishing?" I ask. "La La La Girls in a *fishing* lodge? With fishermen? And killer whales? I'm not sure which species would cause more trouble."

Allison laughs and then narrows her eyes. "C'mon, Mom, just think of it. You swoop in on a float plane and if the fish disappear in one area, they simply float you, lodge and all, to another part of the lake. Wouldn't that be amazing?"

"Amazing," I say. "But doesn't it occur to you that falling from the sky in a plane without, God forbid, wheels, just to land at a remote fishing lodge circled by killer whales *might* be a little more than this old woman can handle?"

"Mom, you are *not* old. In fact, you'll probably get more heads turned by those old fishermen than I will."

"Allison, how you talk. I'm still your moth—"

I start to argue my case, but suddenly my mouth stops working. I'm struck with the surprising thought that brilliant words are dancing in my mind, yet they can't seem to take that simple stroll into my mouth. Dinner arrives and I'm saved from the fractured sense of being a sudden mute. I pick at my meal, all the while trying to locate familiar language, known words, simple thoughts. I'm swimming through dark, slender waters of memory, wondering if I'd ever learned to swim in the first place.

Thankfully, Allison chatters on about her idea to spend a week on a remote Canadian lake. She doesn't notice my quiet flailing, drowning, sinking, which makes me wonder what sort of mother I am to be grateful for her daughter's inattentiveness.

By the end of dinner, my thoughts finally swoop back to me like Allison's float plane; my mouth is once more filled with generous words and unsparing thought.

I brighten. "I guess it could be fun. All right, then, let's give that Nootka place some thought. See if you can get some brochures, and I'll see if my closet holds any come-hither fishing attire to drive those old lodge boys crazy." Allison laughs.

We walk to the car, hand-in-hand, our heads swooning with wine and beer and thoughts of burly fishermen, black and white orcas, and pontoon-clad float planes, lifting, lifting, lifting us.

YOU SMILE. You smile at your daughter as you walk across the parking lot, plastic bags filled with cartons of leftover Chinese food dangling loosely from your hands. Those three small glasses of red wine now color the corners of your lips, making them seem to smile even when your lips have gone flat. You chat to your daughter in chirpy, breathless words, your hair swinging in the wind like the bags in your hands. You place the food on the roof of your car while you unlock the doors. You slide in and buckle up, your lips all the while broadly grinning. You start the engine and press the accelerator like you know what you're doing. You do. You know exactly what you're doing. Then you look in your rearview mirror and you see your bags of food spilled onto the ground behind you—your daughter standing over the mess, her face spilled into the perplexity of having been forgotten.

Suddenly, you don't know how you could cause so many things to crash and spill in such a very, very short time.

I sheepishly drive back and help Allison scoop up ruptured boxes of egg foo yung and gravy, broccoli beef, Chef's special spicy chicken, and dollops of steamed and fried rice. We squat before the headlights of my car, scooping and laughing. We fuss over the spoiled food and the ridiculous sight of it all. At some point, we stop laughing while the silence of embarrassment falls over us like heavy dark shawls across our shoulders. There are no words for a mother who drives away without her daughter or for the daughter who's had to then stoop and pick up the evidence of her mother's unseemly forgetfulness.

I hold a constrained and confused posture on the drive home. When we arrive, Allison walks me to the door and pecks my cheek. Her kiss feels abrupt, as if I should apologize again and again for my terrible slight. I enter the clamorous sounds of an old house that clicks and drips and creaks across my ears. Sadly, the house seems to have forgotten its manners as it chatters on and on in every room.

The house should know I need for it to be quiet just now.

Still unnerved by my unfortunate parking lot performance, I wander to the closet with the intention of consulting my cedar box. It's my new source of comfort and I plan to let it work its magic. I pluck out a random letter as one would pull a tarot card from a Gypsy's deck of symbols.

I select my card and read my past.

My Children:

If I tell you anything at all, I should tell you about poetry. Your MeeMaw taught me about poetry before I knew much of anything else. Of course, it was surprising that a Southern wife of a sawmill worker would have such interest—to teach her small child about poetry—but nonetheless, that was what your MeeMaw did.

Every afternoon we sat on the porch with books spread open like birds' wings in full flight, flashing across an endless sky of words. We read out loud, counting meter and foot, traveling worlds we knew we would never see unless we walked on the legs of poetry. I learned over heat-soaked summer afternoons that, even in its most subtle mood, a work of poetry often walks in rhythm, tapping its words out in some sort of cadence and beat.

Poetry's legs are meant for walking, for dancing—but mostly, poetry is for traveling—to other places, other worlds. To other thoughts and imaginations.

Nearly every day, we sat on the porch, reading sonnets and free verse from the old masters and lighthearted rhymes from the moderns. We marveled over the bravery of every haiku poet and made up our own laughable alphabet poems. With every piece, Ma made me carefully count out each line. Even to this day, before I can befriend a work of poetry, I must study the way it walks, or how it dances across the floor, or if it has the strength to push my heart from here to there.

Poetry isn't like a brother or sister you grow up with and you know their mood simply by the way they drop down into the chair next to you, or laugh with you, or poke at the backside of your arm with their knuckles. No. Every work of poetry is a stranger until you discover its ways. Its benevolence or its malice. Ma once told me that you can never go off with a stranger and expect you'll be brought safely back home. She said it's the same with poetry. You have to know about its character before you can go walking off with it.

I don't know why I never taught you these vital truths. In defense, maybe it is that poets are sadly more comfortable sliding words onto paper, rather than just talking things over like normal folks.

Of course, I struggled over Ma's books, but she sat next to me every day, her arm about my shoulder, guiding me through grand passages of words and thought from her beloved masters. Ma was diligent and urgent in teaching me the language of adults.

Ma's eyes gave her no choice but to be industrious in her lessons; day by day, they dimmed, moving her deeper into a widening swath of darkness.

The doctor said nothing could be done. Ma seemed brave about it and Pa wouldn't speak of it, but now and then I saw her rubbing her eyes, trying to force sight into them with all the panic of the newly blind who walk with their arms extended awkwardly in front of their bodies, clutching at the sky for some sort of bearing.

Ma's only solution was to make me her eyes; at nine years old, I held books in my lap by the likes of William Faulkner and James Joyce, George Moses Horton and Eudora Welty. T. S. Elliott, Mark Twain, John Milton and even Edgar Alan Poe. Southern writers, all—except, of course, Joyce and Milton. Still, Ma said Joyce counted because he was Irish and the South was populated with the hardscrabble Irish, and Milton counted because he was as much a Southern gentleman as any, even though he was nearly older than God and had never spent a lick of time in the South. Still, Ma loved John Milton the most because God (whom she said was only minutes older than Milton) had struck him blind just like God had done to her.

Although we read whatever the traveling library had to offer, Ma mostly loved poetry. She said poetry was the most truthful writing of all words because it takes a brave pen to say what the lips don't have the courage to utter.

Until I found my own brave pen and the comfort of contemporary poetry, I thought much of the poetry we read was strident and unforgiving with its hemmed-in structure and unrelenting rules. Still, I had to admire Shakespeare and Milton, along with others who wrote blank verse with such sparkling, frightening words. Within a few lines, my heart would fall into a poem's rhythm. I was amazed that entire stories could be confined within a fence of ten syllables per line, and yet I was captured by words that seemed like pointed stones meant to pierce the skin and strike the heart.

Even before I knew the technique of scansion and marking accents that show the stressed syllables in each line, I knew that unrhymed blank verse lines, each written all in the same meter, were well more than a simple de-*dum*, de-*dum*, de-*dum* , just as my heart knew it was immensely greater than its own iambic lub-*dub*, lub-*dub*, lub-*dub*.

Of course, the sonnets are another story.

I'll leave that discussion for a different letter because sonnets need a long, unclouded afternoon and a bottle of good wine to get through all their intricacies.

All my love,
Mother

P. S. With all this talk of poetry, I'm inspired to start a sonnet especially for you. Wish me luck with that!

My letter works to distract from the way this day has surged in waves of ups and downs. Now I think only of Ma and how I wish she could have known my Allison and Bryan when they were children, wild as waves whipping up over the shore. How she would have smiled over them, pulling them into the folds of her apron, calming them inside her smiles with the scent of flour and lemon that was always deep within the cloth of that apron.

She would have patted their heads and smoothed their hair with hands that smelled of flour and lemon, just like her apron. She would have loved them dearly and carried on with them as she did with me. Most importantly, she would have sat them down with her beloved writers who were always so deeply entwined within every conversation on her Southern porch.

I wonder if after all these years, heaven placed Ma in my closet so I could read of her now, holding a letter to my breast, rocking it like Ma once rocked me.

I wonder if it's my delicacy, my stupid, stupid delicacy that turns me over and shakes me out like salt and light across the polished floorboards of this old house.

This stupid, stupid delicate, polished body.

What I wouldn't give right now for Ma to pull me into the folds of her apron with her hands scented with pie dough and squeezed lemon, in the midst of my pity and fright, to quietly hold me there until my rolling mind lies flat and emptied from all this catapulting misery. But I roll on.

And I roll on.

Chapter Five

I'm clever. So deliciously clever!

I've discovered that sticky notes can be expanded far beyond the bathroom mirror and refrigerator door. My use of them is genius. I've taken now to carrying a pad of these little ingenious papers in my pocket, along with a ballpoint pen, and when I think to do something in another room, I write a note about it before going there. Then I simply stick the little snippet of paper to the top of my thumb.

If I remember to look at my hand when I reach my destination, I consider it a decidedly good trip.

I invite my children for dinner, confident that an array of sticky notes placed in strategic points will serve as little yellow squares of grace and mercy.

Yes, I'm surely a genius.

I smile broadly as I answer the door and I continue to smile as I pour generous glasses of wine—lighter fluid-flavored Chardonnay for Bryan (the traitor) and a rich-noted, chocolate and cherry cabernet, of course, for Allison and me.

We smile and clink glasses to the day.

Bryan looks at me with eyes the color of blue ice. They are beautiful and I nearly tell him so. I think better of it, though, managing to stay close-lipped about his never-ending loveliness. A mother shouldn't disrupt the manliness of her son, even when his hands—oh, those hands that seemed only yesterday to be colored brown with mud and boyishness—are now cupped around a glass of wine and cheerfulness.

"I can't believe you drove off and left Allison in the parking lot last week," he says to me, grinning and winking with those glacial blue eyes that, within the last couple of years seem to have developed tiny cracks around their edges. "That is so wickedly clever of you, Mom. I couldn't have done better myself."

"Be nice, Bryan," Allison says, wrinkling her eyes. "It was just an accident."

"Accident, my left foot," Bryan says, winking again at me. "I only wish I could've been there to see your face when Mom drove off without you."

Bryan is in Sacramento for his final go-round of interviews and I'm fixing dinner for the three of us—my Southern spaghetti, which means a full half-cup of Parmesan cheese, just as much wine in me as in the sauce, and a good number of shakes of Louisiana hot sauce for emphasis.

The kitchen is in the front, painted soft yellow, next to the formal dining and living rooms with their neutral walls, and wholly separated from the cozy family room (with its one shocking burgundy wall that a friend talked me into and which I no longer have the energy to change). The family room looks out onto the expanse of the backyard that still shows off my Ivan's gardening prowess. The layout is common in the style of this midtown Sacramento craftsman house. Certainly, the kitchen is small and separated from the bustle of the rest of the house, but I'm content while cooking to merely pop my head out now and then to ask how things are doing back there.

Sometimes I wish for a cozy, more modern great room and open kitchen arrangement, but this house is comfortably large and its walls are filled with years of memories and history. I wouldn't give up my house for the world. This is where my Ivan and I lived; this is where we grew our children, with the occasional bowl of lazy goldfish or cage of musky-scented gerbils; where the children wrote their initials in a newly poured concrete patio with delighted little fingers; where we loved and laughed and, on the odd occasion, banged doors and words about some trifling disagreement.

This is where Ivan's prized wisteria still spends lazy summers leaning its arms over the fence as if it's in conversation with the back neighbors. This is a house of spilled grape juice and crayoned wall drawings, a house filled with the aromas of Monday laundry and Sunday chicken. It's my home. I won't be persuaded to abandon its history by either an unfortunate kitchen configuration or the number of steps it takes to travel from one end to the other.

It's my home.

"All right, you two," I say. "I suppose I'd better get my Southern spaghetti on the table soon. When you get busy producing some progeny for me, perhaps I'll pass on my secret recipe, maybe I'll even turn over my special trick for perfect greens. But until I see grandchildren, I'm not letting loose of a thing."

I leave my children, smiling to myself that I've expanded my use of sticky notes to a great amount of my kitchen work.

Today, quite cleverly, I've written out the parts of my recipe steps on a series of sticky notes and, once in the solitude of the kitchen, I shall place each note in order like little yellow ducks waddling one after another down the path of my left arm. As I finish each instruction, I will remove the appropriate paper until my arm is clean and the recipe is done. Wherever I am, I have only to look down to find my next step.

Yes. What a clever girl I am!

I tie on a crisp apron and line my Southern spaghetti recipe stickies along my arm. Before I start cooking, I congratulate my efficiency with an extra sip of red. The kitchen is warm and the wine tastes good.

I hear the laughter of my children from the family room. This is a moment to be recorded in heaven's book of good days. I top off my glass with a bit of cooking wine and begin the first steps of my recipe.

With the stove on, the kitchen heats up quickly. Little beadlets of moisture spring to my skin; my apron sags like a wilted flower tied to my waist. It's the middle of July on a spotless and sparkling Sacramento day. The outside temperature has spiked to 104 degrees and, in spite of this old house's version of central air conditioning, it seems the kitchen isn't far behind the outside heat. I push my melting hair away from my eyes as I stir my sauce and wait for a large pot of water to come to a proper boil for the noodles. I turn on the oven for the garlic bread. My hair falls again and I rub my arm across my steamy forehead. I take another sip of wine and wish the heat away from the day.

I cook. I sip. I cook. I wipe my face with my arm.

I disappear in the heat.

Sometime later (I don't know how long), I find my feet rocking an endless side-to-side two-step in the middle of the kitchen; all my stickies missing from my arm, water nearly boiled dry, the oven practically cavitating from its burning heat, and spaghetti sauce blooping from its pot like spiking red lava.

I'm screaming.

I don't know what to say when my children run to the kitchen and shake me to my senses. I see them turning off the stove and oven, looking at each other with startled eyes and great puzzlement.

I settle under their calming words, but nevertheless, I know my months of lies have been discovered. Most sadly, though, I don't know how I could be so vastly and forever lost without ever having left my soft yellow kitchen.

Chapter Six

I'm in a room that smells of rubber and paper and a thousand dying dreams.

My chair is rigid and cold.

I sit across from a small, young woman with a name tag that reads, *Bridget Ellison, M.D.* When she entered the room, she had with her a large manila folder tucked under one arm. Now she has placed her hands over the folder like it contains a secret that needs careful guarding. My name is printed boldly on the side tab.

Obviously, there has been a mistake.

Bridget Ellison, M.D., is smiling and already I don't like her.

She talks about the heat of August and how she loves the color of my hair.

I struggle to keep up with her pleasantries because my mind is crowded with every man and woman who has ever had their memory questioned.

I'm here only because I had a little kitchen argument with a pot of spaghetti sauce and a few sticky notes. Oh, and the oven.

My beloved Bryan, my pragmatic, leg-jiggling, lawerly Bryan, has now dragged me to see a doctor. Not only that, he seems to be in cahoots with her.

I'm not sure I like him today.

As the pleasantries continue, I discover this is not just any plain doctor. No. I sit across the table from a neurologist who, in spite of her credentials, appears about twelve years old and who does a decidedly poor job of making small talk. Little Bridget Ellison, M.D., indeed!

She is obviously not from the South.

Bryan sits in a chair by the door, his arms folded across his chest. His face is severe with its attorney-in-charge look. I'm not impressed. I am, in fact, miffed with the whole event and can't wait to be finished. After a comment about how I must be so proud of my attorney son, the child-doctor comes to her point.

Her first question feels abrupt and pokes sharply at me. "When did you start noticing problems with your memory, Mrs. Glidden?"

I reflexively poke back at her with my own stick of words. "Well, if I were having memory problems, you've placed me in a poor position," I say. "If I tell you I don't have memory problems, you'll think I've for...um...forgotten that I forget things. If I tell you I do have...memory, you know, problems with forgetting things, I will have taken away your pleasure of testing me this morning."

I smile over the clever logic of my argument. Dr. Ellison returns my smile and nods.

"You make a valid point, Mrs. Glidden, and I'm sure you're totally fine. But it's always wise to keep a good watch on our health, especially as we approach our older, more fragile years," she says. Her voice is soft, but her words are sharp and pointy. They hurt.

I'm about to ask if she's yet out of her training bra, but Bryan's astringent look from under his eyebrows changes my mind. I sigh.

"Of course, these old, fragile years," I say, sliding on a half-smile for the benefit of Bryan.

"Great! Let's get started. I have just a few questions and I promise to be quick." The doctor opens her manila folder. The sudden movement reminds me of a bird opening its wings in startled flight. Something snags deep in my throat.

"Okay, Mrs. Glidden," Dr. Ellison begins. "I'm going to say three words that I'd like you to remember. I'll ask you to recall these words for me in a few minutes."

I nod my head, but I'm still stuck on the image of bird wings splayed open. I look down to my lap and realize my fingers are spread open like wings, ready for their own flight, if not for the fact that they're clutched tightly to my legs.

"Okay, I'd like you to remember these three words. House. Lake. Shoe. I'll ask you to repeat them back to me in a few minutes. But first, I'd like you to close your eyes. I'm going to place an object in your hand and I want you to tell me what it is without looking at it."

I hold out my hand. My lids flutter together and then I feel an object, cool as ice, placed on my palm. I close my hand and roll my fingers over the thing. It puzzles me and before I can stop my eyes, they slide open, narrow windows of curiosity.

A key!

I slam my eyes shut, but not quickly enough. I'm caught. Embarrassment fills my throat and exits as small laughter. "Oops," I say. "I didn't mean to peek."

"That's normal, let's try again," the doctor says. "This time, try to keep your eyes closed." She places another object in my hand and, with the gesture, I think of Ma, her hands feeling every little object around her as a circle of blackness widened inside her eyes. The thing I hold is as cold and round as the circle of dark that invaded Ma's eyes.

I recognize the object. I know the answer. "Oh, it's money," I say, pleasure filling my mouth.

"Very good."

I'm beginning to like this doctor in spite of our earlier go-round. She pulls a piece of blank paper from the folder and hands me a pencil. "I'd like you to draw a regular clock, put in all the numbers and indicate the time as ten past eleven."

I draw a circle and then wish I had a sticky to remind me of the time. "What time did you say again?"

"Ten past eleven."

I'm dismayed. "I'm not much of an artist," I say, stalling for time to gather my thoughts.

"Mom, it's not an art contest," Bryan says. "Just do the clock."

I sigh and look at the piece of blank paper. "Of course."

Then I notice a clock on the far wall. With the devious half-smile of one who's found a way around the system, I copy the clock, my eyes flitting back and forth between my drawing and my model. I worry over my pencil, spilling my breath upon the paper in little puffs of concentration.

I draw my clock.

Even with cheating, I know my drawing is more than pitiful. I'm aware something is terribly wrong, but like everything else these days, I can't figure out how I could be so mistaken. I reach out for another piece of paper.

"No...really, this is very good. You did just fine."

Dr. Ellison takes the paper with my clock and my breath captured upon it and places it on the table. I look at Bryan and notice him looking from my drawing to the face of his watch. His mouth turns slim and rigid.

Dr. Ellison tucks my sad drawing into a pocket in the manila folder and softly folds it closed.

She looks up and fixes her face into a smile. "Next, I'd like you to count backwards from one hundred by sevens," she says, her voice inappropriately animated for what she has just asked of me.

"Count backwards? From a hundred? I can try," I say, speaking slowly, while silently screaming to heaven for help on this one teensy request. "One hundred...ninety...umm." I roll my eyes and look toward the ceiling; heaven is clearly deaf. I begin to feel a prickle of embarrassment in my stomach.

"Oh, dear," I say. "I'm afraid I'm not very good at this. Actually, I'm really awful. That's what those... those little things that make numbers are for. You know those little things that do this, uh, whatever you call it. Um, math! Subtraction! That's it... minus. Minus. Minus." I realize I've slumped in my chair and try to straighten my shoulders. "I've always been terrible with math. But really, I'm very good at finding words."

"That's right, you were a writer," the doctor says. "Many people aren't very good with numbers...so, let's switch to words, then. Do you recall the three items I asked you to remember when we first started?"

"Three items?"

"Yes. I asked you to remember three items."

"Of course. Yes. Three items. One was a...oh, I know this. It was a shoe, right? And another was, ahhh...was it a tree? You said there were *three* words? Oh my, I guess I really wasn't paying attention. Can you give me another three words? Shouldn't we try this again?"

"No, that's fine, Mrs. Glidden. You did just fine. *Just* fine." The doctor pats my arm; I know she's using her hand as a sad offering of consolation.

I also know I'm in trouble.

Failure has rented space in my brain and the payment I receive in exchange is a condescending pat on the arm, followed by a conversation that suddenly turns into talk about me as if I'm no longer in the room. I watch my son as the outer corners of his eyes dip downward and his lips disappear into the landscape of his face like he's beginning to fold inside-out.

YOU TAKE. You take the news with surprising calm. Rather than screaming into the caverns inside your head, you sit like a lady, your hands folded on your lap. People talk around you like you're invisible, but it doesn't matter what anyone says. You look at your hands while you calmly listen to their words. Words like, "Evidence of mild cognitive impairment." Then, "Your mother is relatively young, perhaps early-onset Alzheimer's disease." And, "We'll obviously need to do a full assessment and complete workup before we can venture a definitive diagnosis or treatment plan." You expect to hear the sound of your heart splitting, fracturing into shards and falling to the floor of your soul, but your heart stays in place. Surprisingly, with such a terrifying diagnosis rattling deep within the bones of your head, the most disturbing thing—the thing that hurts most—is how your son's eyes fill with tears and how his chin trembles in a way you haven't seen since he was twelve years old. When the doctor is done with you, she gently ushers you from the room with her patting hand, the manila folder tucked back under her arm. You make an appointment for more testing and then you do the only thing you can on a hot August day filled with bad news and poorly drawn clocks. You take your son out for ice cream.

When we're done with ice cream and bad news and we've again found our brave and stalwart chins, Bryan drives me home.

"You gonna be okay?" he asks. I assume he's anxious to get back to work with its ordinariness of contracts and endless verbiage regarding the movement of water through aqueducts or canals, or whatever it is my beautiful son does for a living.

"Of course. I'm fine," I say. "Go do your water lawyer stuff. That's what you do, right? Are you still a lawyer?"

"Yes, Mom, I'm still a lawyer. But, are you sure? I can stick around if you need me. I could at least make you some tea before I go."

"No. *No*. Really, I'm *fine*." I wave my arm as if waving one's arm through the air clears away any lingering words of disease or imperfect and troubled mothers. "Why don't you and Allison come for dinner tomorrow? We can barbeque something large and lovely on the patio and drink enough wine to forget all about this doctor nonsense."

"Good grief, Mom. Maybe you're not well enough for that right now." Bryan's eyes threaten to cloud up once more.

"I'm quite well. Now get out of here and leave an old woman to her bonbons and Oprah."

With his hands on my shoulders, as if holding me that way might somehow keep me from unraveling, Bryan bends to kiss my forehead.

"Love you." His chin and his eyes barely maintain their decorum.

"Love you more," I say.

"I'll call to check on you tonight," Bryan says.

I wave my arm again, but he's already gone.

The house is dappled with afternoon light that, in spite of my wishes, rudely pushes its way through the partially open blinds. The news of the day has decided to settle into my lungs, making it hard to breathe through the room's watery light. I try to catch onto the air as it leaves my mouth. I think of other, earlier days and I fumble my way to my cedar box. I drift through letters and papers and pull out something written across a creamy, thick, white notepaper that I hope will clear my lungs and strengthen my trembling fingers.

My dearest children:

I wish we'd had a Southern porch when you were young. You should have grown up with a porch—the kind that wraps around the front of the house, with a simple railing and unpretentious stairs leading to a sun-dappled lawn. Magic happens on a Southern porch; I wish to heaven you could have grown up with that simple truth. I wish you could have known the weightlessness of a child's body when it hurls itself from the top step all the way to an explanation of how it got "those awful grass stains" on its knees. I wish you could have heard the music made by fingers pulling the strings of a banjo and I wish you could have sat and fanned your face with folded construction paper on a hot and humid summer night.

One never forgets their porch days, with the sound of fresh vine beans or snap peas crackling in the women's hands, while the shoes of men tap out the songs of Riley Puckett and Fiddlin' John Carson. A Southern porch brings the happy chatter of neighbors from up the road; it serves up plates of fried chicken and fresh-baked blackberry pie. It also holds the wild imagination of a girl on a swing, her Ma's arm curled like a question mark around her shoulders, a book shared between their laps.

Yes, a porch allows for grand laughter and raucous music, as well as countless hours for dithering away a rainy day unfit for anything other than rocking and reading, while the fierceness of clouds pass overhead.

I wish you could have sat on the porch with your MeeMaw as she rocked in her chair, holding a thin book to her breasts, swaying back and forth, as if holding that book and swaying would give her eyes something to think about other than their gathering blindness.

I wish you could have known her audacity.

I'll never forget one day—a rain-promised summer day when the humidity hung over our shoulders like sacks of damp laundry and great thunderclouds filled our lungs with moisture and effort. Your MeeMaw insisted I sit with her on the porch to fan our faces and read her beloved Milton. Specifically, she wanted to hear his poem *On His Blindness*.

She sat plucking snap peas from a bowl, pinching off the stem end and pulling away each pod's tough membrane with one swift movement. Ma's cat (which she naturally named John Milton) lolled at her feet. I sat on the swing, a glass of lemonade sweating onto the floor at my feet, wishing for something, *anything,* other than John Milton's old duddy poetry.

I remember your MeeMaw asking me to repeat the last line of the poem. "Read that last line again," she said, her voice thick with clouds and coming rain.

"The last line?"

"Yes. Say the last line for me."

"They also serve who only stand and wait."

"Read it again," Ma said.

"Again?"

"Yes. *Yes,* Lillie Claire. Read it again." Tears began to form in her eyes.

"They also serve who only stand and wait."

Suddenly, she jumped upright from her chair, flinging the bowl of peas across the porch, causing John Milton the Cat to run off, squalling in displeasure. Her arms flailed in front of her, her blind eyes sprung wide open as if something bright and wild had exploded deep within them.

"I'm standin' and waitin'," she cried. "Oh, dear sweet baby Lord Jesus, I'm standin' and waitin'!"

Your dear MeeMaw pleaded for healing and redemption, the strength of her voice informing heaven that she would not accept her fate with a simple, shrugging sigh. Her moment of truth was dressed in the last line of a Milton sonnet and she cried to God to fix her. She smacked at her eyes with still-young hands wilted from years of scrubbing floors and making pies.

"Jesus, come put your healing mud on these eyes and make them see again," she cried out. "I'm standin' and waitin' for you. Can't you *see* me, Jesus? *Here* I am. I'm right here! Standin' and waitin'. Standin' and wait—"

Oh, I can't go on. I only know that what happens on a Southern woman's porch is sometimes magical and sometimes horrid. But whatever occurs, it must be dealt with sensitively, courteously—and always with a fluttering fan in one's hand. Please try to remember that one thing if you should ever have a porch where you can sit, sipping lemonade, while allowing your gaze to wander over poetry that will scare the living daylights from your soul.

If you ever have a porch, do make sure you hold a proper fan.

Be brave,
Love, Mother

P. S. I'm still selecting words for my sonnet for you. It's difficult, but thanks to the heavenly stars, you love me in spite of my recent shortcomings.

I fold the letter and put it back in the box. I had hoped to find a different piece, a thing of cedar-scented comfort rather than a reminder of heat-sodden lungs and blind eyes and the hell of John Milton. I consider pulling a different letter, something that might make me laugh, but instead close the box and find what contentment there is in the simple mystery of chance.

Somewhere in the world it must be time for a glass of wine.

I place the box back on the shelf and stand in the dim closet, not really anxious to leave the dear space that wraps around me like Ma's arms.

I place my fingers over my eyelids and feel each round hardness beneath. I press sharply into them until I see star-pointed sparkles of light.

With my fingers pressed tightly to my eyes, I pray that what I see—sparkles of bright and dark together—will be etched into the slate rock of my mind and that I will not forget this moment.

My eyes are good.

What they see is good too. I spread a prayer across the walls of the closet. *God, if you're out there somewhere, you probably know that something is taking my mind. But still—please—let me remember this one small thing. Help me to always remember the generosity of good eyes. Oh, and a Southern porch. Please don't forget the Southern porch, because I probably will.*

I leave the closet and go to the kitchen, where I open a bottle of Cabernet that grips my palate with thankfulness that I still remember how to work a corkscrew.

Chapter Seven

Now here I am, my mind crisp and crackling, words springing easily to my lips. I am invincible today.

Yes. The day is brilliant and the joy of it washes over me like a warm summer rain. I feel as if I've circled back from the dark side of the moon and now I fiddle with the bright side of everything.

Angels once again live in my mouth, moving my tongue, forming words out of the crack-hard fissures and crumbling monuments within my mind. I'm told that's the way with this Alzheimer's disease thing I supposedly have—good days here, bad days there. It seems, though, that my days are sectioned into *moments* of good and bad.

This is a moment of good.

Allison and I are sprawled across my bed like teenagers at a sleepover. Her hair smells of fruit and flowers and I swoon beneath its scent. I'm mesmerized by the simplicity of her deep green eyes.

"Bryan tells me you've come down with some sort of disease," she says. "But maybe you just need a nice vacation. So, listen to this. I've decided to forget fishing in Canada and now I'm thinking of a couple of weeks lolling on some beach in Maui. How does that strike you? Grass skirts, little umbrellas in some tall, rummy-yummy cocktail. Bare-chested *men*."

"Oh, well...I—"

There it is—the bad moment! Suddenly, thoughts fidget in my

mind. Doors slam in my face—one by one—shutting out content, meaning and distinction, closing off the soft nooks and crannies of all my delicious words. All that remains are the hard and ragged edges of a dark and empty mind. Entire syllables, usage, syntax and pronunciation are suddenly locked away. Unavailable.

I'm aware that I'm a sudden wild-eyed mute; I hate these moments that come and go like storms on a November Sacramento night.

Thankfully, Allison chatters on, unaware of the clattering chaos in my head. Perhaps the angels that live in my words have flown to some other woman's mouth. I know what Allison is saying, but for the life of me, I can't seem to initiate a sentence of my own. I can only manage puny responsive sounds. Simple yeses, noes. Little sighs and shrugs. Words that should accompany these gestures are simply missing.

I'm swimming through an expanse of mud.

Finally, I stumble across a few small snippets of misdirected thoughts lying on the floor of my brain. This gives me hope. I manage to string together a small daisy chain of words.

"You're a...a...um, a *sweetheart*, dear. Hawaii sounds nice, but what I have won't go away...by...by simply taking it somewhere for a good tan."

"Maybe all you need is some pampering. Look at you. You need a manicure. A facial. A nice coconut-butter massage, and who better to do all that than a handsome native in a Speedo?"

"Allison! How could you say—?"

"Come on, Mom. Maybe you just need to have a good roll in the hay. When's the last time you had some crazy, howling sex? Dad's been gone how long now?"

"Ten years. Still...Allison *Claire!* You're so rude."

I make a juvenile face and stick out my tongue. We look at each other with wide eyes and then burst into high laughter. We roll on my bed like litter-mate pups. We are, at once, young girls again with coltish legs and slender arms, gasping with thoughts about boys and kisses and the forbidden delight of such entanglements.

The door to my mind (which had just moments earlier been so rudely slammed in my face) blessedly opens wide and I'm once again breezy with fresh air and words. I splash memory and language about the room as if there is no end to what I know and this bright and joyful moment will go on forever.

It occurs that this is how things will be from now on. Good days and bad. Good moments hunted and chased down by bad ones like Sherlock's hounds. I'm learning not to expect my lips to stay bright for long.

Afternoon arrives and Allison, even with all her oven-mitted, spoon-churning fumbles, helps me in the kitchen.

Brian arrives late, sputtering apologies and excuses that seem to spill down the front of his shirt. He offers to flip the chicken breasts around the barbeque like he's the man of the house. Nevertheless, he grumbles as he searches for just the right spot of heat.

"I thought we were going to have steaks," he complains. "I really had my mouth ready for something large and beefy."

"Steaks!" Allison wrinkles her nose at the thought. "That's totally unhealthy. Cow meat is just wrong."

"And chicken meat is *right?*"

"We need to think of Mom now. Maybe it's not good for her to have beef. Don't you know that cows stick their tongues clear up inside their noses, for God's sake? How healthy is that?"

"Okay, I'll give you that one disgusting thing about cows, but chickens don't have a lick of sense. Christ, look at the way they flip around even after their heads are pulled away from their bodies." Bryan winks in my direction. "If we want to help Mom, we should at least feed her something halfway intelligent."

My children are off and running with what sounds like adolescent sibling banter; I'm off and running with a lovely glass of red wine and light-filled thoughts crackling through my mind. Yes! Allison and Bryan are mid-squabble and all is right with the world, in spite of my broken brain. I move indoors to poke at potatoes baking in the oven and put the broccoli on to steam. I'm able to figure out the workings on the oven and stove—always a good sign that I'm having a rare moment of excellence.

Bryan works at the barbeque while Allison sits at the table. As I watch from the window, an amused smile still making its path across my face, my eye wanders to the strawberry patch. Due to my singular neglect, they've overgrown themselves this year, encroaching into small cracks along the asphalt drive, widening their influence with flourishing enthusiasm. I make a mental note to whack them back into a proper and more manageable shape.

Sounds drift in and out the open window and I'm happy with that. For the moment, I'm a flat, smooth stone, good enough for skipping many times before sinking down into my mind's brackish pond of forgetfulness.

YOU BLESS. You bless your ears and all they pull into their secret whorls and curls: the delightful banter of your children who could as easily be looped on drugs as they are on trying to best one another in passionate discussion; the tiny scrape of metal as your son slides his chair away from the patio table; the hiss of chicken turned on the grill; the clack of your daughter's high heels across the patio's concrete floor; the movement of fabric, sluicing across your thighs as you walk through your house; the now-and-again silence of calm in the sweet fragrance of forgetfulness that your husband is forever gone and you miss his hands so damned much you would give up your ears and all they know for just one more touch. Still, all is bright and lovely with your ears as they listen to sounds so normal you forget you are now often a reluctant outsider. You assume that soon you'll constantly be paragraphs behind in conversation, not to mention what will happen to your understanding of nuance, your flagging imagination, or that silence will sit on your head like ash. One day you'll have nothing but stillness in your mind. Today, though, you bless your lovely ears because you hear and discern the language of your children, and you tightly embrace the crackle of this bright and sparkling moment. Still smiling because you've discovered your ears, you walk outside and clearly announce that, Damn it, your strawberries can grow in the asphalt if they bloody well want and—furthermore—you've decided to buy a bikini for Hawaii and you'll not hear another word about it.

After we've eaten dinner and the dishes are washed and put away, after Bryan and Allison blow goodbye kisses across the room, leaving me to another silent evening, I once again find myself at my writing desk, scrawling words onto paper. It's becoming harder to select words, to find the order in which they should occur, to spell those words, to especially hold my thoughts long enough to make sense.

It takes a good deal of time to formulate something into a cohesive conga line of words dancing after words, dancing after more words.

When I'm finished writing the day's thoughts (I use the last of my rose-embossed stationery), I take the papers to my closet, fold them carefully and add them to my growing collection of letters. I consider moving the box to a more convenient location, but decide moving it would take away the ritual of reaching for answers in the dim of my closet and, as an adjunct, I might very well forget any new hiding place. I decide life is mysterious enough.

I add my latest letter and then select an older letter to read; it's written on plain vanilla-colored stationery and folded in thirds. I open it and read.

My children,

This morning I sat on the patio with my coffee, watching as one puffy white cloud seemed to snag momentarily on the corner of the eave as it passed on its way to wherever clouds travel on Sunday mornings. It struck me right then—in that delicate and mysterious moment of a cloud's passing—that you were raised by a particularly neglectful mother. That's when a piece of that cloud broke away from itself and found its way into my throat, thickening it and making tears rain from my eyes.

After swallowing that piece of cloud, I considered things in a more rational light, realizing it wasn't neglect I inflicted upon you, but rather my own prejudice of Sunday mornings and their practices. A mother's influence is indeed great! I'm afraid I squandered mine with you and for that I'm sorry.

I could have offered you a different life. Instead of merely breathing in the sweet scent of your hair as I kissed your dear heads throughout the day, I could have filled those perfect heads with thoughts of all the churchy things that live in clouds and prayers and little squares of Jesus bread. I could have passed on stories of the Glad Tidings Holiness Church of Blowing Rock, North Carolina, where I sat with your MeeMaw every Sunday morning. That was her church. Outside it was a simple square structure made of staid and conservative brick and mortar, but inside, that little building was filled with shouting, tongue-talking, arm-waving, Psalm-singing people who swayed as one to what always seemed a frantic, drumming rhythm. People ran up and down narrow aisles, shouting, crying. They danced and twitched and fell to the ground in gob smacked ecstasy. It was amazing.

It was frightening. It was glorious.

The Glad Tidings Holiness Church of Blowing Rock, North Carolina, sang all the way into your MeeMaw's bones. It laid its hands on her. It gave her words that felt like rushing water etching deep pathways into the stoniest of hearts.

She sat in its pews only long enough for the Holy Spirit to take hold and shake her by the neck. Then, she jumped and twitched and danced in its aisles, waving her arms and speaking in strange, nonsensical words. She was slain in the Spirit so often a spot was reserved just for her, where she could crumple to the floor, her arms flickering in little spikes of trembling mystery.

Your MeeMaw's eyes might have been dying, but her wild prayers flung to heaven were as alive as anything ever sent heavenward from the lips and hands of a churchgoing Southern woman while caught up into a visionary cloud of witnesses all crying at once, *Amen* and *Amen*.

Once a month, the ladies of the Glad Tidings Holiness Church of Blowing Rock, North Carolina, passed around tiny cups of grape juice and plates filled with cut-up pieces of white Wonder Bread. Ma said Jesus lived in the bread; he swam in the grape juice. On those Communion Sundays, I would sit in the pew next to Ma and feed her a piece of bread, then hand her a little cup of juice. Afterward, she would sit, her eyes like blue taffeta, little Jesusy prayers falling from her lips, her face mesmeric like an angel's.

She was simply enchanted.

I remember when you were small, I would wonder if Ma was looking down from Heaven to see me carefully washing your hands before we sat at the table and then neglectfully forgetting to show you how to lace your little washed fingers together to thank God for the peanut butter and jelly sandwich you were about to eat. At night, I wondered if she saw that we never kneeled next to your beds, our hands in prayerful little steeples, saying our *Now I lay me down to sleeps* and asking for our souls to be kept or taken, depending upon whether we woke or not the following morning. We did none of those things. We didn't pray. We didn't go to church. We didn't boldly raise our eyes to the ceiling, or bow our heads in humility.

I taught you nothing but the purity of hopscotch. I told you that poets and writers and possibly even mathematicians would one day decipher heaven. I taught you that your heads were always meant for kissing rather than condemning.

I taught you nothing churchy.

Of course, we could have spent our Sundays like your PaaPaw, at the side of a stream with fishing poles sticking out from our bodies. I could have taught you how to thread worms and toss out your line so it didn't snag in a knot or catch under a rock.

I was neglectful there, as well.

I didn't thrill you with stories of how the North Carolina sky filled every morning with yellows and blues and its tree branches dripped down like heavenly green rain. I should have, at the very least, told you about the Blowing Rock. You would have loved it—that large rock hanging out over John's River Gorge like it had risen from the ground, a wild swelling ocean wave, only to be frozen solid into one reckless and furious moment of foam and watery heft. It was said the wind caused the snow to blow upside down and your own words to blow right back into your mouth.

Can you imagine that an entire town was built around a rock and upside-down snow—and yet I told you nothing of it?

It was there that your PaaPaw and I stood one wind-blown Sunday morning, our hair standing straight up from our heads, our voices screaming out for the wind to bring your MeeMaw's eyes back to her. Her eyes stayed blind, of course. But still I stood beside your PaaPaw, our hands clutched together, our voices raw in the wind, our bodies bent and thrust over the edge of the Appalachian Mountains until we took on the same curved and wild shape of the Blowing Rock. It was magnificent!

I should have told you about it all, about how I danced the aisles of the Glad Tidings Holiness Church and also how I fiercely screamed into a wind so brutish it could cause snow to fall upside down. Both places offered magical hope; both gave, in the end, only poignancy and heartless truth. How could I have explained my loss without making it yours as well? I felt that a worse cruelty, so I simply kissed your beautiful heads, washed your tiny fingers and let it go at that.

If you've felt deprived, I hope you'll forgive a mother's irresponsibility. The fierce protection of one's children doesn't come without its unintended consequences.

As I write this, we're well past the time for me to have taught you the stories of heaven and hell. Nevertheless, I hope when your own Sunday cloud comes by to snag itself on the eaves of your houses, or fill your throats with cloudy tears, I hope you'll remember this letter. I hope you'll remember that I'm sorry I didn't have the righteousness to place you in a church pew, or at the very least, show you how to properly hold a fishing pole or how to scream into an upside-down wind. But—when you need it most—I hope you'll remember how it felt to have kisses on your little heads, all throughout the day.

Love,
Your Mother

Once more, oh God, *once more*, I stand in my closet with the knowledge that unseen disturbances are changing the entire structure of my mind. My brain is slowly being strangled. I'm being slowly deprived of my oxygen and I gasp with anxiety.

I return the letter to its proper fold and then to its place in the box, alongside its newest companion letter.

I leave the closet in time to hear the first raindrop of a rare Sacramento summer storm crash against the window. It makes me look up with agony in my heart. It isn't so much that an unusual rain has started to fall, but rather that I'm so stricken by its thunderous presence. I simply don't know what I should do next.

I place my face against the suddenly cold bedroom window. The rain makes me think that time is passing by and I am passing by—and now an odd rain is knocking, knocking at my window.

Chapter Eight

I've abandoned sticky notes that refuse to stay put on my thumbs and arms and, instead, now cleverly journal every idea and whim in small moleskin booklets that Bryan brings to me. I've also taken to wearing slacks with big hip pockets, which I fill with these little notebooks, along with pens of different colors. Ever the pragmatist, Bryan's instructed me with the proper use of these blank books.

I write about every aspect of my days—who called, who did not, how the sky turned lavender at the end of the street, and how the garden now gasps and suffers under my neglectful hand.

Allison, on the other hand, fusses over my bulging pockets, clucking and loudly chortling disapproval of my little books. She's come today to bring me fashion magazines: flipping through the pages, she points one delicately polished finger toward pictures of hollow-cheeked models, sleek and skinny in pants that threaten to fall from their tiny hips.

"This is the new style," she says. None of the fashions appeal to me, nor do they have any practical application for my purposes. "Notice that not one of these pictures shows a woman with notebooks sticking out of her pockets. They don't even *have* pockets."

I bristle. "Without pockets, how can these pieces of cloth then be considered true pants? And furthermore, not one of these poor, underfed girls is over thirteen or suffering from Alzheimer's."

"*Mother!* It's crazy that you and Bryan think you have some feeble old person's disease."

"Honey, it's not what *we* think…it's that rotten doctor who says these things. Blame it on her and *her* tiny little hipless body. I certainly do." I offer a wan smile.

Allison peers over another magazine page. "I still don't think there's anything wrong with you that a little pampering won't fix. See? Now, look at this." Allison holds her fingernails out for my inspection. They feature a spotless French manicure; I coo over them, which makes her smile in triumph. "You should be doing *this* every two weeks," she says, waving her fingers at me. "Twenty bucks and you'll feel like a beautiful new woman."

"Your MeeMaw," I say, "now *she* was a beautiful woman, and never once did she have a manicure. Oh, I wish you could have known her."

"Mom, please," Allison says, her eyes screwing sideways. "You really need to get out of those awful fat woman pants. We only have two weeks before our trip…. Why don't we run out and get you some really stunning items? I have a friend who works in designer clothes at Nordys. You'll be gorgeous. Trust me."

"Your MeeMaw, now, *she* was a beautiful woman. I wish you could have known her."

"You just said that a minute ago. You've said that at least twice now…don't you remember?"

"Ahh," I say.

YOU TRIP. You trip over tangles of things that lie along the path of your memories. For all your vigilance over words that might repeat themselves without your permission, you find yourself once more wondering how you missed some sort of slippery string of thought that threads out from your mind. An obstacle over which to fall. "Ahh," you say when your daughter reminds you that you've repeated a thought. Your ears tingle red with shame because duplicate thoughts keep falling onto your tongue, and "Ahh" is the only explanation you can manage. You picture words looping out again and again, like some crazy spirographic drawing and you can't seem to stop yourself from adding more and more loops, until you have nothing but a jumble of black squiggles and a mouthful of "Ahhs" to mutter in apology. The horror is not that you repeat yourself; you don't mind retelling your thoughts or your stories. Certainly, you understand your children saying, with a roll of their eyes, "Mom, you've already said that twice." It's clear you say things over and over, but still that's not the terror of it all. No. Here's the horror: your brain is breaking and no one can stop it. No one.

"Stay with me here," Allison says, looping words around my neck and pulling me back to her. "Hawaii. We're going to Hawaii. It'll be *good* for you."

Her words feel like her twenty-dollar fingernails have just scraped across the skin of my soul. "I understand," I say, "but I *need* my pockets. For my notebooks."

Allison groans.

"And," I add, "of all the things I shall very soon forget, I hope this conversation is the first to go. You're being rude and it doesn't suit you."

"Come on, Mom. I get it. You have a rotten disease. I know that and I understand…really. Here, I have an idea…if you *have* to repeat something, just keep thinking, Hawaii, Hawaii." She spreads open a hopeful smile and I take advantage.

"Fair enough," I say. "Still, I need *something* to carry my notebooks in. I can't do without them and that's just that."

"How about a nice purse, then? Something colorful." She still carries the remnant of a five-year-old girl wheedling her mother for a new toy.

The childishness of my daughter is off-putting.

Sighing, I do the only thing available to someone in my position. "Fine, then," I say. "We'll go shopping for new pants for your frumpy old mother, and as soon as we're back, I'll wear whatever I want. Deal?"

Allison's lips curl up at the corners like delicious little red-skinned apple wedges. I want to eat them; I'm helpless against her soft mouth.

"Yay, shopping," Allison says.

"Yay, indeed," I say.

Before I'm able to change my addled mind, Allison maneuvers me to the car. By the time we reach the mall, all lingering traces of argument are scrubbed clean. We are once more chattering magpies,

La La La Girls holding hands, smiles decorating our faces. With Allison's encouragement, I buy three sleek, hip-smoothing slacks, not a pocket to be found anywhere. She's delighted. While she trots off to the ladies room, I find two shirts embellished with Hawaiian prints and lovely breast pockets large enough to hold my little notebooks and pens.

Problem solved!

After our afternoon of shopping, we take my packages home. We open the bags and arrange the contents across my bed. I clap my hands and coo over my purchases.

Allison's face gleams with pride for her accomplishment.

After my daughter leaves, I return to my bedroom again and again to admire my purchases, especially smiling over my shirts with their colorful patterns of palm trees and flying birds, their lovely large pockets. Each visit to my room, with its display of clothing and accessories, brings me delight.

On each return, I clap and coo. Only once do I wonder how I came to have this wonderful array of goodies on my bed.

Chapter Nine

Today is travel-to-Maui day and I'm beside myself with joy. I repeatedly check my suitcase, zipping and unzipping, fingering through the contents, making certain all my items are neatly folded and properly tucked away. Finally, I give up and simply let the suitcase speak for itself. I decide that since it's too full to close, I must be done packing. I check my notebook to remind myself what time I should be ready.

Bryan's insisted on driving us to the airport. He arrives on time, checking his watch for verification of his timeliness.

"Where's Allison?" he asks, tapping the instrument that, for him, measures time and character. "I don't feel good about this trip, you know. Allison isn't responsible for *anything*, except for maybe getting to her next manicure on time."

"Hello to you too," I say, waving my son into the living room.

"Sorry, Mom." Bryan reaches down to kiss my cheek.

"She should be here any minute," I say. "Do you want some nice iced tea? I made sun tea this morning before I remembered I'd be gone for two weeks."

"Thanks, Mom, but…really, we really don't have *time* for tea."

"I should go pour it out, then. It'll spoil while I'm gone."

"That's okay. I'll take care of everything while you're gone. Did that list I made help you get everything organized?"

Bryan's question is gentle. Simple. Meant, most likely, to comfort rather than to pry. It occurs that I'm not certain when such questions began. I wonder how long it's been since I ceased to be a mother to my children and how long it's been since we've shifted roles. It was most likely a subtle shift, hardly measurable by any yardstick or passage of time on a clock. Still, in these regretful days, my handsome son, the child whose lips must dip at least a foot in order to find his mother's cheek, now finds himself more parent than son. He comes armed with questions to make certain I'm safe, that I'm staying on the straight and narrow. He asks; I answer. There was a time when I was the questioner: *Did you finish your vegetables? How's your home-work coming? What time does the dance end? There won't be alcohol at the party, will there? Who's driving?* At some point between urging him to finish the peas on his plate and today, it seems Bryan's taken up the thankless task of watchfulness over me and I'm saddened by it all.

I frown.

"Did you follow the list I made?" Bryan asks, hopefulness in his voice. For one brilliant moment, I glimpse a memory of my son, a basketball in his young hands, his legs illuminated by the sun, tossing hoops in the driveway with his father. In that lovely thought, he's not asking about lists or suitcases, but simply if I'm watching him try to make the next basket.

"List? I'm sure I did. In fact, I must have followed it too well because now I can't close my suitcase."

"I'll go see. Why don't you call Allison and make sure she's on her way?" Bryan goes down the hall and soon returns with my suitcase neatly closed with all its zippers in place.

"I checked your suitcase," he says brightly. "You did great…except, I did notice that you didn't have any underwear. I added a few pair from your drawer."

"Underwear." I say it like it's the first word I've spoken all day. I let the word and all its implications hang unaccompanied in the air. What woman in the world forgets to pack her undergarments?

"Did you call Allison?" he asks.

"Allison? Was I supposed to call her?"

"Oh, God, Mother. I don't feel good at all about this trip. Where's your medicine? Did you take your pills yet?"

"Probably. Oh…I don't really know."

"Where's your pill counter?"

"I suppose it's in the regular place…unless I packed it in my purse like I was supposed to." Bryan looks in the cupboard and then into the depths of my purse. He comes up with the blue plastic pill caddy like he's just pulled up a fish barehanded from the bottom of a deep pool. He opens the compartment marked "F" for Friday and scowls. He pinches several pills of varying sizes between his fingers.

"You didn't take your medicine this morning." He rattles the container and then opens the "T" for Thursday and the "W" for Wednesday. He pulls out more pills. "You're three days short of a full load."

"Should I take them all now? I shouldn't be short of my full load, should I?" I offer a bright laugh.

Bryan looks askance for a moment and then laughs with me. For one sparkling moment, he accompanies me in the forgetfulness of unpacked underwear and unswallowed medicine. We sway within the here and now and its sound of laughter bouncing around the back of our throats and the walls of my dear yellow kitchen. For one small moment, my son sees the oddity of his mother's shrinking mind and we're neither of us ashamed.

For one small moment.

Allison arrives then, dazzling and breathless. "Look! I'm the color of Hawaii," she squeals, twirling into the living room.

"You're beautiful," I say.

"You're late," Bryan says, waving his wrist-watched arm toward Allison. "We should have been at the airport twenty minutes ago."

"We're not *that* late and even if we are a few minutes behind, it's not my fault. I had to wait for my toes to dry before I could put on my shoes." Allison shows off a fresh pedicure peeking through open toe pumps. There are sky blue flower petals painted across each large toenail, a perfect match to her flowing pants outfit.

"Well, I hope you don't scuff your cute little toes running through the airport because you're totally *late*."

"Oh, relax, Bryan. You're such a time freak."

"Children, *please*," I say.

Allison and Bryan's bickering begins to slide a wedge into my thoughts and I feel interrupted. Disjointed. There's a hard comma suddenly inserted into my mind where there should have otherwise been a smooth passage. "You're both raining on my Hawaii and we haven't even gotten there yet."

" Mom is right," Allison says. "Total rain."

"Really? Are we going to have rain?" I ask. "Do I have an umbrella?"

"You're okay, Mom. Don't worry," Bryan says.

"Well, *I'm* ready," Allison says.

Bryan scribbles a look of disengagement on his face. "Then let's load up and go. Mom's excited for Hawaii." He winks at me and opens up a smile wide as an umbrella under a stormy day. Bryan's smile causes me to wonder again if I need an umbrella, but this time, I keep the question to myself.

We load our suitcases and our differences into Bryan's car and drive to the airport. Allison's in the back seat wearing her sky blue outfit and flowers on her toes and I'm in the front wearing wonderment on my face that the day matches Allison's toe petals.

At the airport Allison guides me through the process of checking our bags at the ticket counter and then helps me through the security check to reach our gate. She is blasé. She's ignorant of the difficulties within my hardscrabble mind and—oddly—her disengagement seems comforting. She watches with bored disinterest as I fumble my license back into my wallet and shove my boarding pass into a side pocket on my carry-on bag. She is sophisticated and I do my best to emulate her posture. "We're going to Hawaii," I tell the security guard. He is sophisticated too.

We find our gate and locate two side-by-side narrow molded chairs; we wait for our plane, carry-on bags tucked between our legs. Allison busies herself texting. Then she dials a friend to chat while I absently turn pages in one of her *Glamour* magazines. I decide to use the restroom before boarding and motion my intention.

"Watch my bag," I mouth, not wishing to interrupt her conversation.

Allison cups her hand over her cell. "Where are you going?"

"Restroom."

"Okay. But don't be long. They're just about to call us for boarding."

Allison waves me away, seemingly lost once more within her giggly, happy conversation. She tosses her hair like a prancing pony and it's hard to take my eyes from her. But I leave the boarding area and walk down a bustling aisle filled with shops and little restaurants.

I locate the women's room and try to hurry. As I wash my hands, I notice my mind is wild with excitement. It's all I can do to keep from crowing to every woman in the restroom that I'm going to Hawaii and I have a boarding pass tucked into the side pocket of my carry-on bag back at the gate to prove it. I finish and hurry my steps back to Allison.

YOU YELL. You yell at your feet because they turned you the wrong way and now you find yourself on the far side of airport security, while your identification, your pass, your daughter, and your trip to Hawaii are on the other side. No one but your feet can hear you, but you give them a good talking-to nevertheless. When your feet are nice and sorry, you let them take you to the security gate where you find an opening to bypass the area because you don't need to stop again. Surely the guards remember you. Certainly they know your plane is about to leave and you must be on it. But harsh hands abruptly pull you aside. You explain yourself in hurried, frightened tones, but all your words and explanations make no difference to the uniformed woman who pats the inside of your legs and runs a security wand over your body. Tears spill from your eyes as you are taken by your arm to a security room. Young men speak harshly, the same way you earlier spoke to your feet. Your plane is now flying to Hawaii, along with your lovely new pocketless pants and your red, red lipstick, but you are not. You can't stop crying when your frantic daughter finds you and you cry even more furiously when the security guard wraps her arm around your shoulder in a gesture of comfort when all's settled and forgiven. Your own daughter's arms stay unsympathetic as she pulls you through the airport to the ticket counter. Her mouth turns tight as a slash when her wheedling and cajoling to secure another flight go unrewarded. Her voice becomes hurled stones as she hails a taxi, her hair snapping and swinging. Words of anger flow from her mouth. Through it all, you silently chant your new vow, over and over. You'll never trust your feet again. You'll never trust your feet again.

Once inside the taxi, Allison narrows her eyes and gives me her mad face. "How could you do this to me?"

"I didn't…I don't …I don't know how this could have happened. I went to the restroom and then I just…I accidentally turned the wrong way. I'm sorry. How could I have known?"

Allison's eyes are unyielding, their dusky green color now resembling hardened slate. "Why didn't you tell them to just page me… right away?" she says. "If you would have just done that one *simple* thing, we could have made our flight."

"Allison, my darling, I tried. How could I know there'd be such a stink? We'd already been through the security gate, so I just went around. I didn't know I couldn't do that. I'm really, really sorry, I just went the wrong way."

"Wasn't it obvious that you were going the wrong way?"

"No, it wasn't…I didn't know."

I turn toward my daughter and catch her dear hands up into mine. "I'll make it up to you. I *promise*. We'll go someplace even better. We'll go to…Canada. Yes. We'll go there. But, won't you please forgive your dear old mother…for this one horrible mistake? Please?"

For one bright and luminous moment, I watch Allison's eyes soften into what looks to me like heaven's forgiveness in the midst of an unforgiveable offense.

"I'll try," she says.

I realize I've been holding my breath. Slowly, I relax my posture, my shoulders, how my mouth has tightened and pulled downward. "We can do this again," I say. "Next time I promise not to go to the bathroom."

"Sure…whatever. No bathrooms."

After a time, Allison sighs loudly, turning her face to the window on her side of the taxi. "On second thought, no. I'm just too mad at you."

Allison turns inward and silent. Anything left of my sensitivity that's not been already shredded by my daughter's eyes is finished off by my own crashing guilt and embarrassment.

The rest of the ride remains silent. Allison deposits me at my front door and returns to the taxi, her heels clicking down the walkway to serve as her only departing words.

I roll my carry-on suitcase (with my pills, three brand new notebooks and my unused boarding pass tucked neatly inside) into the living room and leave it to unpack in the morning. My larger suitcase with all my new clothes is, of course, on its way to Hawaii.

"Damn it. I really need you, Ivan. Now!" I cry into the emptiness of the house. "Where the hell *are* you?"

I go into my closet and nearly rip down my cedar box. This time, I bypass the normal chance and happenstance of what I might read and carefully go through the letters until I find the one I want. This time, I leave the box on the floor and take the letter to my bed. I read:

My children,

Whenever I think of the difference between what is serendipitous and what is miraculous, I always wonder which prevailed when your father and I first met. Was it serendipity or miracle? I don't know. I only know my head and my heart were forever changed because of him.

Of course, for all the silent, pious prayers to Jesus and for all the words flung into the wind that howled up and over The Blowing Rock, your MeeMaw's eyes continued to deteriorate into permanent blindness.

By the time I was sixteen, her eyes saw only darkness and defeat. She would sit hour after hour in the quiet of her chair, John Milton the Cat ever present on her lap. Now and then she would gamely mutter victory over her eyes, but we all knew she had lost her heart for the fight.

Still, your MeeMaw sent me off to school every day to learn what she could no longer teach. Because she had taught me to read so well and because that translated into everything else taught in school, I had gone ahead of my class. I was to do something that neither Ma nor Pa had done. I would graduate from high school.

The day of my graduation, I announced at breakfast a speech that I had rehearsed for a long time. I was done with school, which left me free to care for your MeeMaw without interruption.

I never got to finish my speech for the commotion that erupted.

Your MeeMaw would hear of no such nonsense. Claiming me gifted, she declared that neither she, nor the God who gave me such giftedness, would stand for anything less than my heading off to college in Boone. Standing up from her chair and swinging her arms in front of her sightless face, your MeeMaw insisted I was not to end up the poor, blind wife of a mill worker.

Your PaaPaw, of course, took sputtering umbrage to that.

The rest of that evening was filled with the question of God's realm in my life and Ma's realm in her household. I wish you could have witnessed how reasoned and civil a Southern house could be, even in mid-argument over the destiny of a child.

Your MeeMaw stood her ground, those beautiful blind eyes of hers flashing like lightning from heaven's hand, her own hand smacking the table like a clap of thunder. Your PaaPaw didn't have a chance over those eyes—or the striking words that issued from your MeeMaw's mouth.

I was given no say in the controversy—thus was the South in those days. Children, regardless their age, were respectful and, above all, obedient. Even in the heat of an argument, children, even children graduated from a higher grade of school than either parent had seen, were expected to be civil and gracious.

And silent.

In the end, the question was settled by your MeeMaw's flawless persuasion and your PaaPaw's quiet acquiescence.

I went off to college.

On my first day at school, I met a young student by the name of Ivan Daniel Glidden—the man who would become your father. You'll need to decide for yourself if our meeting was miraculous or serendipitous. I have my own thoughts, but since I've kept them to myself all these years, it doesn't seem right to talk now about something I'll never be able to prove. In a way, I'm still that Southern girl who stood in the kitchen silently, obediently, wondrously and fortuitously listening to her parents argue about her future.

Next, perhaps I'll tell you about the way your father's generous smile absolutely ruined every good ounce of sense I ever had.

Love,
Mom

There—at last! There it is. The first mention of my Ivan and how it was we came to find each other. I think of Bryan and Allison reading this account and hope they will feel the same sense of wonder I found all those years ago.

I also consider that Allison might (upon reading this letter) realize that some misunderstanding—even a terrific and terrible argument—is something auspicious and meant to let fly.

I crush the letter to my chest, letting tears fall willy-nilly down my face and onto the front of my blouse. At last, I've found my beloved and he lives within a few words written, front-to-back, on two pages of flowered stationery.

In spite of the day with its myriad distresses, I fall asleep with thoughts of Ivan's hands on my body. In the morning, I'm puzzled to wake up fully dressed, my letters scattered in a wobbling trail from the closet floor, and, most disturbing, a suitcase squatting like a small, dark gnome in the middle of the living room.

I write a reminder in my notebook to ask Bryan if I'm going somewhere.

Chapter Ten

It's turned now into those late summer days when the back garden gasps in the heat; I can nearly hear its great heaving discomfort. I go to the garden shed on the back side of the house to find my garden gloves and sun hat. Then I drag out my tools and my little gardening stool, intending if nothing else to clip a few heat-sodden flowers and bring them inside to the air conditioning. I select a few blossoms still fresh enough to grace the kitchen table, scooting my little stool along the edge of the flower bed as I go, placing each cut bloom in a basket. On I go. Clipping. Scooting. Gathering.

I'm troubled by the simple task of controlling where my clipping hand lands. I've lost the ability to pick a spot and then command my hands or my feet to end up there. I suppose some part of my broken brain is causing damage to my relationship to things outside my own body, causing me to move and drift now in confounding ways. Even holding a flower stalk in one hand doesn't keep my other hand from clipping at the blank air beside it in clumsy, empty strokes.

I notice a flower, a long-legged aster, lying on the ground, gasping, crippled now at its knee and sadly a victim of my heavy foot.

"Oh, I'm so sorry, little flower," I say into its purple petals, its orange center. I'm certain it's a childish thing to speak aloud to a flower, but I nearly expect the poor, broken creature to answer. I've stepped on the dear thing, most likely expecting I was stepping somewhere else. I take the mute and dying flower into my hand and try to straighten it at its crushed and broken place. It won't stand and instead falls loosely at its bend, oozing liquid from its mortal injury onto my gloved hand.

"So, so sorry," I say.

"Mom?"

"Oh, Bryan. I didn't hear you."

"You okay?"

"Certainly, dear. But I don't think this poor flower is doing very well."

I add the aster to the bundle of other flowers in my basket—a few roses, their edges curled from the heat, a couple of sun-bleached hydrangea large as lions' heads, some lavender and yellow freesia—all stricken, first by the heat, and now by the clippers in my hand. *So, so sorry.*

I stand. I'm sure there's most likely a look of guilt on my face, but if so, Bryan seems not to notice.

"Here, Mom, let me get those for you."

"Oh, my. I'm afraid I've really mangled these unfortunate little flowers. I'd hate to hurt your nice suit too."

"I'm good. I've got a genius of a cleaner."

"It's nice to see you, dear," I say.

"Let's go inside. It's too hot out here for you."

"Is it? I hadn't really noticed."

I follow Bryan inside and watch as he places the flowers into a vase and pours cold water over their wounded legs. He sets the vase on the kitchen table and we sit down, the bouquet a sad commentary between us.

"I talked to the doctor today," Bryan says.

"Would you like some tea?" I ask. "Or maybe it's time for wine. It must be time for wine." I take off my sun hat, hang it by its strap on the back of my chair and move to rise from the table.

"It's still morning. Really, nothing for me. I need to get back to the office. I just thought I'd stop by and tell you about my conversation with the—"

"Oh right. The doctor...how is she? Dr. Alli...something, isn't it?"

"Dr. Ellison."

"Oh, yes. Sure I can't get you something? Lemonade?"

"No. I just came by to talk to you."

"That's so nice of you, dear." I sit down again. "How's work going for you? Do you like your new office?"

"Mom, I've been there a year and a half."

"You have? That long? My goodness. How do you like it? Here, let me get us a couple of glasses of wine. You can tell me all about it." I stand again and move toward the refrigerator. "Chardonnay for you, right?"

"Mom! *Please.* I just want to talk to you about the doctor."

"The doctor? Well, why didn't you say so?"

Bryan looks up at the ceiling, then back to me. "Here, come, sit down." He pats the seat on the chair next to him.

I shuffle back to the kitchen table. Bryan places his hand over mine as if to keep me pinned to him; his eyes look like the world has jumped into them. "Okay, here's the deal. Your latest MRI shows definite shrinking of your brain. It's especially obvious in the hippocampus region, pretty much confirming what we already know. It's obviously been shrink—"

"Shrinking? My hips? Oh, goody." I clap my hands in mock delight. "Every woman wants little hips."

"Very funny."

"I'm sorry, dear. I know...I know this means I'm still heading downward." I look at the flowers with their heads now slumped over the side of the vase. I wonder how long it will be before their petals fall onto the table, how many days before *their* heads are gone?

"Yes, you're moving a bit southward. It's to be expected, I guess."

"I'm, in spite of it all...I'm okay, though. Are you okay, dear? You look a little peaked."

"I'm all right. It's just that this is really so sad for you...for us. But the doctor was hopeful. She wants to try a new medication...maybe even submit you for a trial."

"I have to go on trial? Whatever for? Did I do something wrong?"

"No, of course not, Mom."

"Oh, good. How about cookies, then? Would you like some cookies? I might have some in the cupboard...I don't know."

"No. No cookies. No tea. No wine. No lemonade. No *nothing*. I just stopped by—"

"I know. Just to tell me what the doctor said. What did she say again?"

Bryan brushes his hand over the petals of the fallen astor.

"She said you're sick."

"Oh, I'm so sorry. I don't know why I'm sick. I mean, everyone gets sick now and then. I remember one time when you had a fever and—"

"Let's talk about this later. I tell you what. I'll stop by tonight and check on you."

"Oh, that would be lovely, dear. I'll make my famous Southern spaghetti. You can call Allison, maybe. I haven't seen her in such a long time."

"How 'bout I bring pizza? Does that sound good?"

"Wonderful." I stand abruptly. "My goodness. I need to dust if I'm going to have company tonight. What time did you say?"

"I'll be here around six. And no dusting, you hear? It'll just be me."

"And Allison?"

"Don't worry about Allison. Here, sit down. I'll make you some tea before I go."

Bryan stands and walks to the stove on legs that seem to have turned into slender, broken flower stalks.

"Bryan?"

"Yeah?"

"I'm okay, you know. I'm okay with being sick…it *is* part of life, you know. It's a shame I'm so clumsy with the flowers, though."

"You should have a gardener. I'll get you a gardener."

"No. I don't need a gardener. Just new feet and, well, maybe a new brain."

Bryan brings me a cup of tea and kisses my cheek. "We'll be okay."

"Of course." I look at the vase. "We'll all be okay."

After Bryan leaves, I drink my tea and talk to the flowers on the table. "I guess we're all going to lose our poor little heads pretty soon, aren't we?"

The silence from a vase of too-late-in-the-summer flowers is my answer.

I spend the rest of the afternoon looking through letters from the cedar box. I find the next letter about Ivan and let its words take me back, back, back.

Dearest children:

Your father, my Ivan Daniel Glidden, was a beauty! On the day we met—my first day in college—he leaned into me with those great blue eyes of his, eyes that could cause a mountain to cleave in half. His was a smile stronger than the wind that blew the upside-down snow at The Blowing Rock. He was a beauty, all right; a third-year student determined to leave behind the simplicity of the Appalachians for the complexity of anywhere else. Your father pulled me into his whirling vortex of life and left me gasping for more. That first day of school, he caught me up by the hand and never let go until the day he died, twenty-eight years, two children, and one massive heart attack later.

Ivan held me close to his chest on the day that Ma died of heartbreak for her eyes and he held me even closer when Pa died just six months later from a lungful of Carolina sawdust and his own blind and broken heart. He helped me box up memories and books and scoop up John Milton the Cat so I could hide that poor old cat in my dorm room because I couldn't bear to leave him behind. When it came time, my Ivan helped me bury John Milton in the yard of your MeeMaw and PaaPaw's silent and ghostly house. Then, he let me cry bitter tears across his shirt when new people moved into the only home I had ever known.

Five days after I graduated from college, Ivan took me once more by the hand to marry me forever and ever, amen. I had no Pa to walk me down the aisle or lift my veil to kiss my face goodbye, so Ivan simply eliminated the aisle. We stood at The Blowing Rock, surrounded by a generous spring wind and blessings smiled from the lips of Pastor Lonigan as we gave ourselves to one another.

I swear I could feel your MeeMaw's eyesight finally blowing up from the bottom of the gorge in time to watch her only child become a woman.

Your father cared for me like no other; I cared for him the same. On the day of our wedding, standing beside The

Blowing Rock, our fingers trembling with the thought of
one another, he brushed the hair from my face with such
tenderness I thought I would die right then. If the wind
had not had the sense to blow upward, it might have carried
me right out over the gorge and far into the Appalachian
Mountains before anyone could have caught hold of the
hem of my dress. I swear, that fierce wind blew into our faces
and forced its way into every crevice of our young hearts. It
caused us to hold to one another until we knew that no wind
we ever encountered would ever be stronger than the wind
from the bottom of John's River Gorge. It made us wrap our
arms about one another until it was impossible to separate
us—through early days of our marriage when I was pregnant
so quickly we had to laugh and gasp and then, through the
next pregnancy that happened so quickly again, we could
only look at each other large-eyed and incredulous. We were
wrapped together completely; there was no crevice for any
wind to come between us, nothing wild enough to pull us
apart—not babies that stole our sleep and consumed every
waking moment, or jobs gained and lost, or the tiny worry
over sniffles and chicken pox, or the larger, fearsome worry
when you two were teenagers.

We held each other tightly through every crashing thing
and every joyful thing. We held each other when Ivan's
job fell out from under his feet and it took three months
of painful doubt before he landed every man's dream job as
Chief Financial Officer at Clive and Ulster. Gosh, they took
good care of your father.

Then, we clinked glasses together when my job as a simple
high school English teacher thrust me upward to serve in
the English Department at American River College. We
whooped through the house like wild hooligans and got
drunk on wine and possibilities when *The New Yorker* bought
one of my poems.

Your father was the skin on my body and the sense in my
days. And so, when his heart suddenly stopped and refused
to come back, I was ill-prepared for the force of death that
causes a woman to suddenly breathe alone. Twenty-eight

years of standing with him arm-to-arm made me notice his abrupt withdrawal along every inch of my skin and deep within my lungs. There is nothing of me that doesn't miss him.

There is everything in me that will miss him as long as I breathe.

You children may think of your father with different thoughts, different memories. Maybe you think of your own little hands caught up in his, or maybe you concentrate on those rare fatherly scowls when you were in trouble and only his withering look could straighten it all out. But he was as good to you as he was to me. He was good to everyone around him and it is nothing but cruelty to us all that he let go of our hands and took hold of heaven's grasp when he did.

I've gone on much too long, so I'll end here.

With gentle love,
Mom

I'm suddenly tossed. Shifted. Turned inside-out and shaken loose from whatever goodness there had been throughout the day. The usual comfort of standing in the center of my closet, of unfolding and refolding my little letters and poems, of recalling the history that has kept my feet like roots in nourishing soil, now twists along the length of my bones. The years it took to reconfigure my life without Ivan are vanished, and the grief of his loss is as present and palpable as if it were just today he died in my arms, out in the yard, under the pecan tree. I remember the grass was flattened and scorched under him as if he had tried to put out a fire with his body.

The letter flutters from my hand; losing my memory altogether might not be such a bad thing after all.

I decide I would be happy if there might be starfish in my brain, sticky-footed creatures frolicking under the surface of all these salt-water tides of tears. Yes, that should be it. Starfish, slowly feeding on my darkest memories, especially those of my Ivan's terrible death, on the grass, under the pecan tree. Sticky, sticky starfish, eating up my words, my thoughts. I imagine them growing larger, more plentiful. Stickier.

Chapter Eleven

A spider has made a messy web in the corner of my bathtub. Somehow, in the privacy of my mind, I know this spider has something important to tell me. No one else would know about the gravity of a spider in one's bathtub. But I know. I know.

I clap my hands for joy. I run to the kitchen where I take hold of a chair and drag it to the bathroom. I place it across from the spider and sit carefully, like a lady. Her legs tremble as I scrape the feet of the chair a bit closer.

I don't know what to do about her and her serious eyes. She is quick, busy with her web, until she sees me. Then she stands tall, waving her front legs like a joyful hello to a long lost friend. Her mouth is a wide declaration, a smile, perhaps. Her shiny black body, like patent leather, seems sturdy, impressive.

I'd like to take her up into my hand, bring her to my lips, but I decide against the gesture.

After all, what kind of a fool converses with a spider? She should be killed and then swirled with the hottest of water quickly down the drain. She might bite. Everyone knows there is certain destruction when a spider takes over the corners and crevices of one's house, leaving webs with flies, stuck and sucked dry. But I can't destroy her. Not with her legs trembling like this, or her mouth opening in surprise at my approach, or the hopefulness that takes up the entire length of her body and spreads out across the expanse of the web she has crafted.

She is magnificent and we are making friends.

"Well, hello," I say in my loveliest lilt. "You shouldn't be afraid of me. I wouldn't hurt a fly, although I'm sure you'd be delighted if I were to serve you a nice large fly specimen for your dinner." I laugh and settle in for a morning's conversation with my new friend.

She tells me secrets.

I hear her. It surprises me because of the constant buzzing that has recently taken over my ears. Sometimes I nearly cry out because of its horrid annoyance. Buzzing, buzzing always. But it doesn't seem such a bother, now that I hear the high, tremulous voice of this spider. There it is, in a pitch just slightly above the night-and-day radio wave of sound that fluxes deep within my ears.

I hear the voice of a spider and I am enchanted!

We soon exchange names and the pleasantries of the day. She prefers her married name, Mrs. Bird, which I find amusing since any bird would snatch her up if given the chance. I mention that she is lucky to have found a spot where she is safe. She measures the distance between us and says she could very well say the same for me. We laugh and laugh over that one.

She dips her head as she mentions she is a widow. I brighten with our common state. As it turns out, we are both widows, with children, but without any close lady friends.

We talk and visit until morning turns itself over to the sensitivity of afternoon and its changing shadows. Reluctantly, I leave Mrs. Bird to her churning business while I drag my chair back to its place in the kitchen. I busy myself with pushing a sponge across an array of dirty dishes. It's a difficult task these days to keep ahead of my own messes. I sweep toast crumbs toward my hand, only to miss and watch them flutter to the floor.

There was a time when I would have rushed for a broom and dustpan. I would have been immaculate. Now, I'm lucky to notice anything amiss. Some might say I've become relaxed, focused instead on things more worthy of my mature status. I know otherwise. I'm, instead, simply incapable of anything more than the most rudimentary tasks. Sweeping fallen crumbs into a dustpan requires a coordinated effort of body and arms I find no longer possible.

I finish the dishes as best I can and move to the living room. There are books and magazines to straighten, although I rarely hold them, much less read them, anymore. It's not that reading has become a trial of wills between words on a page and a mind that is as unruly as that spider web now hanging in the corner of my bathtub. No. I can still read just fine. Rather, I just don't seem to have the interest. I keep reading materials on display for appearances. A woman who reads is, after all, a woman worth engaging in topical conversation.

I want to at least *seem* topical.

I'm nearly done when the doorbell rings. It is Bryan. He holds a pizza box and a six-pack of beer in his hands, a wide grin blazing on his face. "Hey, Mom!" he says, bounding into the living room. "Whatever you're doing has just been cancelled in favor of the most fabulous artichoke and black olive pizza ever made. And beer...I brought beer too."

I clap my hands. "Oh goody," I say. "Pizza and beer with my boy. Life is good to me today. First I meet Mrs. Bird and now here *you* are!"

Bryan's face scrambles into brief puzzlement, before widening back into a grin. "Here, let's get some plates. We can eat in front of the television because if pizza and beer isn't good enough news, there's a game starting in twenty minutes."

"I'll get the plates," I offer. "You go wash up and I'll meet you back here."

Bryan leaves the pizza and beer on the living room table and heads for the bathroom, while I pull plates and glasses from shelves and carry them into the living room. I'm nearly beside myself with my joyful day.

I'm struggling to figure out how to unfold the TV trays when Bryan comes into the living room. He fills his plate with pizza and pours two beers with a practiced hand.

"Here, let me help you," he says. In no time, he has the two trays flipped to their correct positions and snapped into place. "Did you know you had a black widow spider in your bathtub? Not to worry, though. I took care of it."

"What do you mean you took care of it?"

"I killed it, of course. I whacked it with my shoe and washed it down the drain."

"You what?" I ask, my eyes widening.

"I killed it." Bryan shrugs his shoulders as if what he has just done is part of one's every day activities.

"You killed Mrs. Bird?" My voice trembles. "You just killed my only friend in the *world*."

"Mother, you can't be serious. It could have hurt you."

YOUR VOICE. Your voice becomes a siren. It is a guttural utterance that starts low and then continues up the tonal register until you are nothing but a wide open shrieking mouth, scream- ing one word over and over. Murderer, you yell. Murderer! You sweep the two full glasses of beer from your table so that they crash to the floor and form great wet puddles on your carpet that will forevermore smell of beer and malevolence. Then you snatch up triangles of pizza and throw them at your wide-eyed son. You hit him squarely with globs of cheese and the force of words. That was Mrs. Bird, you scream into his face. You have made your son afraid of you and you are now insane with grief for a spider.

"Mom, I didn't know," Bryan says.

I squint at him, my eyes filled with mistrust and tears.

Bryan softens his voice. "Look." He sighs. "Okay, let's fix this. Really." He looks around at the mess I've made. "Let me clean up the carpet and then let's go out for dinner. Okay, mom?"

"All right. But I'll not forget this. No I won't. And from now on, mister, I won't let you in my bathroom. Not for anything." I narrow my eyes to slits. "You can't be trusted anymore. There is blood on your hands now."

I go into the kitchen and grab the sponge. I walk back into the living room. Bryan is on his knees, picking remnants of pizza from the carpet. I throw the sponge at him. "Next, you'll probably tell me you helped Mrs. Spencer move away."

Brian looks up at me.

"You remember Mrs. Spencer from down the street. She gave you a box of sidewalk chalk for your second birthday and you tried to eat it...made you very sick. I should have killed her for that."

"Mom—"

"My goodness," I say, brightly. "We've turned out to be a murderous lot. Do you suppose they have red wine at the restaurant? I could use a glass of wine now."

Bryan holds his brow as if he's not certain it will stay in place any longer. "Sure, Mom. They have wine. They have anything you want," he says.

Bryan finishes cleaning while I go pay my final respects to poor Mrs. Bird. Poor, poor smacked and flushed Mrs. Bird. She might be the lucky one after all.

Suddenly, I feel the shame of a mother who has deeply wounded her child because of a ridiculous misunderstanding. Of course it's illogical to reach for friendship tucked into the poisonous folds of a spider. I know this truthful thing deep within the center of my chest. Nevertheless, she was all the morning had to offer.

Bryan must have cleaned her web from the corner of the tub because there is no evidence that anything was ever there. The only thing left is the regret of a screeching mother who misinterpreted her son's tender deeds.

I go to my dresser where I keep a stack of cards for various occasions in one of the drawers. I select an appropriate card, sign it, and take it to Bryan who is finishing the last of the clean-up. I hand him the envelope with his name carefully printed on its front.

He opens the envelope and pulls out the card. On the front is a lovely pastel drawing of a small outdoor table set with a vase of white lilies and a single empty place setting, all under a sky filled with puffy white clouds. He opens the card to see the inscription printed in flowery lettering. *I'm so sorry for your tragic loss*, it reads. I have signed it, *With deep misery and regret, your mother.*

Chapter Twelve

I've turned inconsolably sad for no good or apparent reason, and I find my mouth puckering, my chin wavering over the smallest things.

And thus, without any particular cause or specific worrisome event, I begin a glorious crying phase with uncommon gusto. I outdo my former notebook stage by splashing grand and plentiful tears over everything and everyone.

Ma would have tsked her tongue and called me a woman of sackcloth and ashes. She would have said I had no better sense than to beat at my own chest. Pa would have told me to stop my caterwauling and go help Ma with the dishes.

Allison—who still seems barely halfway done with forgiving me for ruining our trip to Hawaii—continues to skirt me with countless excuses and repeated *sorries,* while skipping our weekly dinners, our daily phone calls. She punctuates her words with pursed lips and little squinchy lines pulled like drawstrings at the corners of her eyes.

Still, Allison checks on me now and then with quick, pithy phone calls. My beautiful La La La Girl. My sweet pony. My tender friend.

It is Bryan, however, with his little-boy-blue eyes, wide with concern upon his thirty (is it five- or six- now?) year-old face, who calls me daily and brings me boxes of tissues and little French chocolates to make me all better. He hands me his offerings and I break into fresh tears for the tenderness of it.

"I'm sorry," I always say. "I don't know what's *wrong* with me. Why is this happening to me?"

"You're good, Mom," he always says. "No worries." Then he kisses the top of my head because my constant tearfulness renders him incapable of doing anything else.

One day I cry to Bryan, "I don't know why Allison treats me so poorly. I ask her why and she tells me I know. I *don't* know, Bryan. Do you?"

"You didn't do anything wrong. What say you and I forget all about sad things and blow this popsicle stand? There's a new little Italian restaurant on K Street I've been dying to try." Bryan raises one eyebrow in a playful gesture. "I hear they've got a bottle of red with your name on it."

"Really? A bottle of red? With my name on it?"

"No kidding. Go get your shoes on and let's stuff our faces with meatballs and wine. Maybe we'll even do a film noir something-or-other at the Crest Theatre."

I clap my hands in delight and tuck my tears down into my pocket. I slide into my shoes and smile my way into Bryan's car. Halfway to the restaurant, I see a cat the color of Ma's old cat, John Milton, dead and flung to the side of the road. I weep loudly for it. Bryan hands me a tissue and speeds a little quicker to our meatballs and wine.

At the restaurant, Bryan waves away his own preference and orders a bottle of Pinot Noir. The wine is lovely and makes my tongue think of ripe strawberries and raspberries and a smoky fire on a cold night. A rare smile comes to my lips.

I look at the bottle label. "You said this was going to have my name on it, but it says, *Mi Sueño*. Did I…when did I change my name to *that*?" I ask.

Bryan laughs, deep and hearty, from the bottom of his chest. "That's just a figure of speech."

I look again at the label. "Oh, good. I'm glad I'm still who I am. So what does this mean…this *Mi Sueño?*"

"It's Spanish and it means 'my dream.' Isn't that nice? A wine for you named My Dream." Bryan's voice seems to snag on a nail somewhere deep in his throat.

"Well," I say, "I'm afraid I'm all out of dreams for myself, but maybe there are still a few good *sueños* left for you and Allison." I laugh and then start to cry again.

"Aw, Mom. Here...cheers." Bryan holds his glass up to touch with mine.

"Cheers," I say. *Cheers*. An odd word for a crying woman to utter. Nevertheless, I clink my glass with Bryan's and say *Cheers* into his tender eyes.

"How can I fix you?" Bryan asks.

"I'm fine. I'm just...well, I guess I'm really not all that fine, but there's nothing to be done about it." I reach over and pat his hand.

Bryan looks deeply at me. I spend a moment wandering across the landscape of possibilities and hopefulness spreading across my son's face.

"I wish I knew what it's like for you," he says after a while.

"You don't want to know," I say. I take another sip of wine. I shrug. "It's hard to describe. Sometimes I feel good and bright like there's still something in here." I rap the top of my head with my knuckles. "Knock on wood."

Bryan raps his head and laughs. "Yeah, knock on wood."

"Sometimes I remember things, like I have a nice wind at my back, pushing me along."

"Like now?"

"Mmm...like, right now I'm doing okay. At least, I think I am." I look across the room. "See that man over there?" I lean closer, lowering my voice. I point in the direction of a man seated a few tables down. "He probably doesn't know that a single drop of water can travel all the way around the world. I can guarantee he doesn't know reading poetry could save his life or that his tie is hanging down all crooked."

"I don't understand."

"What I'm trying to say is that I still notice things. I still see things. I get inspired and laugh and...obviously I cry. I'm just losing my words to talk about it all. Poof! One minute I could probably recite a soliloquy and the next all those lovely words simply vanish. In a stupid instant, I can't remember a damned thing. I forget things faster than I even knew them in the first place, if that makes sense. Maybe I'm simply growing backwards."

"Growing backwards?"

I laugh. "Yes. A magical way of getting younger, but this is just a terrible way to do it. Keep the wrinkles, but lose the memory of how you earned each one."

"Maybe there's a different medication, something new or more effective. We could try another doctor, or maybe you could qualify for a trial—"

"No, Bryan. I don't want…really, I'm fine. Maybe I get a bit soggy these days, but really…there's not much help for a gummed-up brain. The good thing is that I keep those nice tissue folks happy." I smile, but Bryan's face has fallen from the edge of inspiration and helpfulness.

I look down at my menu and frown. "I can't figure out all these dishes," I say, my voice now flat as a stone. "Will you help me?"

He brightens—at last and without trying, I've given my beautiful son something about me he can fix. Bryan folds his hand over mine and escorts me through the long list of foods. I do my best to concentrate, but I'm stuck on a word that clangs and rings through my head like a loud, noisy gong. It repeats over and over—the same word, banging wildly inside my mind. *Cheers. Cheers. Cheers.* Tears slide again across the rounded curve of my eyes until they fall in fat dots onto the menu.

I'm mad at my eyes. I shake them free of their water and pick up my wineglass.

"What's the name of this wine, again? It's quite good."

"You don't remember? It's *Mi Sueño.*"

"*Mi Sueño.* My, what a pretty name! What does that mean?"

"It means 'my dream.'"

"Well, cheers to your dreams," I say. We clink glasses and I find a small moment of peace within the sound of two glasses touching.

By the time Bryan drives me home, I've found twelve new things to cry over. He leaves me at the door with apologies, another fresh box of tissues and a generous kiss on my wet and snotty cheek. I stand for a while at the door, waving until his car is gone.

I wander to my closet only because it's become my place of comfort and because it draws me there, sometimes many times a day. Often, instead of reading about what sort of person I used to be, I just stand in the middle of my closet, allowing my feet to shuffle back and forth.

Tonight I take down my letter box and finger through my letters until I find the perfect piece.

I read out loud and listen carefully to my halting voice. I still read well, but it's getting harder to decipher my crooked handwriting. Some passages take a few stuttering tries before the meaning is clear enough to move on to the next. Nevertheless, I plod ahead.

My dearest children,

This letter makes my hands tremble before I even set down a word. I don't know how to approach the subject, except to jump in with both feet, hoping not to make too much of a mess of it.

I believe you should know as much about death as you do about life. There! I said that frightening word. Death—that sharp and specific moment between one's last breath and the silence of forever gone.

As much as I'd rather celebrate only how your grand-parents lived (because to think of anything else makes for a terribly sad day), I suppose you should also know about the way your people died.

On my side, your MeeMaw went first. The doctor said it was heart disease, silent and deadly and that nothing could have been done to prevent its horrid and instant conclusion. Your PaaPaw found her in the garden, curled around her favorite rose bush, clippers still in her hand and a look of astonishment on her face.

When your MeeMaw died, I think your PaaPaw—always a worryingly stoic man—choked back his tears so deeply into the crevices of his lungs that those tears puddled right there, which most certainly started the silent growing of what would soon take him away too. I believe he looked at his wife all laid out at the Dignity Family Funeral Home, her hair softly curled, her lips tinted a soft pink, her best dress hugging the curves of her silent body and, right there and then, he just let his soul slip off to heaven with her. There's no other explanation, because just six months later, your PaaPaw died of lung cancer.

He never even told me he was sick, but that's another story for another letter. (I'll work on that.)

Of course, it's possible that death isn't all that bad for the departed, but nevertheless, terrifying for the living. I guess everyone believes in something, though. I know Ma believed in heaven, Pa believed in fishing, and they both believed in love.

On the other side of the family, your father's parents both died young, reaching for each other (most likely) during the slow motion, frame-by-frame instant when a logger misjudged the angle of a curve on one of our mountain roads. Your dad was only sixteen when his parents, your paternal grandparents, were crushed under the very logs that might have made the sawdust your PaaPaw carried home in the cuffs of his pants.

I think about that coincidence every now and then.

Your father told me his parents would have doted on you, marveling over your first steps, your first words, your first mud pies, your first pencil strokes, your first moments of everything. His father was a millworker like your PaaPaw, but for a different company, his mother a homemaker, very much like your MeeMaw. He had one older brother who died of pneumonia before he was born.

Of course, you know your father died of a heart attack in the prime of his life. I can't even go on at all about that.

And then there's me—the one now with the broken brain.

It will cause my death, you know. The good news is that I know how I'll go and, if there is such a place as heaven, I'll surely be once more with your father. With Ma and Pa. Maybe even Ma's old cat, John Milton, will be there. Hah!

Still, I'd rather discuss the way the roses did this year and how their blooms were such a constant delight when I'd bring them in to let their long stems sway over the lip of that cobalt blue vase that I love so much.

I hope I didn't needlessly upset you with this letter, but still, it's important for you to know your past and how it might affect your future. It seems you might need to guard your hearts, your lungs, and your hands on the steering wheel. And now, of course, your brains.

We are your kith and kin. Your heritage. Your good or unfortunate health. If there is any sadness in this backward look, I'm sorry for causing it.

It's said that sorrow doesn't last forever. That's wrong. The sorrow lasts and lasts and lasts. That, you should also know.

Love and gentleness,
Mom

P. S. I hope it helps that I've written this letter on my dearest and most favorite stationery. Don't you love its creamy color?

I stand in the middle of my closet, as still and silent as any grim winter could be; my memories are a flash powder of starlight and magic, blazing white-hot one moment, cold as ice the next. There seems to be a system of hierarchy within my mind now. New, young star memories are born only to die an immediate sparkling death, while the eldest thoughts sit on fat cushions, twinkling like old wrinkled sages.

My thoughts are turning inside-out and what I should know is gone the moment I learn it, while what should have passed away long ago is all I can think of and cry over—again and again and again.

Chapter Thirteen

Now here I am, dry-eyed and trembling after months of splashing and crying over every little thing, I'm finally dry-eyed and upright. Of course, all that warm moisture I made created a favorable climate for bees—loud and bothersome bees—who are now busy hanging a nest in the rafters of my mind. I hear their industrious work as they spread their sticky honeycomb across the hardened wood of my brain. I feel them flying around, gathering all the memories they can find onto their legs, intending only to make jar after jar of some tragic nectar of forgetfulness.

It's no wonder I've always been afraid of bees.

With a chronic buzzing that seems to have settled deep inside the wells of my ears, I begin what can only be called my mad phase. I let words fly through the air much like the stinging insects that inhabit my head. I bellow into the room and to the sky and the stars above.

"Who did this to me? I want to *know* and I won't leave this world without an answer!"

I stand at my window and hurl obscenities at the moon. "You'd better goddamn tell me." The moon is silent on the subject.

I hurl a dinner plate of half-eaten spaghetti at the kitchen wall; it leaves a large dent, red and angry like a bitter bruise. I can only imagine the wall is enraged by my assault, but it says nothing.

I stand in the middle of the living room and let my throat explore sounds and expletives only a madwoman would make.

I rip open the seams of my blouses, scratch at my face.

I'm unfolding, unraveling, and the twisting movement of this slow unwinding of my mind is incomprehensible torture. Still, I won't let this thing happen to me without protest.

I am mad.

Loudly, wildly, soundly mad and the only soul who knows this is me because I hide my anger from my children. To everyone, I am a sweet little woman. To the walls and the moon, however, I am a different story.

YOU HIDE. You hide your broken dishes in the bottom of the garbage can, covering them with yesterday's crumpled newspaper. You sneak shards of breakage out to the trash can during the dark of night when the neighbors are sleeping and only the yard dogs bark to each other about your secret tantrums. Still, in spite of vows to be nice—tomorrow—the moon shrinks from your outbursts and the sun wisely covers its ears. You give each day its bitter tonic of words, each night its dollop of pitiful spite. You make bargain after bargain with yourself to be kind to what's left of your dishes and your sensibility. You call your children and make cooing mother noises, even though they are grown and can look over your shrinking stature without even having to stand on their tiptoes. You don't fool them. Still, you hide. You hide. You hide. In the end—when you become tired of hiding what everyone knows about you anyway—you simply leave your broken dishes in plain sight and allow your lusty words to fly about like tattered kites in a terrible wind.

One day, in the middle of my horrid madness, I decide to be gracious. I invite Allison to come for lunch; I want to plan a lovely daytrip with her.

My effort toward civility wobbles the moment I open the door and see the stubborn posture of my daughter.

"Don't even think about it, Mom," she says brushing past me. "I'm still mad at you from the last time. In fact, I'm probably going to be mad for…forever…and don't look at me with that blank look."

I try civility again. "Good morning to you too, dear. Really, I *don't* know what you're talking about. Come, I made us tuna sandwiches. They're delicious! Here, let's eat in the kitchen and plan our trip."

"There's no way. You *ruined* my trip to Hawaii. Ruined it!" Allison flips her hair across her shoulder. I envy my daughter's hair as much as I envy her snippy spunk. I want to place my fingers inside the dimples on each cheek so I can touch the same spots where angel's fingers once touched. Allison makes it impossible for me to breathe. To regret. To fear.

"Are you saying I should find someone else?" I ask.

"Mom, you know you can't do that. What if you get somewhere and you forget where you belong? Or you lose your passport?"

"I'm only talking about a day trip to the foothills. A little antiquing. Maybe a nice little glass or three of wine in...ah, what's that town? You know, that stream named after that old man?"

"Sutter Creek?"

"That's it! Sutter Creek. We don't need passports to go there, do we?"

"We didn't need passports for Hawaii either."

"Hawaii? We went to Hawaii?"

"Come on, Mom. You made us miss our flight and we never even got there."

"Oh, sweetheart, I'm sure there was a good explanation."

"Explanation? Good God, Mother, you don't even remember what I'm talking about."

"Well, I don't exactly remember the mistake, but I *do* remember the feeling."

"What does that mean?"

"It means, I remember the feeling...I was horrified with myself."

"So?"

"So, do you want to go with me...or should I go with my new friend, Edith? She's a hoot. I think you'd like her."

Allison rolls her eyes; her entire head participates in the slow and exaggerated movement. "You don't *have* a friend named Edith."

"Of course I do. I met her just yesterday."

"Yesterday? You don't go anywhere unless Bryan takes you, and he's in goddamn *Hawaii* for a conference. How ironic is that?"

"Bryan's in Hawaii? How lovely, lovely, lovely." I clap my hands. "Oh goody for him."

"Mother! Come on...who is this Edith?"

"Oh, yes. Edith. I met her right here, in the house. There she was, right in the bedroom…I think that's where we met." I turn my head sideways, hoping a different position might help me remember more clearly. "Anyway, she's my new friend and she's better to *her* mother than you are to me."

Allison looks at me with stiff eyes. "Now you're just being stupid," she says, flipping her hair across her shoulder. "Fine, then. Go with your new friend. Go with *her*." She scoots herself to the farthest end of the couch, nearly crouching like a wounded animal.

"Allison, why are you being so mean?"

"Because you're not like my mother anymore," she says. Tears well in her eyes and her chin takes on the pointed look of a small child in full tantrum. Her words feel like the tips of gleaming needles, piercing and sewing large swatches of anguish onto my skin.

"We used to have fun and now we don't anymore. I constantly repeat the same thing over and over again because you don't remember *anything*! And now you're making up people." Allison becomes a watershed of tears and I reach out toward her. She flinches, pulling away from my trembling hand. "I miss my real mother," she cries.

I find myself across that proverbial wide river, the one that separates a forgetful mother from her less-than-gracious daughter. She's on the side of perfect words and unfailing memory; I've apparently drifted to the ice floe side of forgotten dreams and fallen-down bridges. There is, of course, something contemptible about being on the wrong side of a river without a way to be rescued. I look longingly toward my daughter.

She digs through her purse, pulling out her car keys.

"I'm leaving," she says. "And, by the way, tell Bryan he can do *everything* for you from now on. That is, if you can remember one stupid, simple thing…although I doubt you can."

With that parting shot, my daughter, my La La La friend, my sweet little pony with dimples made by angels, walks out the door.

At least I have a few more dishes to break, more wild words to fling at the sky.

I go to my closet and pull down my letter box. I open the box and scream into it. I close the lid, happy I've captured a small piece of anger and misery inside.

"Hah!" I say.

I put the box back on its shelf and leave the closet.

Minutes later, I return to repeat the opening, screaming, closing, *Hah!*-ing. This at least seems better than breaking the last dish I have left to my name.

Again and again I open and close the box, until finally my eye falls on one particular folded letter. I snatch it from the box and yell at the paper. "So, tell me something else I don't know. Something else I'll forget." I shout into the creases of the paper, across whatever words it might contain. I unfold the letter furiously, nearly ripping it in two. I look at the words and force my eyes to focus. I read.

My sweet children,

I want to tell you about John Milton the Cat. It's time you should know about cats and the magic that lives in their fur. John Milton was a graceful and practiced cat, as if he knew his every footprint before it was ever placed upon the ground. He preferred your MeeMaw's lap to any other place in the house, but when she died, John Milton decided I was next best. It's been said that one does not choose a cat, but rather, a cat chooses you. In the case of John Milton, I was simply the suggestion of a person he loved who was no longer there. He grudgingly chose my lap, but I don't think he ever gave up longing for the fabric of your MeeMaw's skirts to settle deeply into on days too cold for anything else.

It was one of those cold days of unflagging rain after Pa died when Ivan and I dragged poor old John Milton out from under the porch with the idea that we would sneak him into my dorm room. I was all that sad cat had left and I couldn't bear the thought of abandoning him to the cold without someone to love him. John Milton, having other ideas, squalled as loudly as the sky as we drove from the old house in Lenoir to Boone. He refused my lap during the ride and preferred instead to scream up at us from underneath the passenger seat. Now and then, he would reach a paw from under the seat to plead with my legs.

Your father and I argued during the trip.

The strength and force of our words turned the day upside

down. With John Milton screaming under my seat and the argument above, the car was a horrid cacophony of noise. Ivan wanted me to keep the cat quiet. I couldn't. It seemed we each found our own misery.

Suddenly, your father and I stopped talking. I remember pulling in my breath and locking it tightly behind my lips. I believe your father did the same. We didn't really want to fight, so the only expedient thing was simply to dam up any further words and let the day be what it was—one of wincing pain and regret and a cat squalling like a terrible storm.

In spite of John Milton's pleading cries for his own discomfiting day, the car was filled with silence: of unspoken words; of Ivan's hands wrapped tightly around the steering wheel rather than cupped around my waist; the forever absence of my Ma and Pa; the mountains of my home receding behind me.

I looked over at Ivan with his jaw set angry and rigid beneath his skin. I wanted to end the relationship with him right then, but something caused me to look at the softness of his hair and the way the cuffs of his shirt touched his wrists. I looked at Ivan's legs, his eyes. The curve of his neck. His lips. In that moment, I saw the whole of Ivan and my heart broke into a million pieces.

"I'm sorry," I said, pieces of heart making their way to my mouth and causing liquid, teary words to spill over my lips. "I guess this isn't easy on you either."

"Oh, baby. Oh God, I'm the one who's sorry." Ivan looked at me with eyes filled with his own pool of tears. "I'm the one who's sorry."

Ivan reached for my hand and pulled it to his chest so I could feel his own broken heart because of our first fight.

Ivan pulled the car to the side of the road. "Ah, Lillie Claire," he said, holding my hand over his crashing heart. "Look at us in this car…only inches away from each other and yet we've never been so far apart. Marry me. Marry me so we'll never be like this again." There and then, with John Milton grumbling displeasure under the car seat, with the sky around us storming and flashing in fits of rain and blinding light, your father did what he always did.

He took up my hand and fixed our painful hearts.

There! That is what I know of cats and their magic. I'll hold every hope that you will also know the wonder of words that hurt and words that heal.

I'll hold every thought that you'll always abandon hurtful words and concentrate only on gentle words. Healing words. You might also want to think of cats while you're at it. The soft thrum that flutters from a cat's throat is magical, you know.

Please don't forget this, my dears. Please don't forget.

All my love,
Your Mother

I refold the letter in my hand and let its intent fall on my shoulders like a cleansing rain. I gently return the paper to the box. Just as I close the lid, I softly whisper one more small utterance of *Hah!* across the folded paper of my letters.

I then take to my bed, dramatically pulling the quilt over my angry, bee-infested head.

Chapter Fourteen

After screaming my way through each day, I've at last taken on a quieter, more somber tone—a demeanor more befitting a Southern lady.

Most days the house hears only the sound of my voice; the television has nothing to say and music is far too joyful to be appropriate. The house listens to my words politely, intently. I speak more to the house than I do the garden because the house is a place of constancy and solidity, whereas the garden is wild with its flux and flow and movement of things in the wind. The house has integrity, gravitas. The garden, on the other hand, threatens to fling itself into the sky in leafy pieces of foolish disinterest. It frightens me with its flapping, flinging leaves. So I give my words over to the structure of the house, letting it hold them tightly against its upright walls until such time as I may need those words again.

I walk through the house, stepping from room to room as if each is on a string of rosary beads and each beaded room deserves its own prayerful thought. I let myself move from bead to bead to bead, allowing my words to become a nonsensical supplication. *Now I walk me down to sleep, now here I am...now here I am. If I should die, then let it be...and now I walk and now I sleep.*

I would be mortified if anyone should hear me. But it feels I have no choice but to walk in circles, whispering over every step, hoping my breathless words will be remembered by the walls. It's a stupid hope as I continue to dissolve into the terrible oddness of these days.

I tell no one—not my children, nor the sky, and certainly not the garden tomatoes.

Today, when I'm finally weary of my circuitous murmuring and I've nothing more to say to the walls, I throw open the front door and stand very still, just inside the doorframe. The leaves sputter and rustle about in response to the day's rain-filled November wind. I want to listen to the boisterous chatter of trees, if for no other reason than because I'm simply weary of hearing my own voice.

What I hear, though, is not the sound of talking trees, or even the muttering of clouds as they bump into one another. Beneath all the busy vocalizations of the day, I hear a tiny voice from under the bushes next to the porch—a mewing sound so mournful and frightened, it could have come from my own throat. I pull the leaves aside and peer under the bush.

"John Milton!" I cry.

My arms scoop up a dusky gray cat, little more than a kitten, wet and shivering. "Oh, John Milton," I coo into the squirming cat's face. "Where have you been? You come into the house with me right this minute. And just look at you, all a soggy mess. Let's dry you off and fix you a nice bowl of milk."

Joyously, I take the cat into the house, but before I close the door, I look up beyond the trees with their swaying leaves, still clanking in the wind.

"Well," I huff into the air. "You could at least have had the courtesy to also bring my Ivan back to me. You're such a nasty, hateful sky!"

My anger is cured for the day and the magic of a cat in my arms seems a far better conclusion than either grumbling from room to room or throwing my coffee cup to the floor.

I'm still happily bouncing through the house when Bryan comes to visit the following day.

He brings me a stack of new books and offers them to me with hands that once held crayoned Mother's Day cards with his name carefully scrawled inside. He now offers books and magazines filled with such simplistic writing I should be insulted. But his hands are so hopeful in the presentation, I can't help but be moved by them.

He gives me crossword puzzle books and large-print romance novels (a genre I've never liked). He loads my arms with *The Big Book of Memory Boosters for Today's Seniors*, *Cooking for Dummies* and (most embarrassing) a book entitled, *Sweet Submission* with a barely-clad woman depicted on its cover.

My son has no idea how far I've slipped these recent months.

"Thank you, Dearheart," I say, receiving his gifts. I poke at his pockets. "You don't happen to have a nice bottle of something adult in there do you?"

"Of course not. It's only ten in the morning." Bryan laughs and the room sparkles with his voice. "I did think, though, that you might like to take a nice drive if you don't have any other plans."

"Oh, that would be wonderful," I say. "What day is it? Where are we going?"

"It's Sunday, how about Apple Hill? I thought you might like to head up to the foothills and pick out a couple of fresh apple pies to freeze. Thanksgiving's just two weeks away and I'm going to fix my famous turkey surprise for us. So go get ready."

"Apple Hill!" I clap my hands. "I haven't been there in years. That sounds lovely. Oh, my mouth can already taste a slice of their famous pie. I'll need to feed the cat first, though." Bryan looks puzzled; I decide his expression is because he's an attorney. Puzzlement is what he does for a living.

"When did you get a cat, Mom?"

"I've always had a cat. He was missing for a long while, but he found his way home just yesterday...I think it was yesterday, anyway. Poor thing was all wet and hungry. He's probably hiding because he doesn't know you."

Bryan's face is a sudden mixture of moving eyebrows and mouth, dimensions that loom and lurk and manifest into subtle tics that only a vigilant mother would notice. Despite all this obvious facial chatter, Bryan is unreasonably handsome this morning. I start to tell him about his handsomeness, but I'm interrupted by the sauntering feet of John Milton the Cat.

"There he is," I say. "He's come out to say hello."

"Oh my God, Mother. I thought you were just making stories."

"Making stories? I'm surprised at you, Bryan. Don't you remember John Milton?"

"John Milton, the dead poet? I thought we were talking about cats."

I pick up the cat. "Dear, *this* is John Milton." I rub the cat under his chin. "He's come home after all this time…just blew in on the wind." I coo into the cat's small, wide-eyed face. "Oh, and he was such a mess, wasn't he?"

"Oh, God," Bryan says. "Just go get ready."

"Ready? What am I getting ready for?"

"For Apple Hill."

"Apple Hill? Oh goody…I *love* Apple Hill. I haven't been there in years. I'll just go freshen up a little," I say, plopping the cat into Bryan's startled arms. "A woman never knows when she might meet up with Robert Redford, you know." Bryan looks down at John Milton, snuggled deep into his arms and his eyebrows once again go wild across his face.

I think I might explode with the joy of it all.

"Take your time. I haven't read the newspaper yet." Bryan puts the cat down and finds his favorite living room chair. He crinkles open the Sunday paper and pulls out the comics first; the innocence of that small gesture nearly bursts my full heart.

I run to the bathroom to ready myself for our drive. I put on some makeup and when I finish, the sink is dusted with face powder. I reach under the cabinet for a sponge to tidy up and accidentally knock over a tall can of hairspray, which then topples over several bottles of nail polish and a tube of hand lotion. The craziness of it makes me think of dominoes, meticulously stood on end to form an intricate, curling pattern—and how one finger can knock the whole arrangement down—one domino after another. It occurs to me that I've never understood if the fun is in the building up or the knocking down. I decide it's the creation of the pattern that gives dominoes their power. Without such intricacy, there would be no whooping cry for joy when it all comes crashing down.

I rearrange the cupboard and then stand up. A flick of familiarity hits me: sprinkles of powder have poofed onto the countertop. I wonder why I didn't clean up after myself. "You're doing it again, Lillie Claire," I mutter to myself. "Come on, now…think. Think!"

I reach into the cupboard and pull out the sponge from under the sink, careful not to knock anything over. When I'm finished, I decide to do a quick clean-up on the kitchen countertops since I already have a sponge in my hand. I head to the kitchen to wipe the tile when I notice a bouquet of flowers on the counter that I had meant earlier to take to the living room. I scoop the vase up into my hands and head out of the kitchen.

I stop dead in my tracks.

"Bryan!" I cry. "When did you get here?"

Bryan's face is a picture of bewilderment.

"Mom," Bryan says. "I've been here over half an hour. We're going to Apple Hill. Remember?"

"Apple Hill? Oh, goody." I place the vase of flowers on the coffee table. "Apple Hill. I haven't been there in years. I must be a mess, though. Just give me a few minutes and I'll get ready."

"I thought you already did that?" Bryan asks, his eyebrows arched like question marks.

"Of course not, dear. You just now mentioned going. I'll only be a moment." I turn to run to my bathroom. "Yay, Apple Hill," I say, clapping my hands.

Behind me, I hear Bryan sigh deeply into his newspaper. The strange whisper of his breath causes me to think of wet cats and falling dominoes.

Chapter Fifteen

*Y*OU DREAM. *You dream in spiky colors of blues and oranges that float about your bedroom, a picture show of your very own northern lights. Now and then, you wake; you're annoyed with the rudeness of the intrusion, but then you figure someone must be trying to show you something special. So you put your arms behind your head to look at the beautiful lights that sparkle through your bedroom. You lie inside the coolness of your sheets and watch for answers to be spelled out across the ceiling of your room. You drift into sleep again and sometime later you wake to find yourself standing naked in front of your living room window, your thighs burning with the illogical hope that someone might be able to see you through your sheer curtain. Tears stream down your cheeks because you don't understand the lights or your thighs, or yourself any longer.*

The morning is sad with its shadows and wind. Tree branches clack in the breeze like animal claws skittering across the roof. I make my way to the living room to sit in the yellow chair that looks out the large front window with its curtains drawn wide. I've neither the energy nor the will to either change from my robe or properly close the drapes. The early hour has fallen across my shoulders; I remain heavy with the half-remembered shame of showing my nakedness in front of that window during the night. The well-wintered maple tree clattering outside the living room window waves its own naked body at me, causing me to pull my robe tightly against my sorry throat. I'm filled with shock and remorse for my nighttime display and yet, the louder, more insistent thought is that I might again repeat the act. Even John Milton's nose nudging my hand for his breakfast doesn't rouse me from my terror.

Only one thing repeatedly bangs and clangs and thrashes through my thoughts: I'm now afraid of myself.

The morning travels slowly, dragging its shadows around, warming and thawing the night's frosted grass, allowing moisture to slowly trickle down the dark legs of the maple. I remain in my chair, holding my robe tightly against my frantic body. John Milton meows from somewhere in the center of the house. I stay frozen in my chair until my children arrive, the chilly near-noon hour swirling across their coats. I've, of course, forgotten they were bringing lunch—take-out Chinese, complete with steaming won ton soup, broccoli beef, chef's special chicken, vegetables in hoisin sauce, steamed rice, and fortune cookies.

Bryan kisses my cheek, his lips cold from the January day. "You're staying cozy today, Mom? Good for you," he says. "It's a good day to stay bundled up in your robe."

I manage a trembling smile.

Allison bustles past me, a sour look on her face, her arms filled with bags of food. I hear spoons clanking like little bells just before they're plunged into food containers. I hear plates being stacked and then spread out on the table, utensils arranged aside each plate.

There would have been a time when I'd have done the honors. I'd have used my good serving bowls and proper spoons, rather than tossing take-out paper boxes willy-nilly across the table. I'd have set down my beige linen tablecloth or, at the very least, arranged woven placemats, instead of clattering plates onto the bare wooden surface of my polished table. But that was another time when I wasn't so damaged by broken thoughts, when I was able to keep my tables gleaming with oil and carefulness. That was another time when I wasn't so confused and consumed by thoughts of my nighttime nakedness on display for passersby to see.

Allison calls us to lunch and Bryan gently steers me to the table.

We've each remained silent as we waited for my dear daughter's feeble table presentation. When we're seated and food's been dished onto our plates, Bryan breaks the silence. "You're quiet today, Mom. Is everything all right?"

I nod. My lips are pulled into a tight line, refusing to speak for fear of something truthful falling from my mouth. I'm terrified I'll tell my children that their mother stood in the night, naked in front of the living room window, with burning thighs and thoughts wilder than today's maleficent wind.

"You didn't get dressed," Allison says.

Again, I nod. A nod of the head is as much acknowledgement as I'll allow myself. I'm simply and forever afraid to open my mouth. I look at my fork as if I'm busy admiring its intricacies.

"You haven't even brushed you hair," Allison continues. "And your cat is starving. What's going on? Are you ignoring us on purpose?"

I shrug my shoulders and continue to stare at my fork now as if it's a wondrous new thing. I'm pleased it gives me distraction from my sense of faultiness, my midnight indiscretion. I take the fork and poke at my food, but for the most part I'm not hungry.

When lunch is over, Bryan's dear, round hands capture me about the waist. He returns me to my chair in the living room, all the while clucking in my ear about what a nice lunch we just enjoyed.

"Did you like the tea? Allison picked it out. Green raspberry something-or-other." I wonder if he's hoping I'll mirror his face and smile in return.

"Yes, I liked it." I clamp my mouth closed on any further escaping words.

My children take up spots across from me on the couch, one at each end. Again, we find silence and I'm comforted by the absence of conversation. I find new fascination with my hands as they resume a tight hold on the collar of my robe. I'm sure my pose gives the impression of one in deep contemplation, but the fact is I'm simply frightened my robe will once again spill open.

Bryan and Allison have recently begun to talk around me as if I'm not in the room, but today I don't mind. I'm happy to be a peripheral occupant. The wind outside seems to have picked up, causing the shrubs and trees to dance in a wild tango formation across the yard. John Milton, although sulking about the wind and my neglectfulness, finds enough forgiveness to swirl about my lap before settling under my hand.

"So what's up with you wearing that ratty old robe all day today?" Allison says. "You're clutching it like you're afraid someone's going to take it away. And that *cat*..."

"You should make an effort to be kinder," Bryan says. "You act like she's your enemy instead of your mother."

"I'm nice. I put lunch on the table, didn't I?" Her mouth forms a circle of propriety, but her eyes narrow into a slash of suspicion and defensiveness. At last, the sibling bickering of my children is something for me to be happy about.

"Putting lunch on the table isn't nice, it's ordinary. It's just a thing people do." Bryan stands. "I need a beer...anyone want anything?" He moves toward the kitchen on legs that seem nearly angry.

"No, and don't get all lawyerly with me," Allison calls after him. "I know it's just a thing. But, come on, it's still a nice thing."

Bryan returns with an opened bottle of beer. "Okay, okay. But don't you think you could add a smile? Some conversation? A sense that you're with us here?" Bryan sets his bottle on the table. He's blinking. Pleading. Forming his hands into a gesture of concern.

"What do you want out of me?" Allison says. "I'm here, aren't I?" She picks up a magazine from the coffee table, flips it open to somewhere near the middle, then slaps it back on the table. "See? I'm here. I looked at a magazine. I'm engaged."

I consider telling my daughter her rudeness is causing her face to wrinkle and become misshapen, but I'm still too afraid for what words might accidentally exit my mouth.

"Look. Be flippant if you want. But the way you dance around Mom...the way you ignore her is...well, it's pretty mean." Bryan clasps his hands together as if he's in earnest prayer for her soul. "When's the last time you came over without me dragging you here?"

I'm altogether invisible to my children. Strangely, I'm happy for the moment—I'm the topic of conversation without the burden of actually needing to contribute to the discussion. I want to clap my hands for the joy of being forgotten and that thought nearly makes me burst into laughter.

"I've tried," Allison says, squarely facing Bryan. "Since Mom got sick, I've taken her out shopping, we've had manicures. I've taken her to lunches and dinners. I *tried* to take her to Hawaii. But everything I've done for Mom has turned out to be a *disaster!*" The pitch of Allison's voice rises to match that of the steel wind chimes that clang in the wind outside.

Her body is fierce and lunging. I wonder if she knows how she is twisting her face into an ungainly collection of wrinkled eyes and pursed lips.

She picks up another magazine and smacks it back on the table. "She hasn't said a word since we got here," she says, nearly hissing. "She has no thoughts. I don't think there's anything in there anymore. *Nothing!*"

She picks up another magazine and throws it to the floor. "Face it, we've lost our mother. She's *gone.*"

The familiar sting of tears begins to grow. *No, my little pony...I'm right here. Don't you see me? Here...over here!*

"Of course she has thoughts," Bryan says. He spreads his arms as if he were about to give a benediction. "She's not gone."

That's my boy...he sees me.

"Mom thinks all the time just like everyone else...even you. It's not her thoughts that are leaving...not at all...it's her ability to use language. You can call it dementia. Or wigged out, or...or whatever. The point is, Mom is still *thinking.* She's thinking all the time."

"Come on, Bryan. She can't remember one day to the next."

"Okay, granted. But, how does that make her not our mother? How does that make her nothing? Mom *knows* what she loses every day. Can't you see how sad she is right now? Look at her. For God's sake, she's *crying!*"

Allison fumbles with her hands until they match the prayerful pose of Bryan's. Slowly, she pulls her eyes up to meet my face. She sees my face, wet with sorrow for my beautiful and befuddled daughter. She looks at how I'm obviously sad above the folds of my robe that I continue to keep pulled tightly to my neck. She sees the agony inside my hunched and crooked body.

Suddenly, something similar to lightning splitting open a night sky flashes across her eyes. My daughter sees me as if I've just entered the room for the first time this day.

"Oh, God...Mom!" Allison cries, her face crumbling into small pieces. "Mom." Her voice crashes against her lips.

She rushes from the couch, her long legs bending to kneel beside me. She buries her face in my lap and circles her arms around me. Together, we become a portrait of remorse—me with my dark night-secrets and Allison with her daylight tears.

Allison sways me back and forth, her arms tight around my waist, apologies spilling onto my robed lap. "I'm so sorry," she cries. "You *do* know me, don't you? You're still here?" *I'm right here, dear.* "Mom, I'm so, so sorry."

I release the grip I've had on my robe and allow my hands to fall to Allison's head. I stroke her hair. For the first time all day I let truthful words come from my mouth. "There, there," I croon. "I'm right here. I'm right here."

YOU LET. You let words of love drip from your lips until your daughter is bathed and cleansed in the carefulness of your narrow language. You hold your child to your lap and fold your arms like an angel's wings around her slenderness until it's impossible to distinguish mother from daughter. While you're holding her tightly, you lift your eyes in time to see your son tiptoe from the room. You follow him with your eyes. With one on your lap and one in a different room, you find your children are separate, yet nevertheless the same. In your bewildered thoughts, you know no difference between same and separate. When you're through washing your children with love, regardless of where they move through your house, you watch their bodies go away into the night. When they're gone, your eyes travel down to the place on your robe that holds dried tears from your repentant daughter. You vow you'll never allow your robe to be cleaned of the day's emotion. You realize there's not much distinction between repentance and shame, except the first can bring joy, while the latter, if not cured, can be terminal. Oddly, the evidence of the day's mixture of tears on your robe pulls your lips into a brief smile and at last, you're no longer afraid of the coming night.

Chapter Sixteen

"I'm *not* leaving my house," I say. "Not. Not. *Not.*"

My children sit on the couch, their hands tumbling in their laps; Allison picks at a loose thread on her skirt, Bryan straightens invisible wrinkles on his slacks. There's a growing chasm between my ideas and theirs; maybe there's always a wrongful distance between a mother and her children. Clearly, I don't know, but I recognize I'm suddenly in a battle for my future.

I feel lucky to be having a good moment with words coming easily and clearly. Of course, my language skills could simply be propelled by the gravity of the topic. Nevertheless, I use every word that comes to mind in order to argue my case.

"Why would you even *think* I would leave this home, the home where your father lived, where you were babies?" I say. "This is where you grew up. Underneath all this paint is every crayon mark you ever scribbled over the walls when I wasn't looking. I couldn't bear to scrub them off, so I just painted over them so I'd know they are still there. And that front door? We went out that door every morning. I walked you to school with your little hands nestled in mine. Every morning. And then every afternoon, I met you outside your school doors to walk you home again…home…here. How could you even think I would walk out that door now…*our* door…and never come back? No. I'm not leaving."

"Mom, you didn't even *look* at the brochure we brought," Bryan says. "It's a nice—"

"I don't need to look at a brochure to know you're trying to put me away."

Allison's hands fly to her cheeks, presumably to hide a sudden flush of color. "No, Mom. We're trying to *help* you," she says. Her hands barely hide what now looks like streaks of fire consuming the wall of her face.

"By tearing me away from my home? That's helping me?"

"Okay, let's slow down and start this conversation over again," Bryan says, his face softening into the curve of a half-smile. He seems to be running his own internal version of good cop, bad cop. I wonder if he does this when negotiations at his law firm need to be reset. I can only assume this is the look he uses to disarm anyone foolish enough to go against him.

He sighs and moderates his tone. "Look, Mom, you could have someone do *everything* for you. Housework, shopping, the laundry. They have fun bus trips. You could meet new people. You could have girlfriends again." He waves the brochure like a fan. "It's a beautiful facility and you can have your own apartment with your own things. It's beautiful…really."

"It is," Allison says, her smile looking like a wedge of red apple. "We took a tour already and it's gorgeous. We can decorate your room any way we want, and I know this wonderful designer who is totally gifted with small spaces. She uses really soothing blues, muted colors, soft textures. She could—"

"No! I'm not leaving. I don't *like* soft, muted things. I don't like small spaces. I don't want someone else telling me where to put my things. I'm not leaving my home just to spend a fortune to go sit in some tiny, cramped little baby blue, softly textured hole waiting to die. I need my space. I need my garden."

Bryan cups his head and slides the brochure back into his bag.

I've made my point.

"Well let's just postpone the thought of moving until you're ready. In the meantime, we'll get you more help around the house, someone to help you keep up with daily things. The dishes and laundry. The heavy gardening. Kind of keep an eye on things around here until you're ready to talk about this again."

"I don't need help." I place my chin in a defiant pose. "But if it would make you feel better you can send someone over to lop back that yellow…thing…that vine-thing that's hanging over my rose bed and blocking the sun. But I'm not moving and I won't discuss this nonsense again."

With that final, sputtering word, I stand from my chair and head toward the kitchen, leaving Bryan and Allison to clatter about in their seats. Bryan colonizes the couch, while Allison perches on the edge of her chair like a cat ready to spring after a sparrow. I expect they will maintain those positions for at least a few minutes.

I pluck a sponge from the bottom of the kitchen sink and wipe it across the counter.

Even though I've won this round, I begin to cry. Great drops of sadness fall onto the kitchen counter. I dab them up with my sponge and move over to the stove, continuing to wipe crumbs and tears and the misery of every woman whose children think it best to take her from her home.

Whether it's for my own good or not, I can't imagine never having a cleaning sponge again in my hands. I can't think of having my garden shears and gathering basket, my dishes, my furniture sitting out on the driveway to be picked over and bargained down in a yard sale. I can't conceive of never again lying in my bed, listening to the early morning creaks and groans and rustlings of this dear old house. I can't possibly leave behind the pencil marks on the pantry doorjamb where each year's growth of the children was carefully measured and tallied, or where their little handprints were pushed into wet cement as we poured the walkway along the side of the house. I can't be asked to leave the spot where my beautiful Ivan fell to the ground, my arms holding him, my scream keening through the sky as his last breath sighed into the earth.

There is rigorous madness to my arm strokes, a blue sponge creating a ridiculous prop for a crazy woman. The difficulty of a failing memory makes me either obsessively clean, going over and over the same spot like stories that get repeated again and again, or forgetful to pick up a sponge in the first place. Right now, I fall into the former category, rubbing obsessive-compulsively over and over the same spot in a great spurt of muttonheaded behavior.

Soap creeps up my hands, my arms, like bubbles from an ocean surf. I'm reminded of something and I run back to the living room.

"I took you to the goddamn ocean and this is how you treat me? We stood together in the surf, laughing, with bubbles of saltwater climbing up our legs and this is what you want to do to me? Put me away?" I shake my wet sponge at the startled faces of my children, flipping water across the room like a blessing. "You can't hide the ocean we stood in and you can't hide me."

I run back to the kitchen and start scrubbing the counter again. Again and again and again my arm makes wild circling arcs across the countertop. I feel John Milton winding his soft body around my legs, his tail curling like a plant tendril up a garden stake.

I run back to the living room. "And I'll not leave John Milton," I cry. "And you can't take him away either. He's my comfort…and… so there!"

I march back to the kitchen where I find John Milton looking as nonplussed as my children. I seem to dismay those I love these days. My children. My cat. Even myself.

Here is my predicament: I've now become that electric moment between a spark of lightning and its thunderous announcement when everyone counts the seconds between the flash and the boom. My children say something I find disagreeable and I can nearly watch them count in their heads, *one Mississippi, two Mississippi*, as they measure the time until I come crashing down around their ears.

Now here I am, standing in the middle of the kitchen, tears falling onto the floor, drop by drop, when Bryan and Allison come in. Without a word, they braid their arms around me.

"Shhh, Mom," Bryan whispers. "It's all okay."

"We won't make you move anywhere," Allison says. "We'll get someone to take care of you."

"Forever," Bryan says. "We'll make sure you always stay right here. We promise."

We begin to sway a slow, small dance. It's the dance of a broken mother and her frightened children, the tender waltz of a woman who is well beyond anything but her own terrifying and myopic needs.

I dance within the arms of my children. My hand releases the wet sponge; it falls away to the floor and, for now, the notion of moving me from my home falls away with it.

Chapter Seventeen

My head is a box of dust. Somehow I've altogether lost my ability to reason with myself. I'm now an argument with every movement and every sound I make. I feel as if I'm in a paper boat, floating down a sidewalk stream during a torrential rain. Ahead is a sucking drain, waiting to swallow me up, paper boat and all, and I'm paddling to stay afloat in all this water and dust, but it's useless.

I am lost, lost, lost.

Every room of my home is now littered with the evidence of my fractured thoughts. Laundry clutters the floor of my bedroom, trickling in lumpy little piles down the hallway. I stack mysterious envelopes on the kitchen table into towers of puzzlement; my name is on everything, often printed behind little glassine windows. I'm not curious enough to open any of the envelopes, but neither am I ambitious enough to clean them off the table. If, now and then, an envelope should get brushed away and fall to the floor, it is simply left where it lands. Newspapers lie on the front porch until the delivery boy finally stops leaving them. Some days I'm bright enough to bathe, but then halfway through I find myself adrift and splashing. My hair often goes unwashed, as do the dishes.

I no longer make a distinction between what is John Milton's food and what is mine. We eat what we eat. It's all the same and, every now and then, I'm horrified at what I've become.

Colors have turned to varying shades of gray. Differences and nuance between this and that are no longer available to either my senses or my abilities. Every day there are more and more small downward steps—tiny little backward movements that leave me stunned and ashamed. I shuffle, drift, float through time. Now and then I surprise myself by popping up to take a deep breath of clarity before once more diving under the surface of an ocean always stormy with forgetfulness. During the times when I notice how my disposition has turned to become mostly dreamy and unconcerned with ordinary tasks that are part of running a house, I also understand that in the next moment, I'll likely forget what I'm supposed to be doing anyway.

New things don't stick in my mind for long, in spite of the chewing gum and glue that continues to fill up all the little nooks and crannies of my brain. Making sense of little things is now the occupation of every day. Nights are always long hours of anguish.

This head of mine, filled with its dust and gum, is always an unreasonable question mark. A comma. A period. Punctuation that interrupts the flow of every day. At times, I find long moments of brilliance when thoughts are clear enough to provide encouragement to me that perhaps I'm not really so very ill at all.

It's in these moments of sunny thought that I'm strengthened and able to continue hiding the odd nature of my illness. Somehow I'm always able to rise above the clattering fray, to gather my piles of clothes and place them in the hamper, or to scurry through the house with a dust cloth. To quickly sort through the mail. Snip away dried leaves from my potted violets lolling on the kitchen window sill. Take a leisurely soak in the tub, put on makeup. Find my perfume.

But then I always crash, each time slamming harder than before, tearing myself open with the broken shards of this awful disease.

I am lucid. Then I'm not. Still, I manage to hide it all from everyone, because it seems the only reasoned course—just in case I become better.

Just in case.

Allison sends a cleaning lady twice a week, every Monday and Friday. I'm always surprised when the doorbell rings and a woman I don't know stands on my porch with a bucket of cleaning supplies and a mop, begging to be let in.

These women are lucky I'm a lady with a Southern upbringing. I'm convinced they leave with their pockets filled with my things, although I never catch anyone in the act in spite of my chattering vigilance over every sweep of the hand. I stand over them as they scrub away toilet rings and tidy the kitchen. I follow them around as they pick up my clothes and wash my dishes, as they guide a broom across the floor and vacuum the carpet. As they dust, polish, fold the finished laundry, and sweep the floor. I watch over every movement as they spread the scent of cleanliness across the rooms of my home.

They diligently create order from stem to stern, but each new and different woman fails to do the simple task of picking up my fallen-down mind. It's no wonder—and certainly not my fault—that when they're done and packing to go, I yell at them to *never* come back again.

On Saturdays, men come into my yard with noisy mowers and weed-eaters and blowers to whisk away the evidence of my inattentiveness to the garden. When they come, I move to the centermost spot in the house and stand as still as a statue until they finish and reload their equipment into their truck. I don't like their noise and I don't like what they do to my plants.

After the men with their lawnmowers and leaf blowers are gone, I tiptoe outside and lay soft apologies like tiny prayers over my poor flowers and bushes for the horrid assaults they must have endured at the hands of those noisy, grass-stained men.

The Monday and Friday women are difficult enough, but I especially don't like the Saturday men.

On Sunday mornings, my children come to see the handiwork of the labor that has occurred over the week. They cluck and coo over sparkling floors and manicured lawns as if they had made the shine and orderliness with their own hands. Bryan whisks up my neatly stacked mail and places it in a plastic bag; he'll take it with him when he leaves.

He used to spread papers across the table for me for me to sign. One day I signed something so I wouldn't have to sign things any longer. Bryan told me he was putting my money in trust. We argued over that—a great heaving, sighing argument as heated and tear-filled as when he took away my car—but in the end, I gave Bryan control over all paper things and all car things. Now he just takes my mail without comment and I say nothing in return.

I've no idea where my car went (along with my keys from the lettuce drawer that started all this).

I guess today is Sunday because my children arrive, shaking a rainy Sacramento sky from their shoes and forming smiles upon their faces. They kiss my cheek and say *Good morning, Mom,* not particularly with words, but rather with their kissing mouths and patting hands.

"I'm going to stop your newspaper delivery," Bryan announces, his voice as flat and dull as the low-hanging sun that seems desperate to make its way through this morning's heavy clouds.

"Did I run out of money to buy my newspapers?" I ask. "Am I poor now?"

"Mom, you have enough money in trust to live until you're a hundred and twenty. Dad left you just fine…you don't need to worry about money." Bryan smiles gently in my direction.

"Then why are you taking away my newspapers?" I ask. "Those are *my* newspapers and I *want* them. I need them…for…for newspaper things." My voice is high and thin with sudden distress at the thought of losing yet one more thing.

"You don't read them. You don't even bring them in the house."

"Well, I'd read them if they were placed here," I say, patting the top of my coffee table. "They should deliver my newspapers…with coffee, don't you think? They should ring the doorbell. Maybe I'd open the door if people had the common courtesy that God gave a duck to let me know they're here. With coffee."

My children look at me as if I'm a stranger. A stranger with dust and gum in her head.

"So it's settled," I say. "If I *do* have money then I should have my newspapers, with coffee…and maybe a nice blueberry scone." I narrow my eyes. "Or maybe you're not telling me the truth about my money and I *am* poor."

"Mom, listen to me…this isn't about money." Bryan looks wounded as if I've just questioned his manhood. "All this is about is that you don't pick your newspapers up off the porch."

"Then I want you to call the newspaper people and tell them to bring coffee and scones with my newspaper. I'll pick them up then." I punctuate my declaration with one sharp nod of my head.

"Oh good grief," Allison says. She shrugs her shoulders and wanders off to putter around my kitchen. I've apparently made an appropriate point because Bryan says nothing more. He opens the Sunday paper and hides his face behind its pages.

It's often like this that my children avoid me. I don't know why.

Sometime later, Allison comes out from the kitchen and asks me, "Mother, why is there cat food in your cereal bowl?"

YOU DON'T. You don't know why you would have spooned cat food into your favorite cereal bowl, the red one, the one clearly imprinted with the word Cereal on its side. You want to explain how you know your different bowls, but what's the point? To you, it doesn't matter if you feed the cat from your cereal bowl, or if your cereal ends up in the cat's bowl. A bowl is a bowl. Yet, children still question their befuddled mothers, giving well-meaning discourses about bowls and their proper use (according to the words written across their ceramic sides). You're no longer compelled to be perfect; your best response is to shrug your shoulders and walk to the center of your living room. There, you shuffle your feet back and forth and hold your head in a posture of shame, even though you don't know why you do the things you do.

"Mom?" Allison gently shakes my arm, speaking earnestly into my face.

She startles me. "I don't know," I say, my voice echoing her earnest tone. I say my words once more for good measure. "I *don't* know."

I'm not certain exactly what it is that I don't know, but I assert my innocence over it all anyway.

"Don't feed the cat from *your* bowl...and don't you eat from the cat's bowl," Allison says, her eyes wide and serious. "Okay?"

"Okay," I say. I look up in time to notice Bryan's eyebrows flip quizzically before resuming his place in the business section of the newspaper.

"That reminds me," I say. "Do we know what time my coffee and scones are to be delivered? I want to be ready on time. A lady always needs to be dressed, with her make-up on...and certainly, a smile on her face." My children disappear once again behind their newspapers and kitchen doors.

I return to shuffling back-and-forth in the center of the living room. When one's head is a fractured stream of nonsense, the middle of a room is a safer place indeed.

After my children leave—Bryan taking with him a plastic bag with my mail tucked inside and Allison taking the last of my good senses—I go into my closet to comfort myself with another letter. This time I pull out something that appears to be a poem. I say *appears* because it's nothing like the somersaulting poetry of Milton or Poe or Joyce or any of the classic writers.

Strangely, reading is something I still do well in spite of this creeping, gathering illness. Maybe it's because I learned to read at a very young age. I could, perhaps, compare my continued reading ability to an athlete's muscle memory that, once ingrained, requires little conscious effort or thought to throw a fast ball or kick a field goal—or in my case, to read a simple sentence. Maybe, in spite of my silly-willy mind, I'm simply making up for all the reading Ma couldn't do because her eyes were so very broken. I'm not sure which of us received the better bargain, though. I wonder if we each in our own way came to a certain form of blindness. My brain is as blind now as Ma's eyes had been.

What a sad lot we turned out to be.

As I settle the page in my hands, I decide to dedicate today's reading to Ma and her eyes.

My darling children:

Here's a rhyme we used to say now and then. I won't be sorry for its silly words, because if you think about it, apologies ahead of time only serve to diminish the apologetic. Nevertheless, we made up this rhyme when you were little. We recited it instead of prayers because it made you fall asleep with smiles on your little faces. We called it The Finger Poem and as I recall, it changed every time we said it because we could never remember how it—The Finger Poem—went exactly. Here is one way I recall. As you read, try to picture us lacing our fingers together, yours freshly cleaned after bedtime snacks laced with sticky honey and jelly, mine simply enthralled with how I was entrusted with such delicacies to hold. So here it is—The Finger Poem:

Here are your fingers,
Your whorls and your swirls
Your legacies spinning,
Your waves to the world.
So let's paint a party and
Give them grand speeches
We'll sing to the stars
That crawl across beaches.
We'll give them a dance and
Teach them to Jump!
Lace them like zippers
Zarrimp-a-zarrump.
We'll cross them in gestures of
Fortune and Luck
All higgledy piggledy,
Chuck-a-ruck-zuk.
We'll dress them up smartly
In feathers and lizards
And teach them to ride on
The backs of our scissors.
And when they grow old,
And turn wrinkled and bent,
Like ten little grandmas,
We'll wave them again.

With all love,
Your silly mother

I read my poem and decide it is an utterly ridiculous thing. It makes no sense. I think perhaps I should tear this nonsense into a million unreadable pieces, but then I think about the moment when Allison and Bryan might discover this poem. They might even remember our sweet nights of milky kisses and giggle-faces. That settles it. I refold my nonsensical, laughable rhyme and place it back in the letter box where I found it.

Obviously, I'm in no position to judge.

Chapter Eighteen

It's raining. Allison and Bryan stand at my doorstep, shaking out their umbrellas and smiling at me. "Hi, Mom," they say, nearly in unison, like twins. I can't tell if they're sheepish or impish. They seem to be mostly holes of color in an otherwise gray day of clouds and rain and I can't figure them out.

The odd appearance of my children causes me to wonder how whole flocks of heavy-winged birds can fly through trees without breaking a single branch and yet I can't seem to think my way through one simple moment.

"We brought you a girl," Allison says, a bit too brightly, her mouth smiling a little wider than normal. Her hair swings blonde swipes across an otherwise colorless sky.

"A girl? Whatever will I do with a girl? I can barely take care of myself."

"Mom, we're not exactly talking about a girl," Bryan says. "More like a woman."

"And just what should I do with a *woman*?"

"That's the whole point," Allison says. "You don't have to do anything. She'll do everything."

"Everything?"

"Yes! *Everything.*" Allison beams brightly, her red lips creating another hole in the purple sky.

I decide my children are just being playful. Then a small, dark blue car pulls into the drive and a woman gets out. She waves and smiles.

"Here she is now," Bryan says almost too brightly for me to keep up with.

The woman steps from her car, pulls her coat over her head, and runs through the rain to join Allison and Bryan on the doorstep. She has no umbrella to shake—only a face that beams at me. I'm not at all sure what to do.

"Mom, this is Jewell," Bryan says, ushering forward a woman who appears to be nearing her middle years. "She's going to stay here and help you out around the house."

I study the woman. Jewell. Her skin is like velvet. It looks so brown-buttery and delicious, I want to taste it. I don't know what to do with everyone in the doorway, especially my children and a woman whose skin I want to taste, so I invite them in and tell them to sit.

"My children tell me you're now my woman," I say to Jewell. "I can't say I've ever had a woman before. Just what am I supposed to *do* with you?"

Allison fidgets in her seat. Bryan rubs his forehead and utters a wincing groan.

Jewell seems unfazed. "I'm here to help you, ma'am. Cook. Clean up a little. Do the laundry. Whatever you need. I can drive you to appointments and maybe take you out to lunch or a movie now and then." She smiles broadly and looks at me with warm eyes that seem to have melted round holes through her otherwise perfect covering of skin.

"And this is all the idea of my children?"

"Yes, ma'am."

"And you go home at night?"

"No, ma'am. The arrangement is…well, I'll stay nights, too."

"Good God! Am I to sleep with you?"

Bryan leaps from his chair. "Mom! Be *nice*. She'll stay in the guest room. She's here to…she's a special aide who helps people who are sick like you. She's here to help. Okay?" Bryan leans into me with a gaze that leaves me no choice but to settle into my chair. I cross my ankles and fold my hands. Like a lady.

Still, the room has taken on shades of gray, as if I've brought the day's icy clouds into the house to huddle across the ceiling and drip misunderstanding down the walls of the living room. Bryan settles back in his seat, but continues to look at me with eyes as clouded as the day. I seem to be a source of discomfort in my own home and I don't know how to fix the thing I've just broken.

I blink away the sudden lack of color in the living room. "I've never had a woman before. Not even my mother had a woman and she was blind and lived in the South where it was common for someone to have a woman…for cleaning and serving and such. Sometimes they even had a *man*, sometimes both a man, a woman and all their little picaninnies."

"*Mother!*" Allison cries.

The room is sharply quiet again. Gray again.

From the edge of my periphery, I see John Milton stroll into the living room on practiced cat feet. He walks directly to Jewell and jumps into her lap, rubbing his forehead against her chin before settling into the deep folds of her skirt. Jewell strokes the top of John Milton's head. "What a lovely cat," she says.

"Yes," I say. "That's John Milton. He's come home after a long time away."

"He's beautiful. I like cats and…well, they mostly seem to like me, too."

I stand up as if to announce the end of our interview. "All right, children. Thank you for my woman. She can stay, but she can't sleep in my bed."

Allison opens her mouth as if to speak, but only a small sigh escapes. Bryan cups his hand around his forehead and shakes his head. Neither says a word as I head to my bedroom. I close the door and stand in front of it, not knowing what next to do other than shuffle my feet back and forth.

I hear my children talking; I hear them show my woman around the house, opening doors and cupboards, pointing out where things are kept; I hear *thank you* and *goodbye*; I hear the front door close. The silence of my children's absence creeps under my bedroom door.

Sometime later, I hear my woman—my new woman—cooking in the kitchen and cooing to John Milton. The house smells of spices and furnace heat and, strangely, I'm satisfied deep into the core of my bones.

While things are quiet, I decide now is a good time to consult the oracle of my cedar box. I pull out a letter and read my scrawling words, my breath falling in a whisper over them.

My lovely children,

Your father was born with healing hands—hands that could make your skin swoon beneath their touch. His hands were such that I could feel heat rise up from them whenever I came near and diminish when I would leave. There was mystery in his hands. Mystery and healing.

When your MeeMaw died, your father's hands drew me to his chest and calmed the quaking waters within the cells of my body.

Then, when your PaaPaw died, so soon after, it was your father's hands that melted away those mountains of anguish for whole moments at a time.

His hands helped me wander through my college studies of literature and math and the humanities; they helped me study each book page to become Salutatorian of my class, a purple sash across my shoulders signifying the accomplishment. Then, those hands clasped my elbow to guide me through days of uncertainty and decisions after I became orphaned from Ma and Pa.

They held me on the day of our wedding and, only days later, they opened an envelope that spilled out a letter forever changing our lives. In all the years after, it was the only time I saw his hands tremble. He pulled the letter from its envelope and read it slowly. Twice.

After a long silence, he looked at me and smiled. "It's all good," he beamed. "We got the job." He put the letter aside and pulled me to him. He danced me in a slow, swaying shuffle, all the while whispering into my ear. *It's all good, baby. It's all good.* He rubbed my back with those hands that could melt stone and whispered in my ear until I knew everything was good and we were good and nothing would ever be the same.

The following day, we packed our few belongings into the car and drove away from the graves of my Ma and Pa and John Milton the Cat. We left the upside-down winds of The Blowing Rock and the green-blue scent of the Appalachian Mountains that always seemed to carry secrets deep within their hollows and swales.

We left the soil of our roots, and yet everything I knew or ever wanted to know resided in the hands of your father as they carried me across our wedding threshold and all the way to Sacramento, California.

It's his hands I miss the most. His hands and his eyes… and, of course, the touch of his breath on my neck as he whispered into my skin, *It's all good, baby. It's all good.*

I just thought you children should know of hands and their sublime importance.

Love,
Mom

I look down, dumbstruck that all my memories now fit neatly within the fold of my arms. I grab my letters and hug them to me, bringing them to my face so I can smell them, taste them, feel their texture on my skin. I've created a small treasure; I don't know what else to do but hold these letters, my mouth silently moving a blessing over my armful of creations.

Each day I have fewer and fewer memories. I imagine that soon, only the most elderly thoughts will be left. The withered old women, the old crones.

I'm growing quieter now and, ridiculously, words simply fall from my mind, never to be useful again. They just clatter to the floor and break into unintelligent little pieces. The only thing to do with these once-lovely words is to allow them to be swept up and discarded. I guess that's why I now have Jewell—my woman.

She's here to sweep up after my dropped words.

Chapter Nineteen

*Y*OU PACE. *You pace circles through your house, making footprint marks on the carpet where your woman has freshly vacuumed. It is evening and you're crazy with an urgency to move your legs until they take you somewhere safe, somewhere away from your failing mind. You try the front door, but some foolish person has tampered with the lock and you can't get out. You try another door and it's the same story. Locks have been replaced on each door by someone who intends to keep you from your memories. When the sun is completely done with the day and there's nothing left for you to do but sigh at your doors one last time, you swallow the medicine your woman hands you and go to bed. Sometimes, you wake in the middle of the night to once again wander your paths and try your doors, but the story hasn't changed and your memories are still on the other side.*

My woman, Jewell, proves neither to be my woman nor a jewel, like amethysts or garnets or pink topaz would be jewels. No. She clinically documents my endless circles through the house. She measures my food and doles out medicine as if my consumption were a personal opportunity to prove her worth. She locks all the doors to confound me and smiles incessantly to annoy me. Worst of all, she shorts my evening glass of wine, even refusing to refill my glass when it's demanded of her.

"It's not good for you, ma'am," she offers as her only explanation for such ungracious behavior.

"Nonsense!" I say. "And would you *not* call me ma'am?"

"Yes, ma'am."

I sigh. "My wine is my only comfort," I say.

"Yes, ma'am."

"So, you'll pour me another glass? A proper, full glass this time?"

"I'm sorry, ma'am."

"You're a mean woman, Jewell. I'm going to speak to my children about this."

"Yes, ma'am."

"I *mean* it. You'll hear about this from my children. And *stop* calling me ma'am."

"Certainly, Mrs. Glidden."

"That's even worse. Fine, then…call me whatever you want." I sulk into the palms of my hands.

"Yes, ma'am. Do you need anything else?"

I perk up. "A nice glass of wine, if it's not too much trouble."

Every evening it's the same conversation. Every evening it's the same result. Jewell and I have our circuitous routes and nonsensical words until there is nothing left to do but sit in a chair and rub the topside of my legs until my hands become hot from the friction of rubbing.

I sit now in my living room chair, distressed after yet another unproductive discussion regarding my paltry serving of wine. I absently rub my knees, back and forth, back and forth. The television is on, but people are talking too fast the images are flickering from one thing to another more swiftly than I can follow. Flickering, flickering, flickering.

My stomach feels oddly hot; heat travels through me until I feel nothing but sparkles in my arms and legs—in my head. Sparkles! Twinkling pinpoints prick through my body like lights shining through tiny holes in a blue drapery on the backdrop of a stage. It's a Broadway play! I watch with fascination as sparkles of fiery white light travel from my head into my arms and down my legs, down, down deep into my core.

Sparkles, sparkles everywhere.

The sparkles cause me to dance and jump until I fall to the floor, shaking, dreaming wild visions and yet thinking of nothing but prickly spots of light. I am aware, then unaware and then vaguely aware again.

I float and dance like a firefly in a bottle, helplessly beating my wings against a glass.

I hear someone—my woman perhaps—calling me. "Ma'am. Ma'am!"

Then, I feel arms lifting me. Laying me down. Straps are placed across my chest, my legs. Then I'm quickly rolled out into a cold, gray wintry day. I hear more voices invoking my name. A high, wailing siren penetrates my skin and frightens my heart. I see lights again—flickery, flickery lights that fly about inside my brain, behind my eyes. Once again, I'm part of a play, dancing to the rhythm of a light show.

A voice speaks into my sparkly, sparkly face. "Mrs. Glidden? Mrs. Glidden, do you know where you are?"

My lips buzz together; it sounds like bees live in my mouth. The twinkle-lights in my body seem to have burnt out, but the darkness behind my closed eyes, along with my buzzing lips, continue to befuddle me.

"Mrs. Glidden?" Someone in a bright pink T-shirt with *Emergency Room* printed across its front in large readable letters talks to me. "You're at Sutter Hospital. You've had a seizure. We're going to give you some medicine to settle you. I need to start an IV line for your medicine, so I'd like you to try to hold still for me. Okay?"

I try to talk, but my mouth only manages to murmur in sibilant thrums. I nod my head. Soon, the T-shirted nurse probes for a vein under my skin. When she's done, she pushes the plunger on a syringe of cold, stinging liquid into my new IV line.

Quickly I sleep—a darkly dreamless sleep.

When I wake, I'm in a different room. Bryan and Allison hover over my bed like ghosts clinging together until it's hard for me to distinguish between them. My mouth no longer feels like bees are buzzing and singing behind my lips, but still my thoughts are cloudy and unreliable. I recognize another person at the foot of my bed—it's Dr. Ellison. She holds a silver clipboard in her hands and talks to my children as if I'm not present.

"Your mother's had a seizure," she says. "She seems to have suffered a generalized tonic-clonic event…what you might call a grand mal seizure. Because your mother's brain is most likely accumulating a protein we call beta amyloid…this could explain the event. The protein could be collecting and causing a form of plaque. It's thought that this plaque can cause nerve damage in the brain, which you see evidenced in her continued decline of cognitive and motor function. It's not uncommon for Alzheimer's patients to experience seizure activity, but because your mother is still relatively young, we want to keep her here for a day or two for tests to make certain something else didn't cause the problem."

"Whatever you need," Bryan says.

Allison looks down at her hands as if she is inspecting a new manicure, but I see her chin wavering in distress. "Is she going to die?"

"Of course not, Allison," Bryan says. His voice is in full attorney-in-charge, deep-throated confidence. "Mom is *not* going to die." Then he wavers. "Right, Doctor?"

"Well, actually that's a good question," Dr. Ellison says, matter-of-factly. "Although this was certainly frightening for you, your mother is doing well at the moment. We've started her on an anti-seizure medication that will help control further problems. Of course, we want to evaluate her carefully before we're able to completely determine your mother's specific needs. She might be out of sorts for a day or two…that's common after seizures. But she shouldn't have any long-lasting effects and certainly we'll treat whatever other issues, should anything crop up."

"Thank you, Doc," Bryan says. He shoots a look of victory at his sister. Allison continues to look at her hands, seeming to not notice her brother's arrogant flippancy. In spite of assurances that I'm not dying, Allison's chin continues to tremble. *My poor little pony.*

Dr. Ellison pats my knee. "You let your nurse know if you need anything, Mrs. Glidden, and I'll stop in tomorrow morning to see you." I'm still afraid of my mouth, so I just nod my head. Dr. Ellison takes my chart and leaves my children to continue their ghostly, silent hovering over me.

After a while, when I'm settled and drowsy again, my children leave—Bryan first, then Allison. They back away with kisses and promises to come the following morning. Their absence causes me to spend the next hour hiccupping and crying for them to come back. A nurse injects something into my IV which quickly makes me fall into a dreamless sleep, my eyelashes still wet. Confusion wraps around me like a cocoon of unfamiliar, scratchy hospital blankets.

Nurses come in and out through the night. They are noisy in spite of shoes that squish with every step. They turn lights on and then forget to turn them off when they leave. They take my blood pressure and temperature, grimly writing down their findings. Still, everything is done with care. Every movement is accompanied with a question.

Question: "Are you feeling any pain?"

Answer: "I want to go home."

Question: "Do you know your name?"

Answer: "Who are you?"

Question: "Would you like anything?"

Answer: "Yes. My wine. And for God's sake, try to give me a decent serving this time."

In the morning, it's clear I've become a trembling, feckless, gray-haired Alice in Wonderland, complete with pills to make me sleep and pills to wake me up, pink liquids in tiny little cups and still more pills and capsules in a colorful array of sizes and shapes. Bryan and Allison arrive only to wait in my room—again like silent, worried spirits—even haunting my empty bed as I'm wheeled off for another test or scan.

I feel nothing but circling confusion and I worry over it all.

People come and go; I don't know who they are.

I pull at a narrow, bothersome tube sticking out of my arm; someone then ties my wrists to each side of my bed. I call out for help to use the restroom but no one hears me. I soil myself. I cry. I sleep in deep confusion, only to wake even more confused. Faces continue to float above and around me—I'm afraid of these floating images. People talk, but I can't figure out what they're saying. I talk and my listeners can't figure out what *I'm* saying. I'm a foreigner in my body and I don't know what to do. I'm afraid. I'm afraid.

I tell someone a murderer lives in the elevator—I hear him behind the door that whooshes open. I still hear him when the door closes. He is in there and I tell on him.

More pills are brought to me in small paper cups. Twice a day, blood is pulled from my body into tubes labeled with someone's name. I'm asked if it's *my* name. I tell them it is, but I don't know. I don't know.

I don't know.

After three days, I'm released to two people who say they're my children; they smile and coo over me like I'm a newborn, ready to be presented to the world. It appears I've achieved the medical trifecta of a normal brain scan, good blood tests indicating the rainbow of new medications are working, and (best of all) I'm apparently no longer in danger of imminently keeling over again into a heap of quivering motherhood.

Sometime during the wheelchair ride from my hospital bed to the car, I remember the faces of my children. I'm comforted that I'm not in the hands of the elevator murderer.

Bryan helps me into his car with hands as gentle as his father's would have been. I nearly fracture into a million tiny pieces under the gesture. When we reach home, my woman throws open the door and beams brightly at me as Bryan and Allison—one on each side—help me into the house and to the couch where I'm propped up with pillows and covered with a blue crochet quilt.

"Oh, ma'am, welcome," she says. "Welcome home. I'm making your favorite dinner." Jewell smiles and gushes over me like I've just done something important and impressive, rather than having fallen at her feet only days earlier in a frightening heap of a seizure, complete with leg-thrashing, tongue-biting, and eye-rolling terror.

"I'll take my wine now, thank you," I say. My mouth continues to feel broken and slurry, my head still foggy and shattered.

"Instead of that, how about a grand glass of Southern-style sweet tea? I made it especially for your homecoming."

"I see you've lost your charm while I was gone," I say. "Is that your idea of a proper homecoming celebration? Sweet tea? Really?"

"Sorry, Mom," Bryan says. "Wine's not compatible with your new meds. It's either wine or seizures. Take your pick."

"Can't I think about that over my evening wine?"

Everyone laughs as if I've made a very clever joke, but no one answers my entirely reasonable request. Jewell simply wanders into the kitchen to finish dinner. Bryan opens the sports section to read and fret over the latest ball scores (he's a Giants fan, of course), while

Allison putters about the living room, her hands rearranging things in nearly imperceptible increments—an inch here, two inches there.

If I were in my right mind with a generous glass of red in my hand, I'd be able to figure out the analogy of things being moved without actually making a difference. But it seems I've only John Milton the Cat (who's now curled onto my lap) to listen to my sighing disappointment that so many people can now ruin me by withholding a simple glass of sociable wine.

I spend the rest of the evening stroking my dear little cat, who continues to snuggle deep into the folds of my gown. I most likely look as though I'm in thoughtful repose, but in fact, I'm wildly sulking.

I don't know when it occurred that I turned into a child to be ignored, denied, and quite probably snickered over when I'm out of earshot. Nevertheless, this seems to be the state of things, now that I've had this turn of events. It should have made me important, but instead that seizure turned me small.

Maybe tomorrow someone will serve me up something better than a glass of sweet tea, iced with the growing and palpable doubt of who I used to be.

Chapter Twenty

In the months since my small seizure episode, my woman has turned completely and purely evil and I can find no good explanation for her horrid behavior. She now withholds my wine completely, instead handing me an array of pills, all to be washed down with tasteless water. I've developed an embarrassing inability to hold my bladder and the only cure, it seems, is to pull plastic-coated adult diapers up my legs.

"I don't need diapers," I protest.

"They're to keep you a *lady*, ma'am," Jewell says, her lips smiling with illogical assurance.

"There is *nothing* ladylike about these goddamn diapers," I say. "Take them off me. Now!"

"Yes, ma'am," she says. But she leaves the diapers in place and tidies my room the same as she tidies my bottom—without fuss or comment.

I'm angry, but I console myself by concentrating on her one spot of redeeming brightness.

My woman sings.

Great, heaving songs of heaven and joy and Jesus her Redeemer. She sings of nights in white satin and having blues down to her toes, just as easily as she sings about amazing grace and blackbirds singing in the dead of night. Her voice thrills the walls of every room as she moves about the house, cooking and cleaning. When her voice is quiet, the silence of the house begs her to begin again.

She is comfort to the bones of the house and comfort into the depths of my ears.

She helps me remember that my Ivan was a singer, too. He sang into the whorls of my ears and made me stumble with weakness for him. He caused tears to flood my eyes and smiles to spill like rivers of joy across my face. He danced me through the kitchen and sang me into the tangles of our sheets. His songs were tender and lusty and full of his fair-haired musky scent. Long after they left his warm lips, I could hear the melodies, the lyrics, the tempos, all deeply fastened within my mind.

Ivan's songs traveled from his round lips through the skin of my body and all the way into the tiny ears of my babies while they grew themselves to become Bryan and Allison. I could feel their watery dance inside my belly as they swam toward the songs of their father. I too swam toward his voice.

When Ivan died, it must have been the awful silence of his voice that caused my brain to shrivel and die. There seems no other explanation.

Misery by absence of song.

My only hope is that my woman's songs will bring my dying memories back to life. Certainly, the pills she gives me only serve to make me dim and tired. They cause me to shuffle my feet back and forth in paths through the house, making me the thing I've always feared becoming—a doddering old woman in a leaking, wailing, shriveling body.

When Jewel is finished cleaning my room and smoothing my bedcovers for the day, she leaves me to pull at my clothing and fuss at my completely dissolved sense of whatever Southern charm I once might have had.

I would continue to try the doors for my escape from this place of hell, but someone has dug great black holes in front of each door. Now and then, I see my woman pick up the holes and shake them out into the day like small area rugs. Then she returns the holes in front of each door. She confuses me with such magic.

I'm like an old dog now who circles and circles, before finally grunting and folding its legs under its body. Perhaps the only comfort this old dog has is in the habit of circling. Still, I'm a dog smart enough to avoid the holes in front of each door.

YOU FIND. You find yourself in terrible and perplexing unfamiliarity with the world. Forgetfulness settles over everything, especially hangers and zippers, which baffle you with their complexity, their use, their meaning. You can smell the change in yourself like you can smell a coming rain. You know there is great loneliness that rides on the back of rain, so you turn, disquieted, waiting for those slow, first drops to fall. You're more silent now. Words are as gray as the clouds you smell and you are justly startled by the dearth of thoughts you now have. You might consider it all good and a blessing that life has turned simpler, except you stand with your blouse in one hand and a hanger in the other and, for the life of you, you can't figure out the puzzle because the pieces have changed shape since you last put them together.

My woman is spicing the air in the kitchen with some gusty, bluesy song while she fusses about. I sigh and allow myself to be caught up in the song. I tug again at the sticky plastic that covers the outside of my diaper. A diaper, indeed!

I move to my closet and find myself reaching for the comfort of my letter box. I select a paper and let it unfold in my hand like a flower opening in the morning sun. It's becoming harder to read my own scrawling hand, but still, I manage to decipher every word. I spend most of the morning reading and re-reading words and sentences, allowing them to settle into the memory of my bones.

I read:

My children:

Your MeeMaw had the most beautiful eyes ever seen. Even when her eyesight failed, her eyes were clear and lovely and nearly the color of a day in its first morning light—almost blue and almost lavender. It was even more striking that her hair was like the last day's light—almost black and almost purple. The combination made her seem like there was no separation between morning and night.

Ma was also a wise woman who knew things—like precisely how many grains of salt to pinch between her fingers for bread dough, or just when the tender onion bulbs were plump and sweet and just ripe enough to pull from the garden soil.

Pa, on the other hand, was a hardened tree stump of a man. He was bone and grit, formed from the wrinkled clay of generations of lumbermen who chipped and sawed and hauled their days through the sawmills of the South. Pa was lucky he carried all his fingers. "Just a matter of time," he would marvel at the end of every day that all his fingers were still accounted for. *Just a matter of time.*

I must have looked in the mirror early on and decided I took after Pa, figuring myself a tree stump as well. A freckled, sawdust-colored chunk of a tree stump.

Ma caught me one day practicing my endless mirror gazing. I must have been about ten or eleven years old and complaining to myself that I wasn't pretty enough, or tall enough, or something-or-other enough. I'd been pinching my lips, trying to make them look fat and red and grown up.

"Why'd I have to take after Pa?" I complained. "Why couldn't I be pretty like you?"

"Lillie Claire, you hush your mouth right now," Ma said. "If I drop dead right this second and you never hear another word I say, you listen to this. There's never going to be another Lillie Claire. You think you don't look pretty right now? What you look like will change, maybe not so much as you'll notice in that mirror of yours, but you're going to change and you can't stop that. Just remember that who you really are is deep down inside and was set by God. You're done set for life in how God made you."

Ma fixed her near-blind eyes on me like she could see all the way to the center of my bones. She continued. "So don't you go telling God you don't like how you were fashioned. You can't be trying to pinch your mouth and cheeks darker, all the while thinking that makes your soul better. There's nothing uglier than a red-mouthed beauty with a soul shriveled from neglect. Listen to me when I tell you that if you make your heart right, the rest of you will follow right along."

"But when's that going to happen? When's my face gonna come along? When're my legs gonna come along? Huh?"

Ma smiled. "All in God's time, Lillie Claire. All in God's time. Now get yourself away from that mirror and read me this book." Ma handed me her worn and yellowed *Paradise Lost*. "There's nothing like reading about hell to scare you into heaven's ways. Nope. Nothing like that at all."

Somehow, over the next summer, my face thinned, my legs lengthened and little breast buds formed to give me something new to ponder in the mirror.

All through the thinning and lengthening and forming of the woman I was to become, Ma kept me busy with the puzzlement of John Milton's poetry. *There's nothing like reading about hell to scare you into heaven's ways. Nope. Nothing like that at all.*

Oh, my children, I can still hear those words from your MeeMaw. She was right, I suppose. Being frightened of a thing can certainly serve to propel one toward its opposite. For all of Ma's prodding me to fear hell, though, I could never bring myself to likewise scare the living daylights out of you.

Maybe I *should* have folded my arms around you, or pulled you to my lap to read you disturbing poetry about heaven and hell. Who's to know what a mother should do?

Sadly, your MeeMaw didn't have the opportunity to help settle that question on behalf of her grandchildren. I hope then you'll forgive me for my ignorance about this one little point.

All my love,
Mom

I return the letter to its rightful fold and tuck it back into the box. The closet is dark and I feel suddenly unsettled. It's only the low shadows of late morning, but it feels like the dark of hell. My woman is still singing in the kitchen, but her song is muffled through the walls and about as far away as heaven can be.

I go to the bathroom to splash cold water and sense onto my frightened face.

YOU LOOK. You look into the mirror hoping to see your face, your familiar face. Instead, you see the startled eyes of a new woman, winking, blinking back at you. You engage her in conversation, because you're a polite woman and conversation is the congenial thing. She's nice to you. You don't question that she's in your bathroom because that would be confrontational and certainly wouldn't speak kindly of an upbringing that taught you charm and Southern hospitality. So you smile and welcome and extend gestures of conviviality. She seems to know you. She's not at all like your woman who pulls diapers up your protesting legs or ignores your commands by wretchedly withholding your evening glass of red. No. This is a woman of genteel sensitivity whose company you enjoy. You admire her hairstyle, her quick and witty words, her smile that slides easily across her rouged and powdered face. When you're finished conversing with your companionable new friend, you step out to find your woman still singing to the kitchen walls. "Well," you announce to her. "I don't care any longer that you can't find the courtesy to serve me properly. I've just had a lovely glass of wine with my new friend down at the clubhouse. She, at least, has Southern manners." You turn on your heel and return to your room where you spend your afternoon glad in the appearance of your new friend and blessedly unaware that notions of heaven and hell are—at least, for a short and dear moment—far, far from your thoughts.

Chapter Twenty-One

Bryan no longer bothers to ring the doorbell like a proper guest; he has a key and simply appears inside, unannounced and always breathless. I assume it must be his job, which is always compelling, demanding. Exhausting. It keeps him away for days at a time only to spit him out now and then, wild-eyed and panting, always when least expected.

This morning, my son slides open the door and calls my name. Again, he is a surprise.

"Mom," he calls out, his voice like a song. "The life of the party is here."

Jewell answers. "We're on the patio. You're just in time for coffee."

"Excellent," Bryan says, sliding open the patio door. "Just black this morning...I need all the go-go juice I can get."

He bends down to kiss my cheek. "Hey, Mom...how's my favorite gal?"

"I wouldn't know about your favorite gal," I say. "*I*, however, am fine." I throw my head back and strike a movie star pose; I splay my fingers open like a fluttering fan.

"Very cute," he says, sliding his lips across my cheek. I want to hold his soft mouth endlessly to my searching cheek.

Bryan slides a chair away from the table and folds his long legs easily into its shape. Jewel brings a steaming cup of coffee and a white linen napkin.

"Thanks so much, Jewell," he says. "Please, join us."

I look down my eyelids as Jewell flutters briefly and then slides into a chair.

"I like her, you know," I say. "Very much, in fact. But does a Southern lady allow such familiarity with her woman? I'm just asking."

"Of course, Mom," Bryan says, leaning into his coffee. "A Southern woman has *all* her women sit at the table with her."

"Really?"

"Yes. Really." Bryan winks toward Jewell, which abruptly stops me from commenting about Mrs. McKenna who, during my childhood, never allowed her domestic help to "sit table," as she called it. I assumed it was so the lady's conversation wasn't disrupted by either the beauty of their skin or the wisdom in their words.

"In fact, Jewell needs to be part of this conversation because it involves her time," Bryan states.

"Her time is best spent singing. Wouldn't you agree, Jewell?" I reach out and pat her arm. The warmth of her skin soothes my fingers.

"Yes, ma'am," Jewell says, casting a broad smile across the table. "Yes, indeed. More coffee, Bryan?"

He waves away the coffee pot. "Well, if that's the case, then I've found a terrific way for Jewell to have more time for singing."

"More singing time? Goody!" I clap my hands. "We should sing now. Sing something for Bryan. Go ahead, *sing.*"

"Maybe later, Mom," Bryan says. "We'll sing later. Here, look at this. I brought a brochure for the Golden Years Day Center. They have a great daycare program with various classes for all levels of people. They even have dances and daily luncheons." He pulls a folded paper from his pocket.

"Now, why would we have my woman go to daycare?" I say. "She's needed right here. First you bring me a woman that I don't need and now that I *do* need her, you want her to go somewhere else?"

"No, Mom. It's for *you*. Look, look here at the pictures in the brochure. Doesn't this look like a nice place?"

Bryan unfolds a glossy advertisement with colorful pictures of people dancing and eating and smiling. "Why ever would I go to such a place? It's not nice at all. It's full of...of...*old* people. Look at them! I don't eat with old people and I certainly wouldn't *dance* with the likes of these people."

"May I see those pictures?" Jewell asks.

Bryan hands the brochure to her; she turns it over in her hands, looking thoughtfully. "I see what you mean, ma'am. Yes, there are some older people here. Now, here's what I wonder when I look at the pictures of these nice-looking folks. I wonder if they need a young woman like you to show them how to dance Southern style. I'd bet anything they don't know how a proper Appalachian woman does a jig."

Jewell hands the brochure back to Bryan.

"I see what you're doing," I say, pulling my eyes into narrow slants. I push myself abruptly from the table. "You're evil...both of you. Evil! You're trying to get rid of me so you can have my house and my things and my *cat!*"

I turn and head for the patio door. My fingers fumble with the screen door latch.

"See here," I yell. "You've already locked me out of my own home. You've changed the locks. Help...help me, someone!" I call into the sky and over the backyard fence and into a tree where I see a squirrel running the length of a long branch. "*Help* me!"

"Mom." Bryan reaches me in one step. He catches up my wrists at the narrow places where the skin sags away from the bone. He pulls me to him. "Stop this. We're not trying to take your home. How could you *think* that?"

YOU SCREAM. You scream into your head and into the air because you don't recognize the man who, with the web of his large hands, has taken hold of yours like they are tender, fragile birds. You struggle to free yourself. He is a stranger to your eyes and to your heart. You know he has locked you from your home and from your thoughts and he has a woman with him who is in on the dirty deed too. Your eyes scan for escape, but there is none. The man calls you his mother, the woman refers to you as ma'am. You would tell them your true name, your lack of relationship, if only you could remember who and what you are. The man looks at you and his face shatters into a thousand pieces. It's only then you recognize something familiar about the man—the man—oh, there he is! There's your son.

"Mom, it's me...I'm Bryan. Don't you know me? It's *me*." His face pulls into a tight mask of sorrowful skin, redeemed only by wide blue eyes now filling with tears.

"Bryan!" I smile. "Of course I know you, you silly boy. When did you get here?" I lower my voice into a conspiratorial whisper and pull myself up and into his ear. "There are people trying to take me away from my home," I say. "You need to stop them."

"Let's go in the house. Jewell can make us a nice lunch or something...okay, Mom? Wouldn't that be nice?"

Bryan cups his hand around my elbow to help me inside. I know we've just had an awful moment and my heart feels as if it has split apart, causing a chasm to form deep in my chest; it's as wide as anything I'll ever know. I step inside the house, trying to decide on which side of my heart I stand. I hope it's the safe side that still contains at least a modicum of restraint and good charm, although I can't figure out why I should feel so ashamed of myself.

Jewell hurries to the kitchen and soon I hear her stirring a lusty song into the soup pot. Bryan settles me in my chair and John Milton the Cat comes from the nether reaches of the house to find my lap. For the time being, my heart has scotch-taped itself into a ragged, yet passable piece of equipment.

By the time Jewell serves lunch, I'm happy with peaceful thoughts. I've discovered lately that if I close my eyes around these tiny fragments of peace like I'm wrapping myself beneath the blanket of my eyelids, the posture seems to help me feel safer. I hear Bryan shifting carefully in his chair so not to awaken me.

"It's okay," I say. "I'm still in here."

Chapter Twenty-Two

My beautiful, dear children,

I'm not certain how to address this delicate issue except to simply come right out with it. You should know that your mother is a fraud, a charlatan, a complete fake. I can envision you as you read this, shaking your heads in disbelief. After all, we've been so careful during those delicate times when we've needed to hold each other up to the light and peer through one another until we're satisfied that what we see is the truth of one another. We've spent countless times measuring and comparing and filtering through every possible way in which to gauge each other's weight and worth.

In every way, I suppose I was a good mother—except, perhaps, for the one way that most mattered: mathematics.

I want you to remember that it was your father who curled his round arm around you at the kitchen table, your faces crumpled around all those math problems that seemed so much larger than your small bodies. It was your father who walked you through mazes of word problems and equations.

It was your father who suffered your tearful wails of *I don't get it*, while I offered nothing more than well-timed handfuls of tissues and plates of cookies.

On those days when your father traveled for business, instead of urging your little hands to open your math books, I gave you crayons and coloring books. I gave you scissors and glitter, paper doilies and brightly colored sheets of construction paper. I gave you finger-paints.

Sometimes we heaved the living room furniture aside and set up a tent on the floor. We lined it with blankets and pillows and then crawled inside to eat bowls of ice cream and play flashlight wars. We made up rhymes and stories. We baked little cakes and poured chocolate sprinkles over them. We played dolls and trucks until your eyes turned red with sleep. We took up scissors and clicked and clicked them in our hands until we created scores of paper dolls and winter snowflakes.

We made tea parties.

We did all those lovely things. But never—not once—did we ever sit bravely at the table to spread open books filled with frightening strings of numbers and equations and terribly confusing word problems. It was in that regard that I was a cowardly, diminished woman in front of your innocent souls.

For that I am sorry.

I should have prepared you for life with numbers. I should have held your tiny shoulders and taught you how to measure and count and perform the task of what your MeeMaw and PaaPaw would have called *ciphering*.

I meant no harm. Still, I went weak when your eyes widened at the thought of working through problems, especially when there were pages to color and cupcakes to devour and tents to crawl inside.

When your father would return from his trips, you would once again sit straight at the dinner table, books open like butterflies, your eyes set doubly hard at your tasks. I would circle the table without coming close enough to be found out for my neglect.

I hope you'll remember your father's generous hands around your little shoulders, his earnest eyes as they poured over your problems with you and how his face would light with delight when you *got it*. Oh, please remember those things when next you need to balance your checkbook or determine the percentage for a proper tip in a restaurant.

It was your father who taught you those things.

Sadly, I played no part.

With great sorrow,
Your mother

I don't know where to place the regret that seems to be suddenly spilling out of my heart and splashing to the floor of my soul. So much regret, indeed! From where does it all come? And why should a small letter from my own hand turn my face into a grimacing mask of tearfulness?

I refold the letter and place it back with all the other letters that seem now to be nothing more than a collection of all the regrettable parts of my life. I decide I hate them. I want them, each and every one, burnt until they are nothing more than wisps of blackened ash floating into the sky where the wind can carry them off.

I put my letter box away and go to the kitchen where my woman is making some sort of meal. She is working a knife over a carrot, cutting it into round slices, presumably for the dinner salad.

"I need matches," I say to her. "Now, please. Matches."

I pace while I wait for her to accommodate me. She continues to finish slicing the carrot, slowly, carefully, and then maddeningly reaches for a stalk of celery. I march to her side and hold out my hand. "Matches!"

A whisper of a smile enters her face. "I meant to get matches for you, ma'am, but the store was all out."

"I don't believe you. Do you know to whom you're speaking?"

"Of course, ma'am." A smile continues to curl just at the corners of her lips. "You are Lillie Claire Glidden and you want matches."

"That's right. You won't forget that will you?"

"No, ma'am. I'll not forget it." My woman turns to me and allows her smile to unfurl, fully and brilliantly, until I'm bedazzled by its wonder.

"Thank you. I'll be going now," I say. I return to my room where I stand in front of my dresser mirror and sway gently to the lingering breeze of my woman's smiling face.

Sometime later I move to my door and place my ear on its cool surface. My woman's songs spill into the air while she works in the kitchen. I hear running water as she wipes up, then quiet footsteps in rhythm with her song. It sounds like a gospel hymn, but I'm not familiar with the melody. I decide she's making it up as she goes, much like a prayer. Through the muffle of my bedroom door, it sounds like she's singing in tongues.

My woman moves through the house, starting the clothes dryer, straightening magazines, completing her dinner preparations. All the time, she sings. She sings.

She sings.

When at last she softly knocks on my door to announce dinner, I am ready for her. I've washed my hands and slid my reddest lipstick over my mouth. I've put my hair up in pins and straightened my clothes.

Jewell opens my door and smiles at me. "My, but don't you look beautiful this evening, ma'am," she says. "That's a lovely shade of lipstick. And I don't think I've ever seen your hair up like that. Very beautiful, ma'am."

I pat my hair and smile. "It's for you. Because I *love* you."

"I love you too, ma'am. Dinner is served now."

Jewell takes me by the arm and leads me to my place at the table. She helps me into my chair and lays a soft cloth napkin across the front of my blouse.

All through dinner and continuing after, when my woman turns on the television for me, I spin out thoughts of love for her. When she readies me for bed, washing my face, urging me to brush my teeth, helping me into my nightgown, I continue to assert my love. I tell her over and over that I love her. I smile into her face. I touch her hands and pull them to my chest.

I love. I love.

I sleep with murmurs of love dripping from one corner of my mouth—it is wet and slides down my chin and onto the sheets.

Through the night, I sleep and dream the tossing dreams of the forgetful. When my woman comes to wake me in the morning, she stands beside my bed with her hands folded into comfort and helpfulness. But when I open my eyes, I've forgotten all about the night's dreamy vows of love for her. I'm once again soiled with anger. Covered with despair.

My head fills with the heat of fire and remembrance for something very different from the love and dreams that had trailed after me all through the previous night.

My woman leans down to unstick me from the tangle of my sheets. "Where are my matches?" I scream into her startled ears. "I *need* my goddamn matches."

Chapter Twenty-Three

YOU FUSS. You fuss until your woman and any neighbor within hearing range are well aware of your displeasure. You thump and stomp and sigh with great heaving puffs of breath. No one pays attention. For all your efforts, the sun continues its upward momentum, opening the morning and bringing you closer to your first half-day at the Golden Years Day Center of Greater Sacramento. You push your woman's hands away. You stiffen and refuse to let your legs slide into your pants. You fight with the sleeves of your blouse. You twist your head back and forth until brushing your hair is impossible. In spite of your moaning protestations, your woman buckles you and your twisted pants and your wildly combed hair into the car. You proclaim victory over the Golden Center of Whatever-It-Is all the way until your woman spins you into a parking space and you realize you've been had. You'll forever think of her as a clever fox who promises with her grinning teeth and sly winking eyes to swim gullible rabbits to the other side of the river.

My woman steers me through the doorway into a large building; it is bustling with people and bursting with the voices of strangers. They smell of gray hair and muscle ointment. They are a pungent people and I'm terrified I'll be left with them forever. We approach a woman who smiles from behind a large desk. Her teeth are immensely large for her small face. My woman introduces me.

"Good morning, Mrs. Glidden," the woman says, looking at a clipboard in her hands to confirm my name. I wish she would stop smiling so her teeth would go back into her head. "We're so glad you could be here today. May I call you Lillie?"

"No, you may not," I say. "My name is Lillie Claire."

"Of course…what a lovely name," the teeth say.

I narrow my eyes toward her. "Are you a swimming fox like my woman?" I ask.

The teeth disappear for a moment, only to reappear again, more pronounced with laughter sharpening their edges. "No. But I *am* a dancer," the woman says. "My name is Suzanne. Would you like to see our dance room?"

"What for?" I ask. I realize I'm clutching my woman's hand with frightening fierceness.

"They would like you to demonstrate how a Southern lady might dance," Jewell says, her eyes sparkling promises at me. *Such foxes. Such wicked, wicked foxes, carrying me into this river of unfamiliar people.*

Suzanne of the Terrible Teeth speaks again. "Oh, yes. Please. We really need you to show us. Will you, my dear?"

"Only if you'll not call me your dear," I say.

"Well then…that's wonderful," Suzanne gushes. "Follow me, then, and I'll introduce you around."

Again, my woman steers me as we move down a hallway teeming with more gray-haired people—some toddling behind walkers, some bustling on their own steam. One man sits in a wheelchair with a strap around his chest, presumably so he won't fall out, but more likely so he won't run off. The dull oak floor is old and scuffed, like the people who shuffle along its path.

We are a great migration of people; we travel mere blocks away, into the craft rooms and dining halls of senior centers and care homes. We're dropped off by private cars and designated vans with motorized wheelchair lifts and, once inside, we move along a warren of trails that lead us in, but never take us anywhere.

Today, I join the grand migration.

Three-quarters down the hall, Suzanne leads us through a doorway into a large gathering hall. Several rows of folding chairs face an empty area obviously meant for dancing and mingling. Across the dance floor, a man stands behind a folding table, sorting through a stack of CDs. He pulls one out, then places it into a player and presses a button to start the first selection.

It sounds like Appalachian porch music and I suddenly can't determine if I'm a child or a grown woman. I conclude I'm much too young to be among this sea of gray-headed people.

Surely, I've been brought here by mistake.

I inch into a chair next to a window where a swath of light, wide and heavy, falls across my lap; I'm tiny under its weight. Still, the provocative music dives under my skin and lifts me. Lifts me.

Lifts me.

Slowly, I push the sun away from my legs and stand. I shuffle across the dance floor until I'm standing in front of a thumping music speaker. I look for my woman. She stands just inside the doorway watching me. I wave at her while I grab the arm of another woman, a stranger, who seems to be trying to shuffle her feet to the music.

"You're doing it wrong. Here...here's how you do it," I say. I take her hands and together we sway and hop from side to side, trying to keep to the frantic guitar and banjo rhythm. It's faster than our feet can manage, but we do all right.

When the song ends, I look again for my woman. She's gone, but a small crowd of people move toward the dance floor as the music-playing man starts a Carter Family song. Slowly, beat by beat, it feels like home. I'm on my porch, swinging my feet to the rhythm of Pa's guitar. I shuffle and wiggle and jump and hitch until the song ends. Hands touch mine. Faces with frozen smiles float into me.

I'm home. I'm home.

Over the next two hours, we dance to hillbilly jigs and modern country, with the likes of Glenn Miller, Little Richard, and Kenny G tossed in for good measure. Someone brings pitchers of lemonade and a stack of plastic cups for our thirsty mouths. A man tries to dance with me. He's not my Ivan so I push at his startled chest and turn his gray head away. I don't want him to look at me. I make a mental note to tell my woman to find my fan. A Southern lady never attends a dance without her fan to fend off approaching men.

I return to my seat several times trying to locate my dance card.

It seems to be missing and I make another mental note to tell the woman with the big teeth that there are thieves about.

At noon we're shuffled to another room where we're served a hot lunch of meatloaf, mashed potatoes, corn and enough dark, lumpy gravy to drown most of Sacramento. I'm just finishing a piece of lemon cake when my woman taps my shoulder.

"You're late for lunch," I say.

"That's okay," my woman says. "Are you ready to go home?"

"Home?" I stutter. "I thought I *was* home."

"No, but you can come back on Wednesday if you'd like." Jewell's voice gently pulls me from my chair.

"Oh, I *need* to come back. They're counting on me to teach them more dancing steps." I lean toward my woman and whisper into her ear, "They should serve wine with their meal, you know. These people really need to learn hospitality. And they're such poor dancers." I shake my head. My tongue tsks behind my teeth. "Terrible dancers, they are."

Chapter Twenty-Four

Night is horrid.

Night is the unwinding of everything known; every memory, every thought, is somehow fastened to the sinking sun and it makes me frantic. I want to run after what the sun drags down with it. I'm awkward and discordant and I don't know what to do.

Every evening, I wander through the house muttering. *Bring me back. Bring me back.* My woman, the one whose name I now forget a thousand times over, watches me walk endless circles as if I'm a donkey with carrot stick memories dangling in front of me. Round and round I plod my circles, grinding wheat for a merciless master. *Bring me back. Bring me back.*

Sometimes she catches my hand up into hers; she walks with me like we're schoolgirls headed home for the day. We hold hands and she makes up a traveling song which makes me smile as we circle from room to room. After a while, my woman unclasps her hand, leaving me to continue wandering a solitary path, my mouth feeling sad like my school chum is home, but I must continue on alone.

My woman is on the phone, but I'm so busy grinding the wheat to make the bread to feed the memories to grow the grain to make the wheat to make more bread, I pay no attention to what she's doing. I figure she has her own carrot stick to follow.

Sometime later, when my legs are tired and my brain is nothing but sticky shards stuck together with bits of scotch-taped thoughts, my beloved Bryan comes to the door. He hauls a wooden rocker into the house and places it in the center of the living room. My woman looks on with a smile.

"What's *this* for?" I ask.

My woman answers. "It's for the soothing of you, ma'am. For the soothing of you."

"Here, come sit down, Mom," Bryan says, an eager smile spreading across his face. He pats the seat of the chair and looks at me like a boy who has just presented his mother with a wooden thing he has labored over for weeks in woodshop class.

The chair has neither a harness nor a carrot dangling from a stick, so I consider it safe. I run my fingers along the polished wood and then let my legs fold into the contour of the chair. It fits me and I fit it. My body rocks in rhythm to the words I still haven't stopped muttering. *Bring me back. Bring me back.*

I slowly rock, allowing the chair to determine the length of each stroke. With this gentle movement, the mantra from my lips seems to melt into the delicate polish on the chair's arms. John Milton the Cat jumps onto my lap; my hand falls absently across the soft roundness of his head. I look at nothing in particular and think of nothing more important than the perfect shape of a cat's gray-muzzled face.

For one glorious moment, I am soothed.

Bryan smiles at me and my woman smiles at me and John Milton swoons beneath my hand. Sometime later, I stand without a word and carry the cat to bed.

I sleep well, getting up only once to circle through the house to try the doors and rattle the windows. Outside, rain slides down the gutters and patters across the drive. I barely notice the normal confusion of my footsteps across the carpet and I'm blessedly not compelled to cry out for help. On my second round, I realize there's a new chair in the living room. When I run my hand across its back, there's an oddness of familiarity I can't quite make out. I want to ask my woman about the chair and if we'll be adding more new pieces to the house, but she's asleep. I finish my round of the house and slide back into my bed.

In the morning, my woman wakes me. She is smiling. Singing.

She sings, *Goodness, Gracious, Great Balls of Fire*, as she tidies me for the day. She shakes her hips and I clap with delight.

When she's done fixing me up for the day and the last note of her song is left to hang in the air, I ask my woman if she can keep a secret.

"A secret? Of course, ma'am. I'm good with secrets."

"Then come with me," I say. I take her hand and lead her to my closet where I pull down the letterbox.

"What a beautiful box," she says, touching the smooth, fragrant cedar lid.

"My father made it."

"Ah, well, then, all the more beautiful." Jewell smiles. Her face is luminescent in the low light of the closet.

I shuffle through the papers and remove a letter from the box. "Can you read?" I ask, handing her the folded paper.

"Yes, ma'am."

"Then read this to me. It's mine...I...I wrote it, but now I'm...it's getting hard for me to read my own handwriting. It's a bit scrawling, as you can see. But...shhh... you mustn't tell anyone I have you read for me. People think unkindly of the illiterate."

"No one could possibly think unkindly of you, ma'am." Jewell unfolds the letter with gentle, practiced hands that seem to always smell of lemon oil and cinnamon toast. "Shall we go to the other room where the light is better?"

"No," I say. "We stand here...here in the *middle* of the closet. We read right here in the center because this is where the memories are."

"I see," Jewell says. "Of course, then." She settles the paper in her hands while I wait with my listening heart for the words of my memories. Jewell inhales and then begins to exhale words that hold me in rapture. She reads:

My dearest ones:

I don't know how to write this letter. I've started and ended so many times, I've lost count. This is my final try, so I suppose I'll just have to let whatever words that fall from my hand be as they will. I'm writing of when your father died. There! I said it.

We've never really talked about the day our lives ended.

We've bumped against the issue many times. We've held each other and cried our plentiful tears, but we've never really talked it out. We've never talked about how we stood in that hospital emergency waiting room, wordlessly looking into one another's eyes while doctors were in another room working madly (and in vain) to restart your father's silent heart. I remember clutching our hands together, as if by doing so we could rearrange the thing that was really killing us.

After all this time, maybe we should let go of that day. But I don't know how. There's not been a time since that terrible day that your father hasn't been part of every wakeful moment, alive in every conversation, the center in every speck of light.

It would be just like your father to still be part of everything. He always hated to be in the other room away from us, missing some bit of fun. We were like a four-stranded braid, your father always the central cord in everything. Always, always, he was with us.

On the day of his funeral, we stood in the rain, holding to each other, our heads touching, our stiff legs like a tripod, or a three-legged stool. It wouldn't have taken much to tip us over, but we stood as well as we could, while the sky shuddered over our shoulders and ran down our coats. We formed our shaky goodbyes to your father as best we could, whispery and frightened beneath his graveside tent.

At the end of that day, after everyone left us to ourselves, after the food was put away and the sympathy cards were shuffled into a pile to take care of later, when we finally loosened our grasp of one another, we simply untwined and unraveled.

Without your father to hold us together, we had no idea how to braid ourselves together again. A bird doesn't go far if the structure of its wings is too poor to fly. Your father served as the bones of our family and, as hard as we tried, we simply couldn't fly without him.

When it came time for you to leave that evening, I watched your slumped backs as you walked down the driveway, hand in hand toward your cars. I watched you hug one last time, and then I watched you separate. I watched you split apart, your shadows breaking away, your hands releasing.

I was sad for you.

I stood in the doorway, alone, also breaking apart, with the light from the living room streaming across my back and casting my own lonely shadow to the ground.

I was sad for me too.

The failure of our bodies, our shadows, our hands, to hold tightly together was a great sadness we didn't expect. How could we know that we should have stayed braided, that we shouldn't have pulled inside ourselves, grieving, alone and separate, retreating from one another?

In that moment of parting—you two on the driveway, me in the doorway—it seemed we simply lost our senses. We each just flew off into our own dark nights. I've always wondered if you blamed me for your father's death. I suppose that would be normal. Not right, of course, but understandable. I wonder if you still hold thoughts of *what if.*

As for me, all *what ifs* are gone. My own thoughts died with your father. I buried them. I took a rose and tucked every thought and dream I ever had inside its petals and I placed it in your father's hands for safekeeping. I did that just before the casket was closed and wheeled from the mortuary to the gravesite. Then I took my handful of dirt and let it fall from the height of my hand to the depth of his death, sealing that act of releasing the total sum of myself for your father's eternal safekeeping.

So everything—my thoughts and memories, my love, my dreams and desires—everything, is buried with your father in Space 243 at East Lawn Memorial Park.

We've come back a great deal since that horrid time. We have our dinners and clink our wine glasses together; we've done our best to re-twine into something—anything—resembling what we once were. We try. Sometimes we don't do as well as other times. But we try.

I hope this discussion doesn't upset you. It's meant, rather, to give you some long-needed peace. We're as whole as we can be now and that in itself is comfort.

It's good!

I also hope you'll not think unkindly of me for giving away my memories. When I gave them to your father for his care, I honestly didn't think he'd keep them. I laugh now to think that if there's anything you need from me after I'm gone, you'll have to go first to East Lawn Memorial Park and look for your answers in Space 243.

All my deepest love,
Mother

Jewell refolds the letter and returns it to its place. Her eyes glisten. She places the box back on the shelf and then takes my hands up into hers.

"Oh, ma'am," she says. "Oh, ma'am. What a beautiful letter for your children."

"Good," I say. "Letters should be beautiful. Now, do we have any red wine left?"

"Red wine?"

"Yes. I'd like some this morning with my eggs."

Jewell laughs. "You know you're off the sauce now, ma'am. It's not good for you and what ails you."

"I don't know why my children gave you to me. You're not at all gracious," I say. "Not one little bit."

"Yes, ma'am. Yes indeed, ma'am."

Chapter Twenty-Five

Here's what I know: I know my children, although sometimes when their faces turn white and papery and moist with sadness, it seems I don't quite know them at all; I know my woman and the dark whorls of her kind fingers, the low hum of her voice beneath all the scraping and whirring kitchen noises; I know scrambled eggs, although sometimes I forget the name of their color. Yellow! That's it, yellow. I know the constant itching of my legs and how these beleaguered legs need to walk and walk and move and move until I rub and rub them into stillness and indifference.

I know my garden.

I know John Milton the Cat and how he slips into my bed each night to curl his lanky body next to the length of mine. I know my body, except for my hands. My hands confuse me. I know the rooms of my house and how they flow like one daydream into another; I know my rocking chair and its comfort on my neck and beneath the backs of my legs. I know the sound of my feet. I especially know the sound of my feet. My hair seems odd, but I know most of my face. I know my earlobes, the endlessness of a day, the sound of thunder, stars in the night that flash their tiny teeth like smiles over me.

I know my Ivan is waiting for me. Ma and Pa, too. It's hard, but I'm trying to hurry toward them.

Here's what I don't know: everything, everything, everything else.

This morning, my woman leads me into the sparkling daylight of the garden. She says we're going to have coffee and biscuits on the patio and sit quietly while birds peep at us, begging for crumbs to take into their little beaks. I clap my hands. Coffee with the garden birds is my favorite thing.

My woman is kind to me and she's kind to little birds. I add that to my dwindling list of things I know.

The garden is agog with color and movement, light and shadow, deep thrumming sounds. Bees with heavy yellow legs haul themselves from flower to flower. Tomatoes hang low and weighty on the vine. It's deep into summer and they're plenty ripe for their destiny.

Sparrows and small little darkish birds with yellow beaks and black eyes gather watchfully near our feet. They dart about on their little toes like dancers. Jewell pours my coffee and hands me a buttered biscuit. I pinch off a piece and toss it toward the birds. It doesn't land quite far enough from my legs, causing the birds to shuffle sideways in complaint. Their tiny feet dance forward and then back again. Little mouths, like scissors, open and close to snip at a blue paper sky.

I toss out another piece of biscuit; the birds skitter about, a syncopated troupe. Together they move forward until they reach the edge of their stage: my feet, my legs, my knees. Every now and then, one tugs at his feathers like he's adjusting his dancing costume.

I pitch out more crumbs, again and again. The birds flutter in and out, none brave enough to come under my feet, but still peeping hopefulness that the next toss will come their way.

Finally, I give up and look out over the garden. The heat of the day is already shimmering through the air. I say to my woman, "I need to pick the…um…the—"

"Vegetables?" My woman often finishes my sentences for me now. I think my children pay her for that service and I'm happy for it.

"Yes…vegetables," I say. "They'll spoil in this heat."

"Yes, ma'am, they sure will. I'll pick those for you right after our coffee. They can go in tonight's dinner."

"No. It's my garden. I'll do it."

"Truly, I'd really like to do the picking," she says. "Besides, I need to learn how to pick for the day when I'll have my own garden." Jewel smiles brightly. "You can sit here and tell me what to do."

"You mean you don't know how to pick?"

"No ma'am. It's not something I've learned yet."

"Well, at least you make good...good—"

"Coffee? Biscuits?"

"Biscuits," I say. I toss out another piece, once more missing the distance between my legs and the wary birds. "Next time, though, make the dough so it'll reach all the way to these poor starving things. They might like you better."

"Yes, ma'am. I'll remember that...better biscuits for the little birds."

The telephone rings and Jewell goes inside to answer. I'm left to the last of my coffee; the birds are left with nothing. With a shrug of their shoulders, they give up peeping and dancing for morsels and move out into the grass to look for other, more available nibbles.

I look out at my tomatoes, wilting toward the ground, my shrinking cucumbers. My sad little peppers.

YOU RATTLE. You rattle the doorknob that would let you back into your garden. For the life of you, you don't know how you've come to be inside your potting shed, with clay shards and dirt scraping the undersides of your shoes, an uncooperative doorknob in your hand. You are moist with heat which runs from your temples and down your arms. It collects onto the palms of your hands, making the doorknob all the more impossible to reason with. You stand in the darkness of the shed with your wet hands and your wet brain, baffled by it all. All you wanted was to relieve the suffering of your tomatoes, your poor cucumbers. You only needed to retrieve your gathering basket and your garden gloves from the shed—really, a simple, simple thing. Now the door has closed you in and you can't reason your way back to the other side. You flutter your hands and skitter back and forth like one of your dancing birds, hoping someone will hear the small peeps from your mouth. You hear your woman call for you, but she's deaf to the sounds of your feet, your small and frightened voice. The heat sizzles on your body until you melt to the floor. Just before you close your eyes to sleep away the heat, you smile to think how lovely it is to have at least danced like a bird before your death.

Light floods my eyes.

"Ma'am!" My woman's hands fold around my shoulders. "Oh. Oh, ma'am."

She helps me stand and then holds me by my waist, leading me into the cool of the house where she lays me gently on the couch. She runs to make dampened cool cloths, which she pats on my forehead and cups behind my neck, all the time cooing over me. *Oh, ma'am. Oh, ma'am.*

Her hands are like velvet; I love them more than I love anything.

After a time, when I feel less blunted by the heat, I push away the wet cloths.

"Help me up," I say.

"Maybe you should rest a bit more. You've had quite a day of it." Jewell makes her hands into a fan that she waves in front of my face.

"I'm fine…still a bit queasy, but…stop. I'm fine. If you want to be useful, you can stop fluttering your hands around like this."

"Of course, ma'am." She takes one of the damp rags and waves it through the air, making me blink with each pass.

"Please, stop. Here. Go get my…my—"

"Your what, ma'am?"

"You know. My *thing*. In the closet…my…you know, that thing with the paper inside. You know."

"In the closet? Oh! Your letterbox."

"Yes. I always feel better when I read my letters. Go get my letterbox."

When Jewell returns, I let her select a letter. I hope for something new, but, truth be told, everything is new to me now. Everything is a new delight. Everything is a fresh wound.

"Here, this one's on pretty paper," Jewell says. "Let's read this one."

As always, after the selecting, there is the unfolding, the passing of eyes across paper, and then the quiet mystery that settles across the shoulders like a warm robe on a wintry day.

This time, though, instead of the quiet dim of the closet, the reading happens in the living room with sunlight streaming through the windows like shimmering flags.

Jewell settles the paper in her hands and begins to read. Her voice is deep and sultry, as if she is singing my letter. I close my eyes to listen.

My delightful children,

There's hardly anything you don't know by now. Still, there are two things we haven't talked about. The first is how I want my funeral. The second is about the majesty of a sonnet.

Since the first of my chosen subjects might cause you to be sad, let's talk about sonnets and how, when one studies such a thoughtful work, each reading can whisper a different truth. You should know that sonnets can tip your heart and change your soul.

If only I had gathered you up, one on each side and taught you that simple thing, life might well have been different for you. If you had known the wonder of a sonnet's message all neatly wrapped within its fourteen lines, each line ten syllables long; if I had shown you the surprise of each rhyming pattern; if we had thrown our arms about one another as we read the final (and always astonishing) couplet, perhaps your lives would have been greater.

Sadly, I left you to your sidewalk chalk and jump rope rhymes. Of course, that wasn't all bad. Allison, I can still hear your happy voice singing out—*I like coffee, I like tea, I like the boys and the boys like me*—your freckled nose and pink shoulders flashing in the sun, your feet skipping across the concrete drive. I should have recorded your little voice, but of course I didn't.

And Bryan—how I wish I had taken pictures of your sidewalk drawings. Your young fingers were so brilliant; I should have captured everything they did. Of course, there are no snapshots of your drawings, only memories of how I washed your creations away with the garden hose, sometimes grumbling for the extra work you gave me.

How awful of me! Yet, worse than anything ever deprived of you, I never gave you poetry.

If I had done that one little thing, maybe when your father died and left us scattered to our own desperate ways, we could have at least found the echo of his heartbeat inside the tempo of some lonely sonnet. Maybe we could have sat, one of you to each side of me, and found the instructions of life that hide within the elegance of a poem. Perhaps we would have discovered the comfort of words that match the heartbeat and strengthen the bones.

Please, at least now, sit with a sonnet or two and let its words speak to you. I promise you'll find beauty you've never known before. Let that be our gift to each other, now that I'm gone.

I had intended to also discuss my wishes for a lovely funeral, but I'll save that for a different, more instructive letter on that subject. All this talk of poetry makes me want to think of nothing else for the moment. Certainly, no sadness.

And certainly, not now.

With all love,
Mother

"What a beautiful letter, ma'am," Jewell says. "Your children will surely love your writings." She refolds the letter and replaces it in the box. "Oh my, it's almost past your naptime."

My woman takes my arm and helps me to my feet. When we reach the bedroom, I shake loose from her. I shuffle forward and backward, my arms stretched outward, fingers splayed apart, my lips pushed forward, my mouth opening and closing like a small beak.

Jewell takes hold of my arm again. "Are you all right?"

"Of course I'm all right. I'm practicing because the birds have invited me to join their dance tomorrow. I want to be ready."

My woman smiles. "Oh, of course. I'm sure you'll be their star dancer in no time."

"I'm sure to work my way up the ranks." I smile broadly. "But, *please* remember to fix better biscuits. They were very upset with you, you know."

"Yes, ma'am. I'll be sure to remember. Now into bed with you. We're having a lovely dinner tonight and I'll make a nice tomato and cucumber salad, fresh from the garden. I'm afraid your little peppers didn't make it, but dinner will still be good. Bryan and Allison are coming and you'll need your beauty rest so you can enjoy it."

Chapter Twenty-Six

Most of my words now live in cavernous spaces deep in my brain where it's neither light nor dark, neither good nor bad. I can only think it's where the sweet art of existence lives, resplendent with color and sound and lovely, lovely songs. Sadly, though, it's also a place where words enter but never leave. Still, it's also where I seem to spend more and more time each day. Thoughts enter like a piano concerto, lively and in full sustained legato, only to return in diminuendo, a single wavering note in the room. I'm now not much more than a wordless, simple tone, wishing desperately for the return of the bright harmony of language.

The evening brings a cooling delta breeze, which pushes against the backs of my children until they're propelled into my living room, windblown and flustered. They fuss over me with blustery hands and rushing words.

Allison arrives first, fluttering to my chair like a leaf swirling in the wind. She leans down to kiss my cheek and runs her fingers over me, arranging my hair and smoothing my face. I think her hands smell of coconut, but my nose is unreliable now and I'm not certain what scents are what these days.

"You look beautiful tonight, Mom," Allison says.

"Thank you, dear."

"I was thinking you might like to get out of the house and go to lunch with me tomorrow. Would you like that?" Allison's voice is filled with beautiful round textures and endless possibility. "Maybe Jewell might like to go with us too."

"When?" I ask.

"Tomorrow. For lunch."

"Tomorrow? Oh, dear no. I'll be in a dance recital tomorrow."

"What are you talking about?" Allison calls toward the kitchen where my woman is preparing dinner. "Jewell, what is Mother talking about? A dance recital?"

"With the patio birds," I say. "I'm going to dance…I'm in their troupe now."

Allison stops fussing with my hair. She turns and prances to the couch. "Well, that's just silly," she says.

"I see you've forgotten your manners," I say.

"I see you've forgotten reality," Allison says, a frown on her face.

"Well, I *was* going to invite you to the dance, but not now. You're very rude, and birds simply don't *like* rude girls."

"Mother!"

Bryan arrives, wisps of hair tousled by the evening breeze, a supermarket bouquet dangling from his hand. He kisses the top of my head.

"Love you, Mom," he says.

"Love you more."

"You're looking good. Jewell says you had a hard morning."

"I did?" I'm instantly confused. "She didn't tell me I had a hard…a hard—"

"Never mind. You look like you're just fine now. I brought you some flowers. Pink ones…carnations and little purple things with green flaky stuff. I don't know what it's all called."

"They're lovely. I'll have my woman put them in a…in a…you know, that thing that sits on a…on a—"

"A vase? A table?"

"Yes. Yes. I'm so glad you know these things."

Bryan turns and sees his sister. "Hey," he says.

Allison sits glumly on the edge of the couch. She barely waves at her brother.

"Aren't we all sweetness and light this evening. New shoes pinching your toenail polish?"

"I'm upset because Mom's really, really out of it today. She's talking about being in a dance thing tomorrow."

"A dance recital, dear," I offer. "With my friends…the birds."

"See what I mean? She's just off."

Bryan pinches his eyes together. "Nice talk," he says leaning in like a lawyer as if she's a hostile witness.

"Well, it's *true*." Allison's eyes pull tightly at their corners like a drawstring purse.

My woman comes out from the kitchen. "Dinner's almost ready. Bryan will you do the honors and open the wine for you and your sister? Ma'am and I have some special Martinelli's tonight."

Bryan seems relieved to be distracted by something other than his sister's pinched eyes and distasteful manner. Allison goes with her brother into the kitchen. "We need to talk," she says, following on Bryan's heels. I lose the sound of their voices as they round the corner into the kitchen.

I wonder if I ought to join the conversation, but the thought passes. Instead, I busy my mind with anticipation for my dance debut. I decide to ask Jewell if she'll have time to sew a costume for me. I bemuse myself with thoughts of costume drape and design and how I shall look when I'm dressed as a bird.

I shall be a masterpiece of feathery beauty.

I practice holding my lips into the shape of a beak while the table is set and steaming dishes are carried from the kitchen.

The bustle and noise of dinner preparations crumble the infrastructure of my imaginings; I'm suddenly disoriented. I stop rehearsing how to work my mouth. I've forgotten where to place my hands, my thoughts, what few words I have left to me. John Milton the Cat rubs against my leg and I feel somewhat soothed. I'm happy for his soft company.

After dinner is placed on the table, my woman comes to escort me to my seat. I'm comforted by the simple act of walking to the dining table, my children seated and waiting, a candle flickering, serving platters and bowls filled with steaming food. Bryan and Allison seem to have finally made peaceful eyes at one another.

My children sit across from me, their faces milky and sweet. My woman sits next to me; she minces my food into small bites and helps me understand the confusion of my cutlery. I don't remember if I'm supposed to use my right hand or my left. All around me, happy conversation swirls across the table. I'm unable to keep up with the swiftness of thought, the rapid exchange of words.

I think and think and think until it seems I've broken my mind and broken my heart and nothing is left except the thought that I'm so very, very broken everywhere. I hear words now only in abbreviated and nearly impressionistic forms. It's like looking at a canvas, each color vibrant and significant, but for the life of me, I can't put the colors together to form the whole of the painting. I understand some things and—for the rest that is beyond my grasp—I simply let them hang like not-quite-ripe fruit to be picked some later time.

While I wait to catch hold of a kernel of something, I wrestle with my fork and blink at the food on my plate. I look at my children, wishing to notice something better than Allison's tomato-red blouse and Bryan's mouth, busy with food. I want to join myself to them, laughing and clinking glasses over the dinner table. Instead, I'm stuck (as always) trying to figure out the tines of a fork and language that, more often than not, befuddles and eludes me. I'm like a child interested in the perplexing conversations of adults.

Allison digs through her bag for a tissue and takes the opportunity to show off her new purse. "Isn't it darling?" she says. "It's Van Gogh's *Starry Night*. On my purse."

A memory whirls through me like the midnight blue sky and wild yellow stars swirling across Allison's purse.

"*Starry Night*," I say, clapping my hands. Suddenly, I have words. Sentences begin to pour from my lips.

"I love *Starry Night*. I always thought it looked just like the night I brought your father home to meet your MeeMaw and PaaPaw for the first time. What a night that was."

"You remember that?" Bryan asks.

"Of course, dear. It was just before the end of second semester. May third, three years before we married. Your father got all decked out in his best clothes. He was so nervous, the poor guy. You could have fed him lightning bugs for dinner and he would've swallowed them whole if he thought it would make a good impression. It was a beautiful spring night, frogs singing for joy that it was chicken on the table and not their big, thick legs. Your father's hands were so sweaty; my goodness, he had to wipe them on his pant legs before he could shake hands with your PaaPaw. By the time we finished dinner and headed for the porch, your father must have lost more pounds worth of worry than he gained while politely eating every bite of your MeeMaw's enormous chicken dinner.

"But when your PaaPaw brought out his banjo, Lord, didn't your father run to the car to grab his guitar...a smile finally on his face. You remember how well your father played guitar, don't you? Let me tell you, there's nothing better than a porch night on a warm Carolina evening, with a banjo, a guitar and a couple of well-fed men picking out *Poor Ellen Smith*.

"Your MeeMaw and I sat on the swing, our toes tapping with the music, smiles of satisfaction on our faces. And all around us were stars...stars just like those on your purse, Allison. It was a starry night, all right, smiling down on us...and all was well. Your father was the first boy I'd ever brought home to meet your MeeMaw and PaaPaw. And the last boy, come to think of it. I suppose it was the stars that made everything right. Of course, your father's handsome smile helped some, too."

I look back at my plate and resume poking at my food. I seem to have used a month's quotient of words and I'm once more silent as a ghost at the table.

"That was a lovely story, ma'am," my woman says. "Really lovely and told with such an authentic accent. I've never heard you speak so...well, so Southern."

YOUR EYES. Your eyes drift up from the table in time to see a secret look pass between your children. You've seen that look before, that startled exchange. It's a swift widening of the eyes, the jaw lowering only enough to elongate the face without causing the lips to part, a slight rise of the eyebrows. It causes your heart to sag. You can't blame them for their silent mockery, but you'd so much rather have your children look at you with favor for your wisdom rather than with rolling eyes and near laughter simply because your brain is sticky and there's nothing you can do about it. You're aware of the inventory of your losses that add up daily. You know. You know. Before your eyes fall sadly back to your plate and the difficult task of working the fork in your hand, you do what every mother would do—you bless your children with every ounce of forgiveness that is left within your fragile, falling-down mind.

After our meal is over, after my children toss goodbye kisses onto my cheek and my woman takes me by the arm to lead me to bed, I find my mouth has taken to trembling. A small whimper escapes my downhearted lips.

"Is something wrong?" Jewell asks.

"I think so, but I...." My eyes begin to water. "I don't know how to *say* it."

"I have just the cure for all that ails," Jewell says. "Let's get you settled in bed and I'll read one of your letters."

"No. I'm tired of letters." I place my lips into a pout. "My birds...I want to dance with my birds." I begin to cry again.

"How about we read one letter for the birds and then we go to sleep so you can be ready for your big day tomorrow?"

"The birds are bored of my letters."

Jewell laughs at my assertion.

I sigh and dramatically toss my head to one side. "Okay, just one letter," I say.

When I'm settled under the softness of my quilt, my woman retrieves the letterbox and fishes around for a new letter.

"Here, let's try this one," she says. She unfolds the paper, careful that it will remember its creases. Before she begins to read, she places one hand on my forehead and strokes my hair away from my forehead. She continues to stroke my hair as she reads.

My dear hearts,

Oh, you kids! You have fought and bickered over every little thing from the time you were babies. Even riding through most of every day in my arms, straddled one on each hip, you still managed to poke and hit each other, if not with your round little hands, at least with your words and neener-neener taunts.

I suppose I should tell you why I allowed you to behave like little tyrants and boors with each other.

You'll laugh over this, I'm sure. I allowed your sibling rants because I wanted you to know the joy of having someone else to fuss with. Your little fights were—if you can imagine this—music to my ears.

I didn't have a brother or sister to spat with.

Have you ever wondered how different your life might have been, had you not had each other? I don't know why I should ask you, except that I recall wondering about such nonsense now and then when I was a child. I remember one particular day when a heavy, pelting rain kept me indoors. I was suffering from the kind of boredom that causes a child to sigh and whine and press their young face to the window, as if doing so would change the weather and the mood.

I seemed always to be a lonesome and impertinent girl who sighed at the rain and cursed my fate to be an only child. With a sibling or two (I thought), I would have had someone with whom to play a game of pick-up sticks, or at the very least, had someone to bicker with.

Thank the stars you had each other. Thank the heavens (while you're at it) that you still do.

Your MeeMaw should have had a dozen children clambering after her apron and PaaPaw should have had at least a couple of little sons trailing after him into the woods to hunt squirrels and gather fallen wood for the fireplace. I could have had sisters to braid my hair and fight over which color ribbon to wind into the coils and brothers to take me frog gigging at night, or wrestle with across the lawn on sun-sparkled days.

And—here's the best part—you would have had many aunts and uncles to send you birthday cards with money tucked inside. But alas!

Still, I never heard Ma or Pa begrudge me as their only child, and a girl at that. Still, it seemed odd, in that day and in that place, that our home should be nearly childless, except for me. While other homes were resplendent with wild and noisy children, ours was a home of quietude and orderliness. I guess God knew Ma would lose her sight before I was fully grown and a blind mother to a band of children would have been a cruelty.

I wish you could have seen the satisfied and puckered mouths of the other mothers, clucking after their brood of children, counting all the little heads to make certain everyone was present. It always caused me to wonder if there was something wrong with me that God should see fit to keep me alone and less a child than I would have been, had I been one of many. An only child grows into an adult well before her years catch up to the fact. In that odd way, it seemed I was always older than Ma.

And so I remember that one day—that one rainy, face-pressed-to-the-window day, when I was as irksome as any child could be.

After the third time I sighed as if the world were coming to a rainy end, Ma ushered me from my perch at the window and sat me next to her on the living room couch. She pulled her weathered Bible from the pocket of her apron. She placed it on her lap without opening it and then recited several of her favorite Psalms aloud as if they were flickering candles pulsing under the warmth of her breath. Now and then, she punctuated a specifically important concept or lesson with one pointed finger. By the time she finished, I was changed under her recitations of gratitude and kindliness.

Now here's the point of this letter: It's not that you have each other and that you continue to bicker and banter even now. No! That's what brothers and sisters do—they stick out their tongues and say rude things to each other.

My point is that it saddens me terribly that I never pulled you from your own rainy-day windows to whisper the Psalms into your little ears, rather than letting you discover your own amusements. But then again, your MeeMaw was special. She may have been destined to become blind, but I'd like to think that whoever God might be, *She* made up for it by giving your MeeMaw a mother's wisdom far beyond her years. To your detriment, I was as immature as any mother should be allowed.

You certainly have my permission to read the Psalms, as

well as any other book that you want—even girlie magazines, if that's what floats your boat.

Love as always,
Mom

My woman grins at me before refolding the letter, pulling my covers up high enough to touch my chin, and then lowering the light. It's not long before I hear her singing in the kitchen and I'm soothed to sleep within the deep folds of her song. Tonight I sleep nearly three hours before waking.

Somewhere in those narrow hours between sleep and wakefulness, my legs forget how to walk on their own. My feet have lost their knowledge of which is left and which is right and how to step one foot in front of the other. These legs have turned to spindles suddenly unable to swing over the side of the bed. To stand. To walk.

I don't know whether to scream in protest or be glad for my legs and their newfound independence from my body. I wiggle around hoping that I'm only having a momentary glitch, but it's soon clear my legs have given up on me for good. I lie straight-legged and surrendered under my covers, consoling myself—if I can remember this new thing about myself— that I'll at least now stay in bed through the night. It's small comfort, but when one's legs suddenly and completely fall silent, there's not much left to do but sift through the ashes and concentrate on being free from the limitations of an old woman's halting gait.

To think I could have danced with the birds is a foolish thought, indeed. So, good riddance to my recalcitrant limbs, I say. Go ahead— let them be sticks, still and silent like tree branches in winter. It'll perhaps do this family some good that we're all free of the ill conduct of my midnight wanderings.

On the other hand, graceful, fan-fluttering acceptance is more than can be expected when half of one's body turns to putty.

Chapter Twenty-Seven

So now I've become much like a tender birch tree, beaten down so often by the wind I no longer try to stand upright, but simply bend the way of the prevailing wind whether the wind is blowing or not.

I've seen them.

I've seen the trunks of sweet birches arching low in the Appalachian woods, agony waving across their shivering leaves. Obviously, the poor spindly things just gave up under the wind. I know how they must have felt as their branches could do nothing more than rub across the ground, giving off a miserable sound like a thousand beetle shells scraping over the dirt.

I'm now a person who requires tedious care. My own prevailing wind has bent me in half.

I don't know how long I've been sick.

The Chinese pistache in the front yard has grown large and I don't know when that occurred. There is room now for several birds to gather on its lengthening branches. Other things have changed as well. John Milton the Cat has thickened and settled into a body that appears almost paunchy and middle-aged. I see threads of gray sewn onto my woman at the temples and streaked throughout her hair. The rose stalks have grown thick as my wrist and the walls of the house are turning yellow and pale with age.

It seems that since I turned ill there have been several seasons of summer, each followed by a long and rainy winter. Still, I can't be certain of the truthfulness of anything.

What I do know is that a long time has passed since I began to fail. Now a creeping weakness has journeyed into my legs, my arms, my body, settling all thoughts of my ever getting better. My legs are withering like stumps of fallen trees; they're no longer able to stand on their own. I've fallen into disrepair and no amount of care or watering or feeding can cause me to be upright or whole again.

Today, Bryan brings a wheelchair for me and I cry.

He tries to make it better with a bumper sticker that reads, *Honk if You're Horny.* My woman blushes all the way through her cinnamon-colored skin. Bryan laughs. I tell him I don't understand what the words mean. Bryan sobers his face and peels the sticker off.

"There, Mom," he says, crumpling the sticky paper in his hands. "We should make this the Queen's carriage, rather than the street-walker's cab." I still don't understand, but I mirror his smile and that seems to make things better.

Bryan and my woman help me from my bed. My body—bent as low as those sad birch trees forever wounded by chronic winds—folds easily into the shape of the chair. Bryan and my woman smile over me.

"Beautiful," Bryan says. "You're an absolutely regal-looking queen in your beautiful new chair."

"Very lovely, ma'am," Jewell says.

"The hell with you both," I say. "It's a wheelchair, for God's sake. I want *out* of here."

Bryan looks wounded. "I'm sorry, Mom," he stammers.

"Get me out of here." I raise my voice. "Get me *out* of here."

"Relax," Bryan says, using his stern lawyer voice.

"Relax, hell. You try relaxing in this...this ridiculous...thing." I try working my legs to stand, but it's no use. They've forgotten themselves completely.

I start to cry out again, but I'm surprised by John Milton the Cat who jumps onto my lap. It seems he likes the chair. I decide not to argue any further and simply let the branch of my hand bend toward the softness of his gray fur. My woman takes the opportunity to wheel John Milton and me to the living room.

Somewhere during the journey between my bedroom and the living room, I decide to like the chair, but only because of the cat.

Bryan apologetically smiles his way out the door. After my woman moves herself to the kitchen to prepare today's menu, I realize my predicament. I'm a still-youngish woman with a progressive brain disorder, stuck in a wheelchair with a cat on her lap. I try to remember how this occurred, but few words come to my memory.

It seems life is now more-than-spare and I can't help but wonder whether my current state is a blessing or a curse. There is something, of course, to be said for an uncomplicated manner of living. At least I'm not saddled with the complexities that plague other women my age. There is no sense worrying about a wrinkle on my face when I have trouble locating the words that might describe the event that could have caused the line.

I spend the next moments working to remember how I traveled from my former vibrancy to this current state. I manage a mere stipend of simple words and allow them to float through my mind:

Lettuce

La La La Girls

A whistling moon

A yellow shirt

Notes on a mirror

Letters in a box

Bewilderment

Memories

Breaking

Another glass of red

Sticky, sticky starfish

A spoiled trip

Piteous

Behavior

My Ivan

Longing

Stripping

Sparkles

Banging

Crumbling

Evaporating

A sonnet unwritten

A cat comes home

A singing woman

Fluttering hands

All the dancing birds

Darkness

Arms

Lifting

Cradling

Frightened legs

A rolling chair

An elegant awareness

A falling leaf

Such few words for one who once was a poet. A writer. A wife. A mother. Where it was once flowing water, language is now constricted, abbreviated. Mere drops of watery thought. As a poet, I should be delighted. Every poet wants only the essence of thought, the merest of words to tell her story. Nevertheless, a poet shouldn't be stripped of nearly every one of her words in order to tell that tale. She should be able to select and weigh the gravitas of each word in connection with its importance to the others around it.

There should be choices.

She should—at the very least—be able to make sense, if not to others, at least to herself.

The maddening thing is my full awareness of all the blanks. I'm slowly being stripped of my color, deconstructed day by day, word by word, ability by ability. The incomprehensible thing is that I continue to know all the things I can no longer do or say or contribute.

I'm aware.

I look down at my legs. They are thin as twine, as are my arms. They surprise me with their simmering uselessness, but I let them be. I've learned that it's of no consequence to argue with the failures of a once-lovely body when the brain has other intentions. I sit quietly with John Milton the Cat under my hand. The windows are open and the curtain sheers drift and snap with the breeze, waving themselves like white flags of surrender.

The front door comes alive with my beautiful Allison. She's wearing a white dress and floats into the room like a cloud on a breeze. She drifts onto the couch, wrapping the cloud of her dress around her slender legs.

She looks at me. "Bryan told me," she says. "A wheelchair."

"Uh hum." I nod my head. My brow is furrowed with worry for myself.

My hand moves from John Milton to the arm of the chair. I don't know why, but even with a newfound freedom from the burden of lengthy conversation, I feel ashamed for my answer.

I'm also ashamed for the chair and for my trembling legs.

"Do you need anything?"

"New legs?"

"Oh, Mom." Allison's chin trembles.

The breeze from the windows goes slack, and the curtains settle back against the walls. Allison sighs; we sit together silently. She stays a while and then rises to float away, again a beautiful cloud in an endless sky. Before she leaves, Allison walks behind my wheelchair and wraps her arms around my shoulders.

"I'm so sorry." She whispers into my ear, leaving a tearful mark on my cheek. "I have to go now. I'll come and check on you tomorrow. I'll bring some magazines for us to look at."

"It's okay," I whisper back. "Oh, look! You rained on me."

After Allison leaves, I realize I've cupped my hand around her tear to hold it tightly to my face.

I hear my woman's throaty voice singing from the kitchen. The breeze returns and my curtains fly as flags once more. After a while, I go back to thinking of words and wondering when my children might ever visit me again.

I think it's been a terribly long time.

Chapter Twenty-Eight

My woman wakes me, trilling into my ear, "I heard from a little bird that today is your birthday." She sounds like a singing nightingale and I'm instantly confused.

"That's not true," I say. "I've not discussed my birthday with *any* bird...ever!"

"You're right, ma'am...actually, it was your son, Bryan, who told me. Your children are coming for a special dinner tonight. We'll make your favorite chicken with mashed potatoes and gravy."

I clap my hands. "Oh, goody. Yes. Well, then...yes, it's my birthday. I'm sure it is." I crook my finger and motion my woman to bend her ear closer to my lips. "You're forgiven for your lie," I whisper into her startled ear.

After I'm washed and dressed and combed into something resembling a proper birthday girl, after I am wheeled into the living room, after a Happy Birthday foil balloon is tied to my chair, and after the television is turned on to provide its illogical white noise of game show companionship, my woman leaves me for her kitchen chores.

I sit in my chair, happy it's my birthday and I have a balloon bobbing above my head, announcing that lovely fact. I clap my hands and smile. It's my birthday!

Slowly, however, as someone might carefully shift from one hip to the other in their chair, over the next hour, my mood turns. It occurs to me that even with a silver and pink balloon tied to my chair like a buoy marking my place, I'm drowning and there's no one to pull me up and out of this black water lake into which I've fallen. I'm a small, fragile presence held by the silence of gravity and the stillness of coming death.

Surely, this isn't right.

My shoulders slope, my neck is rounded into a crescent shape of defeat. Birthday or not, I'm a body filled with the gathering terror of one soon to die—maybe today, on my birthday—and I don't even know how old I am.

How can it be that I don't know my age?

The icy water of dementia curls around my feet, swirls up my legs, covers my chest, and flows over my head. Yes. I'm drowning. Yet there's no pain, unless I count the agony of all this terrible forgetfulness.

A breeze from the open patio door fills my mouth like the first gasp of brackish water. I suppose one in my position will either sink or swim. There is no simple straight line that marks the difference between alive and dead. I'm as dead sitting alone in front of a flickering television (that's now dinging loudly, *winner, winner, winner*) as I would be if I were lying on a bed the moment after my last breath.

Slyly smiling at this simple insight, I decide dying would be an appropriate response to my birthday. Appropriate, indeed!

With great effort, I turn my chair and paddle my feet and arms until I propel myself across the living room to the kitchen door. I keep at it until I find my woman, who is bent over a broom, sweeping up flecks of dust from the kitchen floor.

"I'm ready to die now," I announce. "I've thought it through and I've decided. I'm a burden in this chair and I'd like you to kill me now."

Jewell straightens and turns to me, looking over my small and crumpled body. She smiles. "You don't mind if I finish my sweeping first, do you?" she asks. "It's hard to concentrate on killing people when the kitchen floor is only half done."

"You're laughing at me...I can tell. You shouldn't—"

Tears sting the back of my eyes as I plunge my chin forward into the pose of one consumed by stubborn resolution. My hands fumble toward my chest. "Look...in here," I say, patting my breastbone. "I mean it in here. I want to die. On my birth...it's my birthday and I want...don't I get what I *want* for my birthday?"

Jewell sets the dustpan down and stands the broom against a corner cabinet. She moves to my chair, kneels beside me, and takes up my trembling hands into the warmth of hers.

"Can you feel this, ma'am? Can you feel my hands around yours?"

Water breaks over the dam of my lower lids. "Yes, but shouldn't they be around my neck? You can't kill me by holding my hands."

Jewell looks down at our fingers that are now entwined like ivy across a trellis. She flips her eyebrows and looks around the kitchen like she doesn't want the walls to hear what she is about to tell me.

"I have a secret. There is magic in my skin," she leans into my ear and whispers. "Magic." Jewell elongates the first syllable until the word sounds like, *maah-jic*. "Right here in the skin of my hands. You've asked me to *kill* you. But my hands—these *magic* hands— they only know how to bake special birthday cakes with ingredients so magic themselves that just one bite will make you feel better."

"Stop it...I want—"

"I know you're sad today. But your children would be so disappointed if I killed you on your birthday...before your party. Let's just put that idea off for a different day. Okay?"

"I don't know," I say. "Maybe." Reluctance rides the edge of my voice, but for the moment, I'm talked out of the attractive notion of my woman's hands tightly circled about my neck.

Jewell returns to her broom. "I'm almost done with my morning chores," she says. "Would you like me to wheel you to the patio for some fresh air while I finish?"

"Mmmm," I say, nodding. "It's still my birthday, though, and I still want to die."

"Yes, ma'am...I *know* you do." She places her hand softly on my shoulder; her stout, warm fingers feel like a fire burning through my blouse. I pull the heat into my bones. Her touch is divine and I hold on to the promise that later—maybe even tonight—she'll be kind enough to slip her magic hands around a pillow and crush it to my face.

Jewell wheels me out to the patio where she leaves me to watch several peeping birds as they peck their way across the yard.

YOU PASS. You pass the rest of your morning watching small dark-winged birds. They bob their way through bright-faced flowers looking for snippets of small bugs or fat caterpillars, clinging tightly like prizes under green garden leaves. It's obvious the birds see that you're nothing more than an oddity slumped in a chair. They continue clacking their small beaks against stems and leaves. There is gladness in their feet as they hop from leaf to leaf, their heads turning this way and that as they listen for the scatter of breakfast. They dance with unspeakable joy tucked into the sleeves of their wings. They make you ashamed for wanting death to swoop down upon you. Your shame makes you want to die all the more, but still, the day goes on and the birds continue on their way and your heart somehow finds a way to sing and weep for it all.

By the time my children arrive, each holding a little bag filled with the weight of a small gift hidden under crinkled tissue paper, I've stopped asking my woman to kill me. The distraction of my chattering Allison and my somber Bryan delight me and, for now, I forget my throat and how I so desperately want someone to squeeze their fingers around it until it forgets to take in air.

Instead, I clap my hands with the pleasure of my children. Their bodies are warmth and comfort and I'm fascinated by their arms and their legs and how they move and gesture. Their mouths are mesmerizing and they shake their heads and laugh with abandon. The late afternoon light seems to have settled across their skin, helping me follow and translate their movements into meaning.

The Happy Birthday balloon tied to my chair bobs above my head like a celebration dance. I'm at last in love with the day and, in spite of the few words still available to my lips, my heart is filled to bursting.

My woman bustles about the periphery of the room, setting the table for dinner and pouring glasses of wine, offering beer or tea, all the time humming under her breath. She seems enlivened by the presence of my children.

Allison approaches me on legs that seem to dance across the room. She dangles a gift bag in front of my face. "Guess what's in here," she trills. "Guess."

I shrug my shoulders, a mute gesture that telegraphs the effort guessing would take. I'd like to remind her about the hardening cement of plaques and tangles that are currently taking up the whole of my brain, but I haven't the foggiest idea about the words it might take to explain.

"Don't make her guess," Bryan says. He has moved to the couch where he sits folded tightly like a closed umbrella. "Mom can't guess things anymore. Just let her open her gift."

Allison's eyes flash momentarily and then settle on the simpler, more reasonable course of trying to engage my face. "Never mind him, Mom. Here, just open it up." Allison grins wildly and places the bag on my lap. I allow my fingers to fumble through its confusing tangle of curly ribbon. Within seconds, I give up on figuring out the complication of a gift bag. I grab hold of a corner of tissue paper and pull. The thin paper tears apart in my hands and tears suddenly travel across my eyes like a swift-moving storm.

"I can't do this!" I cry. "You're making me do things I can't do. Why are you all so cruel to me?" I launch the bag from my lap and it lands with a dull thud on the floor. "Why are you making me do these *hard* things?"

"Jesus, Allison. Give her a hand." Bryan talks into the neck of a beer bottle he's half-drained in only a few seconds.

"Here...let me help you," Allison says, shooting her brother a quick scowl. She picks up the bag and straightens its folds. Without untying the bow or removing the tissue, she plunges her hand inside and pulls out a narrow length of silk material.

"Look, Mom. It's a handmade scarf I got from this fabulous little online Etsy shop. Don't you just *love* it? Look! It has little hand-stitched birds along the edge. I know how you love little birds."

"It's so pretty," I say. I reach out and take the scarf into my hands. The fabric glides softly on my skin and I rub it across my cheek. I smile the mouth-only kind of smile that besets one in my state—the Alzheimer's Mask.

"Bryan, aren't you going to give Mom your gift?" Allison asks.

"Just waiting for you to finish irritating Mother to death," Bryan flashes. He stands from his seat on the couch and crosses over to me. Kneeling, he unties the ribbon from his gift bag. He pulls out the tissue paper and opens the bag for me to peer inside.

I clap my hands. "Oh, goody!" I say. "It's lovely. What is it?"

Bryan pulls a small book from the bag. "It's a memory book for you, Mom. It's filled with pictures of us all…here, look." Bryan opens the cover to reveal pages of pictures, each one marked with a caption. Every page is decorated with clever cut-outs and stickers. "A colleague of mine does scrapbooking in her spare time and she did this for me. This one is all pictures of me. I have two more books…one with all pictures of Allison and one with pictures of you and Dad."

I point to a picture on the first page. "But who is this *little* boy?"

"That's me, Mom. When I was just two, I think."

"You," I say. "Oh…it's you?"

Bryan ignores my confused eyebrows. "I also have a DVD that we made that has all the pictures set to music."

"You're in a *movie?*"

"Well, that's a good way to put it. Yes. Very much like in a movie." Bryan produces a larger bag that contains two more books and a plastic DVD case. "Here are the two other books, and I'm sure Jewell can help you start your DVD any time you want."

"Yes, ma'am, I sure can," my woman says from the edge of the room. "Now, come eat, everyone. Dinner's on the table."

Someone wheels me to my place at the table. My Happy Birthday balloon still floats above me. Hands also float around me; they place a napkin over my blouse, cut my food into small bites, help me stab a piece of chicken with the pointed end of my fork, dab now and then at my chin. A birthday cake with white frosting and a single purple candle occupies the center of the table. Everyone is talking and smiling across my cake—my beautiful birthday cake. A few times, I locate a word or two to interject into the conversation, regardless of the appropriateness to the subject at hand. I roll these snippets of words around in my mouth and then toss them across the table for everyone to hear.

Bryan relates a story about a water law case, detailing its complexity and how it's probably going to go down the drain in spite of all his good efforts. "Hahaha," I laugh. "I'm so happy about all this." Bryan looks up, his fork hanging from his hand like a misplaced punctuation mark, his words stunned in mid-air.

Allison dusts off the silence and begins to chatter on about a new boutique she wishes I could see, offering to take me there one day soon. I clap my hands and shout into the startled ears of everyone, "Lord Tennyson...*Break, Break, Break*. If you could peel back the edge of his grave, I bet he smells like dirt by now." I grin at my cleverness with my mask of a smile that refuses to allow my eyes to crinkle and sparkle. I clap and show my teeth and beam over my birthday cake with its one purple candle.

The room grows quiet but I'm giddy with my birthday and my floating balloon and the faces of my children that rise above their chairs like puffs of cloud over the landscape of the dinner table.

"Well, let's have that cake, then...shall we?" my woman says.

"Good idea," Bryan says. "Here, I'll light the candle. Ready, Mom?"

"We're going to light my cake...and Lord Tennyson stinks like dirt!" I clap and laugh.

My children leave shortly after the cake is cut. Both leave their pieces uneaten on their plates, with excuses that it looks delicious but they are late for separate events. They brush their lips over my cheek and leave with apologies that next time they'll stay to help clean up. My woman waves them away. There is gentleness in her eyes as she ushers Bryan and Allison to the door, even though they probably don't deserve her hospitality after not eating her magic cake.

Jewell seems not to mind.

She cleans the kitchen while I watch my new DVD. I don't know why Bryan would give me a video filled with images of little half-familiar children, but they are charming and I find myself grinning broadly by the time the video ends.

After the DVD, my woman readies me for bed. Before she leaves, I ask her to bring my birthday scarf and tie it around me. "Is it still my birthday?" I ask as she places the silk around my neck.

"Yes. It's still your birthday."

"Good. That means you still have time to do me in...and with my new scarf. It has birds on it, you know. So, hooray! I can still die on my birthday."

I watch my woman stifle a laugh. "Now, why do you want to die on your birthday?"

"So I only have to remember this simple day, you foolish woman. Just make sure I'm not buried next to Tennyson. Poor fellow smells, you know." I clap my hands and laugh at my joke.

"Yes, ma'am. Let's talk about dying tomorrow, though. It's been a long day and I'm very tired. Aren't you tired now?"

"I guess. Where's my balloon? I want my balloon."

"Right here, ma'am...still tied to your chair and ready for tomorrow." My woman turns out the light and leaves me to a night of vividly colorful dreams of balloons in the sky, a frosted cake in the center of a table, and a blue scarf with little embroidered birds fluttering and squeezing around my neck.

Chapter Twenty-Nine

A wheelchair measures the depth and breadth of my world. I've watched my world shrink from wide as the sky to small as a sink basin, then to something like the bowl of a cracked and weathered teacup. Now, it seems my world fits in a thimble. My woman helps me into my wheelchair each morning and she removes me from it at night. The balance of the day, I sit wherever I'm placed: sometimes the patio where I'm entertained by peeping birds, their feathers, now and then unfurled in abandoned delight; sometimes the garden where my woman coaxes young tendrils to shoot up high from the earth with nothing more than her hearty songs and a trowel; sometimes the living room in front of the whirring television; sometimes cozied up to the dining table where my woman urges me to take in spoonfuls of things like ham hocks and beans, washed down with sweet tea and pills. I eat very little of what's offered, but I swallow the sweet tea without much complaint.

It is, after all, sweet.

During the long afternoons, while my woman cleans the house or folds laundry, I doze in my chair, my head lolling, drool stringing from the corner of my mouth, John Milton always on my lap. We are one another's warmth, a symbiotic relationship of fur and fabric and the skin of my hand that, all combined, comforts the both of us. The weather's cooled for the year and each day descends a bit deeper into the chill of winter; my woman keeps my legs covered with a soft quilt.

There's not much I talk of now. I've quieted, much like a still water well that may either be sweet or brackish, depending upon the mood of the earth.

Bryan and Allison visit often. They take turns seeing me; sometimes I know them, often I don't.

To help, Jewell has made signs with large lettering that read, *Hi Mom. I'm Allison, your daughter*—or—*Hi Mom. It's Bryan, your son.* Oddly, I can still read these simple placards and their use helps me feel less confused about who is standing in front of me with a sheepish grin and a bag of taffy or horehound candy that—I'm told—they get from the Internet.

I don't know what that means, the Internet.

I'm comforted, though, that I can still read simple words and I can make out the significance of those words.

My Bryan! My Allison!

My woman has other tricks to keep me soothed, not the least of which are soft tunes she loads into a CD player, usually just moments ahead of any coming distress. I don't know how she figures out when to play music for me, or when to soothe my forehead with a cool cloth. Or when my quilt needs to be snugged again around my legs.

Bryan (according to his sign) is usually content to sit across from me, reading the newspaper or watching a ballgame. He seems to know conversation is out of the question. Simply having him nearby is conversation enough. He's become like a sturdy tree, silent and steady in the wind. His branches lean toward me, but he seems happy enough to let me be silent or find my voice as I'm able.

Allison, on the other hand, clatters on about girlish things while she brushes new color across my fingernails. She tries to embellish my plain and lengthy days with her whimsical thoughts and worldviews. She's the chattering magpie to Bryan's stoic tree. They approach me differently, but their visits are the delight for which I live.

When my children leave, it's as if my heart will break. "Come back again," I manage to say during our goodbye hugs and kisses. When they're gone, tears slide from my eyes. It seems the closing of every door signals the tragedy of forgetfulness. It's hard to hold the knowledge that—only moments earlier—I'd been the recipient of grand smiles and kisses from one of my children, approaching me with fistfuls of flowers or small, white paper sacks filled with exotic sweets.

The moment they leave, I forget they had just been with me.

Every goodbye is heartbreak. Every hello is celebration. The endless hours between are excruciating. My days are now divided between what is lost and what is found. What is joy and what is grief. What is now and what is not.

The worst thing is that I'm vastly aware. I simply can't wrap words around any of these flickering moments. Most words are gone. My eyes now serve as my voice. They are the watchers of what passes. My eyes cry. They wait. They follow and mimic and then move on to the next event as though nothing's ever preceded by anything; nothing's ever followed by anything.

I'm in some grand and ever-immaculate sense of the immediate.

I listen to the chattering of my heart; I hear it clearly because everything else within me is so largely silent. I try to pray behind closed eyes like Ma would have done, but God is nothing more than a vague cloud.

I wonder what will happen when I finally lose the last of these slim and narrow words that still bubble up now and then from my throat. How can I be assured that the loss of letter and syllable will not matter to heaven? After all, how will the angels gather up my words to be recorded when they are no longer uttered? For someone with no answers, it seems there are far too many questions.

I wonder if there's consequence for my side of things if I should feebly forget everything I've ever done. How can I be certain if I was bad or good? How does God forgive what is not remembered? Oh, this quiet, darkening brain of mine. It's all so shameful. Oddly, I also feel shame for my continued heartbeat, my breath, my simmering uselessness.

Now here I am, a small and winnowed woman, spending my days a tragic sleeper with open eyes. I call out. I hear answers. But nearly and utterly gone is the back-and-forth of words that would indicate literate conversation. The connection is almost irretrievably broken.

I'm little more now than a mysterious, rain-filled cloud in a rolling chair.

YOU GLIDE. You glide through each day, seated in your wheelchair as if you've never known any other way. The only evidence of your movement through the many hours is contained in narrow tracks across your carpet and the footprints of someone who pushes you from here to there, and then—at the appropriate time—back again. Your mind is filled with large blank sheets, nothing written on them, nothing recorded, nothing remembered. You try to hold your thoughts, your water, your bowels. Nothing stays. Nothing works. Eating is difficult, as is transferring from your chair to your bed. Dressing is done for you by your woman, bathing as well. There is nothing private on your body, nothing left for your modesty to claim. You think someone has died in your home. In a moment of inspiration, you realize it might be you.

My woman comes to me. "You're crying, ma'am. Are you ill? Do you hurt anywhere?"

I shake my head and manage to let two words whisper from my mouth. "My babies."

"Did you forget Allison was here today? She fixed your nails up again nice, ma'am. Purple this time."

I look down at my fingers. "Oh," I say. I smile over the purple polish on my nails.

"And Bryan will be here for dinner tomorrow."

"Good," I say. I manage a smile.

"Your arms are cool, ma'am. I'll run get you a sweater."

My woman leaves me. I sit in my chair with John Milton the Cat warming my lap, while the afternoon chills my arms. When my woman returns, she finds me crying.

"Are you all right?" she asks. "You're crying again."

"My children," I say. My lips tremble with sadness and regret. "They never come. Do I have children?"

"Yes, ma'am. You have two children. Bryan and Allison." My woman tucks my arms into a light blue sweater with generous sleeves that make dressing me an easier task. "Are you hungry, ma'am?"

"No." I notice my hands. "Look! I'm pretty."

"Yes, ma'am. You're very pretty. Beautiful. Would you like to sit on the patio while I get a few things done inside?"

I nod my head and my woman wheels me outdoors. As always, we leave tire tracks and footprints on the carpet to mark our course, like breadcrumbs littered behind our path to help us find our way back. Jewell leaves me on the patio while she works on her chores. I'm little more than a narrow stillness along the course of a dwindling afternoon, quiet tears serving as evidence of a single repetitive thought—everyone has left me.

I'm alone, except for my little birds and even they have become a distant rattle of feathers in the trees. A westerly breeze stirs, causing the tree leaves to chatter among themselves like the birds they hide. Soon, I give up trying to understand my thoughts and let them simply stir in my skull like soup in a pot.

Chunky, liquidy soup.

I let my eyes close around unnamed observations; my head lolls toward my chest in sleep. The sadness of my inability to clutch onto the simple words is more than I can bear. Sleep is a simpler, sweeter way to pass the time.

Somewhere in my dozing, I open my eyes. The stillness of my body, my hands with their purple fingernails, my hollow-boned legs beneath a soft cotton quilt, my gnarled, sleeping head—all this must have given me the appearance of a tree. For when I look, a bird—a little brown-tipped bird with a small peeping mouth—is sitting on the arm of my wheelchair, calling welcome to his friends.

"Come," he calls. *"A perch for us. A lovely, birdie perch for us."*

One by one, birds come to pay their respects. Some dance for me in an impromptu recital in front of my chair. I'd like to clap for them, but my arms are frozen in place. Little brown sparrows come and go, dancing and flitting, chirping unabashedly into my ears, clicking their small beaks across my hands, my earlobes.

The afternoon stretches on, lengthening the shadows across the yard, cooling the day with its gathering delta breeze.

When, at last, my woman comes to fetch me for dinner, she finds me clear-eyed and smiling. I'm covered in little peeping, fluttering birds. I'm still and quiet as an old oak in the sun, except for my right foot, which softly taps to the rhythm of all the dancing birds.

Chapter Thirty

Here is how I fall asleep: like a leaf flung into the sky by a great wind, only to shudder to the ground far from the comfort of my small and tender branch.

It is always painful.

I am out where it is too great a reach for what is familiar, where dark, skittery things pull at my skin, where the moon burns my eyes. The unavailability of sleep pierces every night for those who are forgetful. I think it is our eventual ruin.

Death by forgetfulness is maddening.

Time slows until it feels as if each day lasts a year. The clock on my bedside table is a useless tchotchke; it's been some time now since I've been able to decipher what it's trying to tell me. Its glow serves as nothing more than a blue nightlight, illuminating my tossing and turning through the night.

I'm of little help to my woman now. It's been some time since I've been able to assist in my bathroom care, my dressing, the transferring of my body from bed to wheelchair. Even keeping somewhat upright through each day is more than I can manage. I'm a ragdoll, nothing but flopping arms and legs in a useless collection of disorder.

Terrible clouds of dark sadness engulf me. My arms have forgotten themselves; my mouth is slack and spongy. I know I've turned into a hard case, but I'm stymied by my efforts to move, confused by my own flesh. Still, my woman hums over my body with melodies that feel like lullabies under my skin—sweet, gentle, warm, washcloth melodies.

I have a new living room chair now, a soft, green medical recliner that looks out over the front lawn. The chair is wide and adjustable, which gives my tender body opportunities to rest this way and that, turn a bit here and tilt a bit there. I lie on a puffy, white lamb's wool hide, which is supposed to help keep my body from breaking down into pressure sores.

It's like sitting on a warm, white cloud, except I'm not yet in the heavens.

Each morning, Jewell heaves me up from my bed and into my wheelchair. She then steers me to the living room and hauls me from the wheelchair to my lounger. Every evening brings a reverse course. It's a tough slog for her and I'm sad for what I put her through.

We're now in the midpoint between morning and evening, the quiet time when chores are done. Jewell pulls a chair next to me, careful to not jostle me. She no longer turns on the television. Its cacophony is more than I can bear these days. Instead, she plays old music, softly, until I'm soothed and rocking to its rhythms. *Porch music*, she calls it. It's mostly acoustic guitar or fiddle, some Glenn Miller, a sampling of old Southern charm. The Carter Family, Jimmie Rodgers, The Cowboy Ramblers. Now and then, a soulful, hands-in-the-dirt Gospel hymn. She always sings along with the hymns; they lie across my body like soft blessings.

Today, my woman seems wistful. She has a blue hardcover book in her lap. The cover says, *America's Greatest Poetry*. She opens to a random page, placing one gentle finger under the first line of word—something Ma would have called "Bible dipping." She begins to read aloud. Although I can't keep up with the words, I'm soothed by the meter and beat. She flips back and forth through the book, alighting now and then on something that catches her eye.

I close my eyes to better feel each selection.

After a while, my woman closes the book and just sits next to me, her soft hand caressing my arm. My skin is fragile, easily broken; her touch is whispery like feathers. She is silent, but her hand is like some faraway memory and I'm all the better for it. We begin to rock together as she rubs my arm. She hums to a Mother Maybelle Carter tune and I'm delighted, as much as there can be any delight left in this frail and broken mind I still miss so much.

I sleep.

Sometime later, when stripes of afternoon shadows fall across me like prison bars, I wake to find a young woman has replaced Jewell in the chair next to me. She is sitting upright, her hands clutching a little purse to her chest, her eyes watery green.

I can't remember her name.

It makes no difference; my mouth is too stubborn to let words form anymore. Her name, I suspect, is too complicated with its syllables and all its myriad history. I know her, though. In the cells of my body, I know the woman who sits next to me with a purse grasped in her hands and a look of devastation on her face. I know this woman with her long blonde hair and her long-legged body.

I look at her like she's the first person I've ever seen in my life and I'm fascinated by it all.

I'm sorry for my constant Alzheimer's mask of indifference. Even my face has forgotten how to articulate feelings with its eyes, its expression.

We simply look at each other.

"Hi, Mom," she says.

"Ahhhh," I answer. My voice is a whisper; it's the best I can do.

"I came to spend the evening with you," she says. I can tell she is trying to keep the inflection of her words as bright as her clothing.

"Whooooo?" I ask. Again, my best.

"It's me, Mom. It's Allison, your daughter."

"Alllliii—"

"Yes."

"Ooooo. I lovvvv—"

"I love you too. I brought fingernail polish and I thought we could just be girlfriends tonight. Okay?" I watch Allison's eyes fill.

"Hmmm." I nod my head, trying so hard to articulate something important to my Allison. My beautiful pony.

In the background, Emmylou Harris sings: *I would rock my soul in the bosom of Abraham; I would hold my life in his saving grace. I would walk all the way from Boulder to Birmingham if I thought I could see, I could see your face.*

I decide to let the music tell her what I want to say.

For the next hour, Allison holds my hands and paints color on my nails as well as my world. All the time, she chatters on much too quickly for me to follow. She doesn't seem to care that I'm only able to smile with my mouth. She doesn't notice it's impossible for me to track her wildly traveling trains of thought.

All I know is that for one small moment, she is once more my La La La Girlfriend.

I'm glad she doesn't see how much I struggle. But through the music, my beautiful Allison simply brushes color over everything, turning her head this way, holding her tongue to the corner of her mouth as she creates. Today, she paints me pink.

She paints me pink.

Chapter Thirty-One

Someone cups their hand gently under my chin and pulls my face up to meet theirs. It's my woman. My Jewell. She tells me my children are coming and I need my face washed, my hair brushed, my red sweater snugged warmly around my shoulders.

I smile at the thought of my children seeing me brightly wrapped in red. Few things pleasure me now, but some events still have the power to enchant me. Wearing red for my children is one. My head dips toward my chest, but contentment nevertheless moves across the stoop of my shoulders.

I'm washed and brushed and sweater-wrapped in warmth. Then I'm transferred from bed to wheelchair to day lounge chair—I try to help lift my weight, but still, I hear my woman groan under the effort.

My poor woman!

My children arrive. I feel kisses, hands patting my shoulders, smoothing my hair. Words are murmured into my ears. I smile, but my head refuses to turn upward to greet them properly.

This head droop is recent and unremitting.

I seem to be stuck in the reflective pose of one who might be deep in prayer—hands folded, head bowed, my mouth silently moving as if small but important words were crossing the threshold of my lips.

I hear my woman offer cups of steaming coffee. I hear a man say, *that would be great.* I hear a woman say, *oh, no thanks. I'm trying to stop. But I'll take a cup of tea, thanks so much.* I hear the movement of fabric, the shuffle of shoes and then a spoon tinging inside a cup. I love my good and gracious ears for all they hear. I only wish I could convince my face to rise from its perch on my chest to join the conversation.

"I'm so glad you came over," I hear Jewell say.

"Not a problem," Bryan says. His voice sounds thin and worried.

"I wasn't doing anything anyway," Allison adds.

"Well, I'm going to get right to it," Jewell says. "The way your mother is…she's become fairly helpless. It's getting too much for me now. It's very hard to move her by myself…hard to take care of all her very specific needs."

Allison sputters. "Jewell, you can't…we *need* you."

"What?" Jewell says. "No, that's not what I mean."

"Well, what is it?" Bryan asks. "Do you need more money? A raise?"

"No. You've always been very generous. I've been with you…your mother…what? Five, nearly six years now?"

"Oh my God," Allison nearly squeals, her voice rising like a siren. "You *are* leaving."

Jewell begins again. "Please, wait…listen—"

"What is it we can we do to convince you to stay?" Dearest Bryan, always the negotiator.

"All I need…that is, what your mother needs is some extra help. I have no intention of leaving your mother. But it's time to do for your mother what I can't do alone, what I'm really not qualified to do. She needs stronger medication, something to help her sleep better through the night. She's only swallowing a few spoonfuls of broth now. She doesn't really communicate much, and you can see she's not sitting well in her chair any longer. I think she may be suffering and she simply can't tell me."

"A night person, maybe?" Bryan mulls aloud over Jewell's suggestion.

"She's suffering?" *My dear sweet Allison.*

"To tell you the truth," Jewell says. "I think we're both suffering. Your mother needs constant care now. She's quiet at the moment, but it's not always like this. It's amazing how such a small woman can have such a big voice in the middle of the night."

"Why didn't you talk to us sooner?" Bryan asks.

"I didn't want to bother you until it was really necessary. But now ma'am needs round-the-clock care and that requires more than I can do alone."

I imagine Bryan tapping his chin with his index finger. Thinking. "I wish you *had* said something sooner. We can certainly get a nurse or a qualified aide who can give her whatever she needs, someone starting tomorrow night."

"Yes. Absolutely," Allison says. "*Whatever* you need."

I hear Jewell exhale, as if she's been underwater a long time and is just now able to breathe again. "Bless you. Bless you. I don't know what to say."

"Nothing to say," Bryan says. "It's a done deal. Would someone here for an eight-hour shift give you enough rest?"

"It would feel like heaven. Thank you so much." Jewell tips her head to one side. "There's one more thing, though—"

"Anything," Bryan says. "We're so clueless at this…anything you need. Anything at all."

"Have you kids discussed the idea of hospice care? In my assessment of ma'am, I think she could easily qualify now. I've worked with hospice before and…well, they're absolutely the very best at helping people like ma'am."

"Are you saying that Mom is…is…*dying?*" Allison asks, her voice rising into a siren of distress. She twists her fingers into a tangled knot. My poor little pony. I want to reach over to stroke her hair, but of course I don't.

"Hospice isn't focused on dying." Jewell walks to me and softly cups her hand under my chin. She smiles into my face. "Certainly, we're all going to go some time, but hospice is focused on allowing folks like ma'am here to *live* their days with dignity. And then… when the time comes, the hospice nurses simply help keep folks stay comfortable while they're looking for that soft place to land, all surrounded by love and family. Oh, and I have it on good authority that they sing too." Jewell winks at me and straightens my sweater before returning to her chair.

Bryan and Allison nod at each other. "That sounds really nice," Allison says. "Absolutely. We can have them here too."

"They'll do their own assessment of your mother's needs, but I can make arrangements on your behalf, if you'd like," Jewell says. "Their nurses are nearly the best, highly trained and absolutely wonderful."

"It sounds like we're all settled, then," Bryan says. "We trust you to do the best for our mom. Now maybe I'd better have another cup of that go-go juice before I get on the road."

"Of course. More tea for you, Allison?"

"Thank you, yes. Thank you for everything."

I hear my woman scurry around. I hear liquids being poured into cups and glasses. The talk then moves and changes and shifts; night settles in and I doze across their words.

After a while, I rouse in my chair to hear the sounds of my children gathering their things to leave. Their feet move toward me. Again, kisses land on my sagging cheeks. Again, careful hands brush across my fragile shoulders. *Love you, Mom* is whispered into each of my ears. Feet move toward the door and the sweet scent of my children vanishes once more.

I wish I could remember their names.

Beads of moisture are quick to find my lashes. It occurs to me that I was unable to participate in any of the entire day's conversation. I couldn't raise my arm to offer the coffee. I didn't smile or gesture or add a moment of Southern grace. No. Instead, my face retained its flat slate pose of indifference, while my mind continued to race in circles and paths, trying to locate something—anything—that might be conversational in nature.

I failed wildly.

I think it's been a long time since I became a piece of porcelain statuary—a relic—to be wheeled from one room to the next, always talked over and around. Of course it's hard to see what may still be alive inside my body, my mind. This pernicious silence, this chronic inactivity, would give anyone the notion there's nothing here anymore. The way my body droops, slack and inanimate within the confines of my chair—anyone would reasonably think I've merely wandered off to somewhere else, someplace that has no structure of thought, no literate understanding, no reasoning.

I'm not certain when people first began to talk around me, rather than speaking with me. It's been some time now, I suppose. Perhaps one day, I simply decided I should be a rolling artifact, wheeled around the house like some *objet d'art*, forever more to be a symbolic statement of meaning rather than a functioning mother. I don't blame my children.

It's difficult to converse with hardened clay.

Nevertheless, I wish this weren't so. Even the frozen need a word tossed in their direction now and then. Perhaps the final gift I can give my children is an understanding, an agreement, that they can talk around me and I'll not hold a grudge over it. After all, I'm really the only one to know of my disappointment.

When I'm done moping about people ignoring me, I open my eyes in time to see sparkles hovering in front of me. They are fascinating—beautiful red and yellow sparkles! They float in front of my eyes like twinkling stars in the room. I reach out to touch them. To grab them. To place them in my mouth. I eat the sparkles as if they're popcorn. They nourish me and satisfy my heart. They busy me.

I'm still eating sparkles when Jewell comes to me. She's finished cleaning the kitchen and folding the last of my laundry. I'm afraid she'll be glad to be done with me and my dirty clothes, the home-made soup I never quite seem to swallow without choking on the diced vegetables, my endless bathroom needs. My terrible moods.

My throat chokes. "Help me," I whisper.

"It's off to bed with you now," my woman says, carefully transferring me to my wheelchair. "We've had a busy day, what with so many birds come to pay their regards and then your children tonight. They're certainly a blessing, those kids of yours. I'm sorry I never had kids, but then I'd have missed out on the likes of you, ma'am. Yes, that's for sure...I'd have missed out on you."

She uses a warm cloth to wash the day off me, but it does little to renew me to a better state of mind. That damp washcloth does nothing to keep me from swirling down a soap water drain toward the center of gravity. Still, my woman takes extra care tonight. She rubs lotion on my shoulders and down my back.

When she's done, she folds the sheet carefully over the rougher blanket edge so nothing will irritate my brittle skin. She smoothes my hair with her hand and caresses my cheek. All the time, she sings over me, her deep, sultry vibrato seeping into what remains of my fractured thoughts. Tonight she sings *His Eye is on the Sparrow* as soft and breathy and beautiful as the heavens she sings about.

When she's done singing, the room turns quiet. Soon, I hear the movement of a book, its cover opened, its pages being turned, the quiet selection of something. *Hey diddle diddle, the cat in the fiddle.* I know this. *The cow jumped over the moon.* The moon—I know about the moon and how I once whistled to it and how it whistled back. I know that moon.

My lips feel as if they may be smiling.

I rise on one elbow. One inch, I rise.

The little dog laughed to see such a sight and the dish ran away with the spoon.

I try to clap my hands in joy.

I fail.

I fall back to my bed as my woman begins to sing once more. She sings, *Twinkle, twinkle, little star.* My eyes are tightly closed; I desperately look for the stars my woman sings about, for the heaven that holds them high above my bed, flashing and glimmering.

I can't find them.

My woman's voice becomes softer and softer. She rubs my arm and strokes my head. She sings about stars.

She sings.

As I fall asleep, I'm filled with bath time melodies and children's nursery rhymes. I carry my woman's voice with me, down a deepening corridor and all the way back to the dreams of a once-again child.

Chapter Thirty-Two

*Y*OU HEAR. *You hear a woman screaming, crying, grunting in the dead of night when the thunder in her brain is louder than the sounds from her lips. You'd like to leave her to her ceaseless noise, but you're apparently tied to her miserable body. She is you. You've forgotten most things now; only the most tattered and ancient thoughts remain. Still, you're aware of your children who visit you, always with bouquets of flowers and dread puncturing their eyes as they tiptoe toward your bed. You're aware of their words, the shaking of their heads, the whispered conversations with your woman in the hallway. You know you now have two more women, one who comes each morning, writing notes on a clipboard and softly reporting to someone on her cellphone. Then, there's a younger one with wide eyes and a firm hand who comes in the evening to change your sheets and bathe you. She rubs your body with lotions because your skin is breaking into pieces. When she's done changing and bathing and rubbing, she rewards you with ice cubes for your cracking lips, a slither of lemon Jell-O to soothe your throat. Still, even with ministering hands gracing your body, you shudder under every draft that brushes your shoulders, every light that floods beneath your flickering eyelids. When the day is late and your room is at last quiet, you hear the sun sighing as it slides down the edge of*

the sky. You sigh with it, as if it's a song only the two of you know.
Every day, your woman—your first woman, the one you've come
to love as much as your children—slips into your room to read
aloud from your box of letters or from a book of poetry or prose. It
no longer matters what she reads. Every word is new. Every story
is fresh. Every refolding and closing is a splintering loss.

It is late afternoon. I can tell by the shadows that fall across my
bed and hold me down. The hospice woman, the one with soft brown
eyes and careful hands, has finished my morning care and is gone for
the day. I like her. I imagine her to smell like vanilla and coconut,
but it's been a long time since I was certain about scents. She is kind
to my body, even kinder to what might be called my essence. She
sits beside by bed, holding my arm and writing on a chart she has
made up for me. Yes. I like her—she is gentle like my woman and she
makes certain that I'm as close to comfort someone like me can be.

I lie in my bed looking much like a little balled-up fist. In spite
of the hospice nurse's cooing words and soft touch, it's still impossible for me to get comfortable. Although my bed is changed and
smoothed daily, it takes but a moment for me to rearrange the sheets
into a jumble; my covers are either too warm or too cold. My nightgown is always a crumple of fabric under me.

There's not much left in my arsenal to let my needs be known, so I
often just moan, softly into my hands. Sometimes, though, I cry out
with great, heaving vigor.

I know everyone does their best. I have three women now and I'm
rarely alone. There is always a quiet fussing about, making certain I'm
warm or cool, cleaned up and wiped down, that I don't stay in my
own filth for more than a few moments. That the temperature of my
broth is tested before it's scooped into a small plastic spoon and held
to my lips. That my hair is dry-washed, my body cleaned with soft,
warm washcloths before my skin is coated with lotions and salves.
Everything is attended to with tenderness and courtesy.

Still, anticipating the needs of a wordless woman takes more than
most can give.

Sometimes whispery conversations are held in my doorway.
Instructions from one woman to the next. *She seems listless today,*
or *She was able to get a few spoonfuls down.* I know which woman is

in my room just by the sound of her shoes as she moves toward me, how I'm touched, whose hands are slow and careful and who rushes through my routine. I know who lingers and who bustles, whose voice pierces my skin and whose words bounce away before I can figure out their meaning.

Now I hear my woman, my Jewell; her approach is soft like the small wing beat of sparrows. I hear the breath of fabric as she sits next to my bed, the whisper of her fingers unfolding one of my letters. "I'll read to you now, ma'am," she says. Late afternoon is the only time I'm alone with my woman and I relish these moments.

My eyes are closed, my body not much more than lines and angles poking through the sheets. Somehow, I know it's the last letter I'll ever hear; I'm too far gone now and so I hope it's at least one of my better pieces.

I'm awake. I'm aware, but most of my body is closing like windows before a storm. I have only three words left to me: *Hey!* and *Help Me!* Sometimes, when I'm electric with energy, I let my three words spill out in ever-widening circles of sound.

As always, the chaos of deep shame for my illness pulls me apart, small pieces at a time. On my bedside table is a small pot of pink geraniums in full flower; I no longer recognize their pungent aroma. I'm ashamed of my nose. I'm also ashamed that in spite of John Milton's comfort and companionship, my hands find it impossible to return any small gesture of love. I rarely recognize people and I'm saddened there is even a need to try.

I should simply know.

The worst of this shame is that, were I able to do so, I would still hide my infirmities. I'd still be deceptive. Until I turned forgetful, I was never a liar. Now every moment that ticks by on the clock and every breath that shudders through my chest marks me an insensible woman still desperately trying to hide her frailty as if I were a drunkard, hiding empty bottles.

Sadly, I'm the empty bottle I hide.

Soon, my night woman—the young one who smacks bubblegum all night—comes to do her job. I'm glad for the medicine, which winds me quickly down into a mostly dreamless sleep. Nevertheless, I'm sad that Jewell is now in the other room until morning.

I don't remember my name.

Chapter Thirty-Three

These memories are the last to go—the rising of the breath like hands lifting the body toward heaven; the circuitous route of blood through the body like a cycle of rain to nourish the earth; the opaque flutter of eyelids, separating the light from the dark; the smacking of lips; the feeble attempts to swallow. Dreams, too. Dreams are the last to go and it is within these dreams I find myself like the moment just before a star is birthed, a dark point of nothing that becomes something amazing within less than the blink of an eye. I imagine I will soon become a baby-blue star, winking on to pulse and twinkle overhead—a new pinprick of light inside a very old universe.

I'm living just behind my eyelids.

Sometimes I'm still, slack-jawed and looking to any observer as dead as any woman could be, seeing nothing and hearing nothing. Sometimes my eyes are open and I moan. Mostly, I appear lifeless as a ghost under the sheets. Right now my hip is feeling pain; I want desperately to turn to my other side.

Oddly, it's the pain that lets me know I'm still alive.

Now here I am, a stillness in my bed—my knees and my feet, my hands and fingers, the leading edge of my chin, each part drawn into the center of myself. My back is rounded, my neck lowered to my knees, like a question mark or, maybe, a near-circle. Everything is rounded now, pulled toward the middle, nothing angular or jutted out, except for maybe my left elbow, which is trying to fold itself in as well.

I still have thoughts, but there are no words to accompany them. Now and then, I grunt in response to something around me, a light left on when I'd prefer the room to be dim, an abrupt moving of me during the changing of my linens or soiled clothes, the prick of a needle into my fragile skin, the countless interruption of hands moving over me, turning me, fixing something amiss with my bed. Or with me. I am aware (always) of my woman, my Jewell, who rubs away the beginnings of any sore on my skin and applies ointment to keep my lips from cracking. She hums over me with sounds like the thrumming of a thousand bird's wings.

For her, I feel love.

It seems the time has come for me to tumble and fall toward whatever landing I shall find. It is evening and the shadows fall with me.

The day is ripe for falling things.

My children come to hover over my bed, their hands folded like steeples over little finger chapels. I'm aware of their tears, the sound of their whispering voices, the soft clearing of their throats, and the occasional flutter of their nervous laughter. Allison has brought candles and she busies herself around the room with the lighting and wick care. My woman tiptoes in every now and then; she adjusts my covers if they've slipped; she rests her cool hand on the inside of my wrist; she feels the heat of my forehead. Her eyes are moist.

It appears I'm dying.

This dying would be painful but for the medication. I sleep. I wake. No one notices the difference. My body takes signals from my brain, but my beautiful, gummed-up, sticky brain has well forgotten its way.

My organs are now doors, closing softly, one by one.

I lie on my right side; one hand is under my cheek, the other lies across my narrow thigh. My fingers are splayed open like a fan—the only indication of the agony of falling, sinking, being crushed by the great weight that is this dying.

I grieve the loss of my body, although no one could possibly guess the depth of my sorrow because I'm so very still and silent.

My breath is ragged now, shallow, occasional; it seems there's not much left of it. I want to push myself upward, high upon my elbows, to rise above the life draining from my limbs, my failing organs. I wonder if the next time I open my eyes, I might see a different place. A field of beauty perhaps, filled with wild California poppies and green, green Carolina grass. I wish for something—anything—to hold onto, some lovely thing that will carry me through this moment.

I hadn't expected to die today, but I suppose I'm as ready as I'll ever be.

I feel Bryan now, my precious Bryan, rubbing my feet. His hands are strong, his fingers too quick as they knead into my fragile skin and brittle bones, but I can't tell him to stop. All words are gone. Despite the strength of his hands, I find comfort in his touch. He is sad for my state and I'm long past rising to fix him with ice cream and a mother's perfectly placed words.

My Allison, my lovely prancing pony, sits beside me. Her hand is on my shoulder, but only barely so. She was always afraid to touch me after I turned ill. I could never fault her for that. A mother with a failing mind is certainly a fearful thing.

Allison speaks. "Should we say prayers or something now? What should we do?"

Bryan answers. "I don't know. Whatever."

"I don't know any prayers," Allison says.

"I don't know any either."

"Well, we should do *something*." Always my kinetic Allison, she would need movement of some kind to soothe this raw and searing moment.

"What would Mom want?"

"I don't know. A churchy song? She always liked music."

"Then go ahead and sing something." Bryan returns to kneading my tender feet.

"What? What should I sing?" Allison asks.

"Who cares? It's not like you're taking requests in a piano bar. Just sing something nice. Maybe something Mom would like."

After a moment, I hear Allison take a breath. She leans into my ear, her hand still on my shoulder. She begins to sing. *Oh Lord, won't you buy me a Mercedes Benz.*

"Allison! What the hell kind of song is that?"

"Well, you said a churchy song. It's the only song I know that says Lord in it."

"Oh, God." I imagine Bryan rolling his eyes, considering the logic of the song. "Well, fine then. Janis Joplin it is." His fingers resume rubbing my feet. Again, I want to tell him to stop, but there are simply no words left. Not one. Sometimes, there's nothing left for a dying mother to do but offer up her tender feet to somehow fix her sorrowful son.

Allison leans into me and starts again. *Oh Lord, won't you buy me a Mercedes Benz. My friends all drive Porsches, I must make amends. Worked hard all my lifetime, no help from my friends. So, oh Lord, won't you buy me a Mercedes Benz.*

Wait! I know the song. I hear the words. There is familiarity. There is something about the rhythm, the rhyme, the meter, Allison's wavering, slightly off-tune voice. I hear the music and something within me, guttural and primitive, responds to the music.

"Look at Mom," Allison says. "She's smiling...and I swear, she's singing along."

"That's crazy."

"Seriously. Come see."

Bryan leaves my feet and moves beside Allison. "Oh my God, she *is* smiling. She likes it. Sing some more."

"Sing it, too," Allison says.

"You're doing fine. Keep going."

Allison leans close to me again. *Oh Lord, won't you buy me a night on the town. I'm counting on you, Lord, please don't let me down. Prove that you love me and buy the next round. Oh Lord, won't you buy me a night on the town.*

"That's all I can remember," she says.

My children become silent. Reverent. They touch my shoulders, my hands. They peer into my face. They smile and coo as if I'm a brand new baby.

"That's so amazing," Allison says. "Who'd have thought that Mom liked Janis?"

"Yeah, who'd have *thought?*"

Oh, there is something to be said for a dying woman's final look at what she is leaving, when every bit of strength is gathered, when all movement is collected and coiled into one final wild and splendid thought. Nothing but this last moment is significant and counted in a mother's book of days. Simply, there is only glory in knowing a mother's children are present.

This is my last breath, my final look, and in spite of the void inside my head that has stolen from me everything I ever knew—every memory that defined the woman who once was Lillie Claire Glidden—I know I am ready.

I now can see what a baby-blue star does the moment just before winking on into its new existence. She looks squarely into the faces of her beautiful children. She sees their hands folded into little churches, she sees tears of astonishment ringing their eyes, and she hears the last of a silly Janis Joplin song floating from their mouths. She looks at her babies.

And she smiles. Then, in a papery whisper, she sings. *Oh Lord, won't you...Oh Lord, won't...Oh Lord....*

The soft light of candles flickers across the room; my children have never before been more beautiful, more wondrous. Their eyes shine, their lips smile over me. They smell of candle wax and prayerful hands. They are luminescent!

Just before my eyelids flutter closed and my lips fall slack and motionless, just before my heart becomes still and damp inside my chest, I see the arms of my children fold around one another. They lean and touch their heads together, a quiet, simple gesture, but one that gives me peace. And peace.

And peace.

Epilogue

YOU LAUGH. You laugh because your refrigerator door is standing wide open like some silly mouth and you remember how it all started with your wallet hiding in the crisper under the lettuce. You remember everything now, every day of every year of it. You especially remember that day—that first day you knew for certain something was wrong. You didn't know a sticky tangle of something was secretly growing in a small fold of your brain, but you knew something was amiss. That first bees' nest in your brain must have nestled itself around the judgment cell, because from that day forward, you were nothing but a lamentable cylinder of tears and sticky notes, of fallen-down dreams and misplaced thoughts. You're at peace now. Everything lost has been restored. Still, you look at your empty refrigerator with its door propped open and its crisper drawer pulled out and your mouth says the same thing it said seven years ago. Hah! you say. Of course, no one hears you. You're very dead now. You look around your house—your sadly empty house. You leave no footprints, but you are very much here. You turn your head to look beyond the refrigerator door.

What remains are walls, stiff with silence. The light is stunted by closed draperies, yet still a strong early afternoon sun finds a way to creep along the edges of the empty carpet. Most of the furniture is gone; their footprints in the carpet give the only clue of where things once stood. A chair here. There, the sofa, square tables at each end. A coffee table, and over there, a floor lamp with a heavy round base. In front of the window with a view to the patio (empty now of birds that used to dance and peep every day) are indentations from the medical recliner, returned to the equipment store, most likely. The cupboards are mostly cleared of their contents; only a few odd boxes still stand open in the kitchen. The house has been only lightly vacuumed and, here and there, I see a missed paw print from John Milton, whose lanky body now lolls over the furniture in Bryan's apartment.

The master bedroom, the only room yet to be packed and gutted of its contents, is softly lit. If it were a conversation, the room could be described as gentle and pleasant, almost warm and affable. Certainly it belies the prayer candles and tears that occupied every corner of the room just four weeks earlier.

Bryan stands at my dresser, packing nightgowns, underthings, a small green velvet-lined jewelry box containing a set of matching wedding rings nestled inside a felt envelope, several pairs of well-worn socks, a few sweaters, Ma's Bible with its fragile onion-skinned pages and notes along the margins. The items seem so few. So precious. Bryan's hands have the tenderness of a son, yet they still contain the thick clumsiness of a boy.

Allison picks through my clothes still hanging in the closet. Her hands are different from her brother's—more delicate, perhaps more apologetic. She folds each piece, letting thoughts of better, earlier times be captured within the creases before settling each garment into a large box boldly marked, *For Charity*. She recognizes the blouses and slacks purchased for that failed trip to Hawaii. Her eyes are watery, choking her throat. *Don't cry, Allison. Mom's right here. Everything's okay, my sweet pony.*

When she's done with the hanging items, Allison turns her attention to the upper shelves. Among the purses and boxes of shoes, she finds a handmade cedar box.

I nearly clap for joy when she pulls the box down and finds it spilling over with neatly folded papers and letters.

"Bryan. Oh my God! Look what I found," she says.

"What? I don't have time—"

"No! It's Mother. She wrote us letters. And poems, too."

Allison takes the box from the closet and spills the papers across the bed. "Look," she says. "Mom wrote all these things for...for *us*."

"I need to get back to the office this afternoon."

"Can't you be nice just once? It's Mom, in this box—"

"Oh, all right, all right...I'll look." Bryan pulls a letter from the pile. He opens it carefully, as if to damage the paper might cause great harm somewhere in the universe. He opens one, flattens it and then opens another and another.

He scans the words, a lawyer's habit. "Maybe we *should* read them," he says. "Look. A lot of them have dates. Let's put them in order and start with the undated pieces first, then read the dated letters in order."

"Don't you think we should just read whatever? Like serendipity?"

"You wouldn't know serendipity if it bit you in the ass."

"What if she can hear us? What if her spirit or her ghost is here and she's listening to you spouting your mouth off?" *How precious that Allison would think to include me in this moment.*

"Well, then she's listening to your spouting too."

Yes. Yes! I'm listening. Spout, my children...spout!

"All right," Allison shrugs. "Your idea is good, let's read them in order."

When the papers are collated, Bryan picks up the top letter. "Do you want to read, or do you want me to start?"

"You read. I'm too nervous."

Bryan looks down at the letter and begins to read it to himself.

"Out loud, please?"

"Oh, God. All right." Bryan looks at his watch.

Without chairs in the room, they settle onto the bed. Allison fluffs a pillow and settles back on it, eyes closed, hands behind her head. Knowing his time plan has been altered for the day, Bryan sighs with resignation and begins to read.

My dearest Bryan and Allison,

I don't quite know what to say to you. Given this illness (so new and surprising to me), I don't know what to say to myself, for that matter. Apparently, I'm sick. It appears I won't get better. What should have been my time to grow beautiful wrinkles; to let the skin on my hands turn to crepe paper and gray hairs spread across my head like fairy silk; what should have been my time to gather you around the table over coffee or wine to offer a mother's wisdom on those days you needed it; what should have been my time to pass on stories of my generation—well, it's all now moot.

Instead, we're looking at a quickening of my mental death. A hurried step into memories lost and confusion found.

I know I've nothing to apologize for. Some people simply get sick. Still, I'm so sorry. I'm so very, very sorry. I'm sorry especially for what I'm surely going to put you through. But you're strong. Please, for my sake, stay strong.

The oddest thing is that I know within the moment of each loss exactly what it is I'm losing. I'm aware of it at the beginning stage of this mesmerizing and confounding disease; I expect I may very well be aware right to the very end.

I've read about my illness. My brain will turn gummy and tangled with sticky cobwebs. I'll lose my language, but apparently I won't lose the feelings that prompt whatever utterances should reasonably occur. How sad for those of us who have to go down this path.

Our memories are stolen.

I won't talk aloud about these things. It's simply too cruel for a mother to burden her children with her gathering frailties. It's certainly not the Southern way. I come from a proud father and mother who suffered their own delicacies with silent mouths and hopeful hearts.

I can be no less.

Instead, I'll write my thoughts to you. Letters. Little poems. A mother's thoughts. They'll be something I hope you'll treasure. I'll struggle over them, just as I'm agonizing over this first letter. I'm tempted to tear it up (of course), and find another, better way to occupy your memories of me. But I'm a writer. A poet. It's what I do and it's what I'm losing. Words. I'm losing my words.

But until all my words are gone—until I'm gone—I'll continue to struggle in telling you all the things still left to say.

So here goes, my dear loves. Try not to fight over who gets

to keep the letters. Perhaps I shouldn't say that, but I know you well enough to know that you will. Just make copies, for heaven's sake, and be done with it.

Oh, and don't worry about me now that I'm gone—but if you need me for anything—I'll be with your father, singing and dancing and living on in his arms.

All my love,
Mother

Bryan looks up with tears in his eyes. He places the letter upside down next to the stack of unread letters. "You read the next one." *Oh, my dear, dear Bryan. Sometimes the stoics break and split most deeply.*

Allison reaches for the next paper, a poem. She reads it, her voice hesitant and quavering through to the end, her head nodding to gain the subtle rhythm in the piece. When she's done, she places it upside down on top of the first letter. In unspoken assent, Bryan and Allison take turns reading, turning each letter over one by one at the end of each reading.

On they go throughout the afternoon, laughing, pensive, sometimes tearful. Occasionally they launch into grand commentary, remembering long-forgotten events, before moving on to the next piece. They lose time, even as the day's shadows lengthen and stretch across the room.

At some point, they scavenge the kitchen boxes and find a bottle of cooking wine, a bent corkscrew and a couple of paper cups. *I smile that it's a lousy red, but a red, nevertheless.*

When at last they come to the final paper, dated nearly two years before my death, the end of the day, as well as the end of my letters, has crept into their eyes. Bryan and Allison look at the last entry.

"Do you want to do it, or do you want me to go ahead?" Bryan asks, his throat thick with wine and memories.

"You do it," Allison says, pushing the letter toward him. "You hold together better than I do."

Bryan takes the letter in his hands and lets his eyes settle on the words. "Okay, hold your breath. Here goes." He reaches over and takes Allison's hand and together they walk the landscape of my final letter.

My children,

It now takes all I have to find only a few words. They're all nearly gone. This shall be my last to you, my loves. It's taken well over (oh I don't know how long) just to write this. Years? A lifetime? I don't know. But today, or yesterday, I thought of your MeeMaw again and how she would gather me under her arm and how we would together read her favorite poetry. Always that ancient, John Milton, as you might guess.

So, my last thought to you shall be no less a gesture. Please feel my arms around you now, both of you, one to each side of me, as if I were reading this to you myself.

One last thing—and I hope you don't mind—instead of simply copying one of MeeMaw's favorite pieces (which, of course, would be something Milton, or maybe Eudora Welty, or even something dark from Poe), I've worked on a sonnet of my own for quite a while now. That's what I'd like to give you as my last gift. The words have not come easily or well. I'm afraid, I've even made quite a mess of it in some spots. But I hope these last words give you comfort, or pause, or even admonition as they fill your ears and fall into your hearts.

So here, my dears, is my sonnet to you:

On My Memory

My arms are empty of words I would hold.
They've spilled from my grasp and now all my life's
Thoughts are gone and my heart cries unconsoled.
Such wintry agony, a thousand knives
Of half-gathered memories, dying fresh
Within wisps of thought on a broken night.
As murmurs of love fall soft from my breath,
You fade, my dear roses, paled by night's light.
Yet don't think of me, my clattering words.
No! Hold to the thought that somewhere in time
Love will return us, not set us apart

Like small buds plucked, a new bouquet. While I'm here
Emptying thoughts to spare room for your tears,
Come sit with me now and read of my years.

—Lillie Claire Glidden
(your mother)

And there it is, my dear children. An imperfect sonnet,
but I think I counted the syllables right—I'm not certain.
Don't tell anyone, but I may have even made up a word or
two to fit the scheme. It would seem I'm too far gone to be
any better than that.

Still, my last words come from a mother's guttural love,
from some visceral place that not even I understand.

My words, my poem, even my love—all are imperfect.
Still, I hope you'll hold these thoughts close to your hearts.
Also, my dears, hold tightly to each other. I need for you to
do this, so that for what one of you might forget, the other
might recall.

Please. If nothing else, now in this moment—simply take
each other's hand, much like when you were children filled
with innocence and wonder.

Yes, go ahead. Do it now.

Take each other by the hand. Then remember me—all
that you are able. Yes, remember.

And remember.

My love forever,
Your mother

*YOU LEAVE. You leave now to the place that is waiting for
you. Your children know everything of you and you'll forever
know everything of them. Their vision of you will always be
that of your final moments. Your agony. Your sad forgetfulness
of their names, their faces. The hushed and failing light as you
left them. But they've also captured an image of you and their
MeeMaw and a grand Southern porch where life was filled with*

lemonade and poetry and their PaaPaw's hands striking chords on a scratched-up old banjo.

You'll visit your children now and then, especially when your daughter marries again and has a late-in-life baby son that gives her—and you—such joy. You'll watch your son as he flourishes in his career, then falters with too much wine and sympathy for himself. You'll try to whisper in his ear, but he's stuck in the bottom of a glass and his ears are deaf. You'll visit him more often than anyone.

You'll visit Jewell now and then too. You'll watch as she hums over a new woman. A woman older than you were, but one who loves her just as you loved her.

One day, you'll turn to find John Milton on your lap and you'll smile at his gray muzzle and wizened yowl. You'll spend grand and glorious eternities with your Ma and your Pa, singing Poor Ellen Smith across the skies. You'll join your beloved husband and welcome him to you as you never did in your living body. Yes, you'll leave your children. But you'll never really leave.

No, you'll never really leave.

The leaves of memory seemed to make a mournful rustling in the dark.

—Henry Wadsworth Longfellow

About the Author

AUBURN MCCANTA is an award-winning writer and poet. Raised in Portland, Oregon, she remembers thinking her mother's garden was a place so green, petals fell from the sky and flowers grew in every pathway. McCanta's father was an advertising director whose work transferred the family from the rose gardens of Portland to the Sonoran Desert of Phoenix, Arizona, where she now lives with her husband and two giant dogs. She serves on the Arizona Alzheimer's Task Force. *All the Dancing Birds* is her debut novel.

Auburn McCanta serves as an Ambassador for the National Alzheimer's Association. Until either a cure or an effective treatment is found, Auburn will donate ten percent of all book proceeds to the National Alzheimer's Association for the care, support, research, and advocacy of Alzheimer's patients and their families. Thank you so much for your help in this urgent need.

Acknowledgments

I T ALL STARTED with a brilliant neurosurgeon, Dr. Cully Cobb, who removed a brain tumor—a large and terrifying brain tumor. With drills and saws and various home improvement tool belt items, he gave me another life and a grand interest in all things concerning the brain. Thank you is not nearly sufficient.

I am in awe of the generosity of my husband, Dan, who told me over and over until I finally believed him and fully shared his enthusiasm that my story was worthy, the writing was good, and the effort would touch people in a positive and loving way. To Dan, I am most grateful.

I cannot thank enough the many people and their caregivers who allowed me to visit, who befriended me and unabashedly showed me the baffling nature of Alzheimer's disease. They taught me about its outward behavior, as well as its inward fragments of thought that flicker like beautiful, inextinguishable lights, from its onset all the way to its end. Thank you for helping me to hold up a flag of hope on your behalf—yours is a profound and humbling message.

My deepest thanks and gratitude to those who suffered through my early drafts, who listened to me natter on endlessly about this improbable idea of mine, who then encouraged and pushed me to carry it out, to be a better writer, to be true to my words, to be unapologetic, to find my feet when I thought they were lost, who talked me off the roof, who joined me in finding the bottom of a bottle of wine, who lent me their courage when I was fresh out, who shared their wives with a blubbering writer, who restored my spirits over a glorious week in Montana, a week in Nashville and then, another week in Sacramento, who chided and cajoled and believed in me when I didn't believe in myself, who told me to point my chin toward the future (I tried my best to place you in alphabetical order—Sorry, I'm not very good with hyphenated, complicated-name people and I placed my female friends before their husbands. I'm bad that way): Shelly Alcorn, Mark Alcorn, Susan Springer Butler, Chuck Butler, Cynthia D'Amour, Linnea Knowles, Leslie Kohler, Daniel Kuhn, Anne Ornelos de Lemos, Drew Myron, Lisa Berry-Nicholson, Kevin Nicholson, Marlene Phillips, Esther Garrett Powell, Russ Powell, Anne Roseman, Paula Silici, Kristi Smith, Dawn Teo, and, of course, the Bunco Ladies of Stetson Valley—one of these days I'm going to win!

Thank you to the generous, slow-dripping, honey-voiced woman of the Blowing Rock, North Carolina, Chamber of Commerce, who leisurely guided me through an introduction to the people and music of the Appalachians and, when our conversation was done, made me pine for a plate of grits and eggs. I wish I knew your name.

Grand and hearty thanks to The Editorial Department. Your support, guidance, editorial genius and copious handholding made this a better book than I could have ever dreamed of creating.

Thank you, Marcanti Clarke Literary Press!

Thank you to the woman who—when she found out the subject of my book—hugged me close and whispered in my ear that she had just been diagnosed with Alzheimer's and she needed my book so she would know herself in the future.

Finally, thank you, Wilson—you are an impossibly dear Labradoodle and pet therapy dog who loves all the little ladies and gentlemen we visit. If you were so inclined to shed, your curly white coat would be infused in every page of this book.

Reading Group Guide

Lillie Claire Glidden appears befuddled by her early forgetfulness and develops a number of coping behaviors that serve to both hide her memory lapses and adapt to them. How does Lillie Claire purposely hide her memory difficulties, and does this mean she is clever, or that she is in denial? Why would a person try to hide being forgetful?

Lillie Claire seems to enjoy very different relationships with each of her children. Is it reasonable to expect that the dynamics of mother/adult child complexities would create different responses in the way Lillie Claire interacts with the characters of Bryan and Allison? Does the immature sibling rivalry that has continued into adulthood obscure and stunt the ability to recognize their mother's shifting behavior?

After Lillie Claire's memory craters in a failed attempt to cook a simple dinner, her son, Bryan, takes her to a doctor for evaluation. Why do you think her son, and not the daughter to whom Lillie Claire seems closer, would be the person to address his mother's health?

When Lillie Claire receives her initial diagnosis of Early Onset Alzheimer's disease, her response is to cheer up Bryan by stopping afterward for ice cream. Do you find this a reasonable response? Why do you think Bryan is visibly upset, while Lillie Claire appears to more easily accept such a tragic diagnosis?

Lillie Claire writes poems and letters to her children and keeps them hidden in a box in her closet. Why do you think she doesn't share her writings with Bryan and Allison? Do you think it is possible for a person with Alzheimer's disease to be able to continue to write and read?

When Lillie Claire's forgetfulness ruins a planned vacation, Allison's response is overwhelming anger. Do you think there may be a deeper issue guiding Allison's protracted lack of forgiveness? What is the catalyst then that prompts Allison to see Lillie Claire through a different lens, finally allowing for understanding and a mending of their relationship?

When the children bring a full-time caregiver for their mother, how does the character of Jewell provide a tempering and calming influence in the home? Does Lillie Claire benefit from remaining in her home with a private caregiver, or would she be better cared for in a nursing facility? Why do you think Bryan and Allison give in to their mother's wish to remain in her home?

As Lillie Claire begins to struggle with language skills, she invites Jewell to read aloud her private writings. Does this change the way Lillie Claire responds to her memories and ultimately to herself?

As she deteriorates, Lillie Claire anguishes over her diminished function as a mother. She laments this loss and, in a fit of regret, decides to burn all her letters and poems. Why would Lillie Claire consider destroying works she has labored so hard over and has dedicated as the final gift to her children?

Lillie Claire is often soothed by her cat, John Milton, and amused by the birds who visit her patio each day. Why do you think Lillie Claire responds so positively to the presence of her cat and to the little birds that she believes perform choreographed dances across her patio?

As Lillie Claire declines and her language turns more deeply inward, are you surprised that her interior dialogue is more intact than she can display to others? Could this understanding influence how one might navigate a conversation with someone who suffers from Alzheimer's disease?

When Jewell breaks down and asks Bryan and Allison for more help, do you think the children should have then moved their mother to a care facility with round-the-clock care? What option would you choose?

All the Dancing Birds is ultimately a story of profound love and enduring acceptance. How did the characters mature as the story progressed? What possibilities might the future hold for Bryan and Allison?